Acclaim For the Work of
MAX ALLAN COLLINS!

"Crime fiction aficionados are in for a treat…a neo-pulp noir classic."
—*Chicago Tribune*

"No one can twist you through a maze with as much intensity and suspense as Max Allan Collins."
—*Clive Cussler*

"Collins never misses a beat…All the stand-up pleasures of dime-store pulp with a beguiling level of complexity."
—*Booklist*

"Collins has an outwardly artless style that conceals a great deal of art."
—*New York Times Book Review*

"Max Allan Collins is the closest thing we have to a 21st-century Mickey Spillane and…will please any fan of old-school, hardboiled crime fiction."
—*This Week*

"A suspenseful, wild night's ride [from] one of the finest writers of crime fiction that the U.S. has produced."
—*Book Reporter*

"This book is about as perfect a page turner as you'll find."
—*Library Journal*

"Bristling with suspense and sexuality, this book is a welcome addition to the Hard Case Crime library."
—*Publishers Weekly*

I told Letterman to pull over.

He did, then nodded toward the bridge. "Should I leave the headlights on?"

"No. It'd just make a target of me."

He shut off the beams and the bridge's mouth turned black and unwelcoming. I got the nine millimeter out and slipped from the car into the night.

I entered the sheltered structure slowly, cautiously, wood groaning under my feet, sparse moonlight filtering in between slats, my back to a creaky wall. I went all the way to the north end and stayed low, gun ready, as I came out. I looked around the low brush on either side of the road.

Nobody.

I returned to the car and got in. "No sign of a soul," I said.

We rumbled through the rickety bridge and then pulled off to the left as we exited the north end. From the back seat I yanked out the duffel and then the two of us, like gangsters in fedoras and topcoats dragging a dead body, lugged the eighty-five pounds of money to the underbrush just past the north end of the bridge.

"All right," I said. "Now you head back."

He blinked at me. "You mean we head back."

"No." I lifted the nine mil. "I'm waiting for these bastards..."

The BIG BUNDLE

by **Max Allan Collins**

A NATHAN HELLER NOVEL

A HARD CASE **CRIME NOVEL**

A HARD CASE CRIME BOOK
(HCC-156)
First Hard Case Crime edition: December 2022

Published by

Titan Books
A division of Titan Publishing Group Ltd
144 Southwark Street
London SE1 0UP

in collaboration with Winterfall LLC

Print edition ISBN 978-1-78909-852-5
E-book ISBN 978-1-78909-853-2

Design direction by Max Phillips
www.maxphillips.net

Typeset by Swordsmith Productions

The name "Hard Case Crime" and the Hard Case Crime logo are trademarks of Winterfall LLC. Hard Case Crime books are selected and edited by Charles Ardai.

Printed by CPI Group (UK) Ltd, Croydon CR0 4YY

Visit us on the web at www.HardCaseCrime.com

For my grandson
Sam
when the time comes

AUTHOR'S NOTE

Although the historical incidents in this novel are portrayed more or less accurately (as much as the passage of time and contradictory source material will allow), fact, speculation and fiction are freely mixed here; historical personages exist side by side with composite characters and wholly fictional ones—all of whom act and speak at the author's whim.

*"The evil is in the people,
and money is the peg they hang it on."*

ROSS MACDONALD

THE BIG BUNDLE

BOOK ONE

Kansas City Shuffle

October 1953

CHAPTER ONE

A middle-aged man taking stock of his life is to be expected. But for this to be my midpoint, I would have to make it to 94, and anyway it was the ghosts of my past haunting me, not my conscience, which after all was the nine millimeter Browning automatic I still carried all these years after my father killed himself with it—when I disappointed him taking the Outfit's money to get ahead on the Chicago PD.

As I write this I'm closer to 94 than 47, which was my age in October 1953 when I caught an Ace Company cab outside the Kansas City Municipal Airport. The cabbie was colored, which in a city where the population was 10% that persuasion might not have been a surprise. Still, Negro hackies didn't generally work white areas, though airport runs could make for a decent fare and those who didn't like the driver's shade could take the next ride down, and those who didn't give a damn got a smile and a nod and no funny business like unrequested tours of K.C.

And I didn't need one of those—I'd done jobs here before. The airport was five minutes from a downtown whose "Petticoat Lane" on Eleventh Street had smart shops and patrons who could afford to frequent them; around Twelfth and Main were the usual stores and palatial movie houses, a few blocks east was a civic center whose plaza included two of the taller buildings, the Courthouse and City Hall, with the massive bunker of Municipal Auditorium to the southeast.

Everything was still up to date in Kansas City. They were giving my toddling town a run on the meat-packing and agricultural fronts. They had an impressive art gallery, fine arts museum

and kiddie-pleasing zoo, and the industries included steel, petro-
leum, and automotive manufacturing. And one once-booming
local enterprise that had faded since the '30s had made a big
comeback recently.

"You in town about that kidnapping, boss?" the cabbie asked.

He was grinning at me in the rearview mirror. He looked
like Mantan Moreland but with a flattened nose; that and his
cauliflower ears made him a former prizefighter. Yes, I'm a
detective.

"Why would you think that?"

Now he was looking out his windshield, which was my pref-
erence.

"Address rang a bell," he said.

"Ah."

"Anyway, boss, I read about you—you that private eye to the
stars."

Life magazine had done a story about me when I opened my
L.A. branch.

"Don't recall your name, though," he said.

"Nathan Heller," I said.

"Chicago, right?"

"Right."

"...So what's Alan Ladd like?"

"Short."

"What about Mitchum?"

"Tall."

That made him laugh.

For the record, I was an inch shorter than Mitchum and
weighed around two hundred pounds, my reddish brown hair
going white at the temples, and "almost leading man handsome"
(the *Life* writer had said). I made up for the "almost" by being a
success in my trade—president of Chicago's A-1 Detective

Agency. By way of evidence I offer the court my Botany 500 suit, Dobbs hat and Burberry raincoat, lining in—it was cold in Kansas City in October, and the sky was trying to make its mind up whether to rain or snow.

We rumbled across the Missouri River by way of the upper deck of the Hannibal Bridge.

No laughter now, as he asked, "You gonna help get that little boy back?"

"Do my best."

"I got a boy that age myself."

"So do I."

"I believe somebody took *my* boy, I kill his ass."

"So would I."

He laughed again, but the sound of it was different.

Just under a week ago, a bit before nine A.M., someone rang the bell at an exclusive Catholic elementary school here in Kansas City. A young, inexperienced nun answered and found a plump, pleasant-looking (though agitated) woman on the doorstep; about forty, the caller looked respectable enough in a brown hat, beige blouse and dark gabardine skirt. The woman even wore white gloves.

She presented herself as the sister of Virginia Greenlease, whose six-year-old son Bobby attended the school, and said she'd just rushed her sister, who'd shown signs of a heart attack while they were out shopping, to the hospital. Virginia was asking to see her son. The nun—new at the school, barely speaking English—fetched the child and turned him over to the woman calling herself the boy's aunt. The boy went along dutifully, hand-in-hand.

Later that morning the mother superior's second-in-command called the Greenlease home to check on how Mrs. Greenlease was feeling.

Mrs. Greenlease, who answered the phone herself, said, "Why, just fine."

The first ransom letter came a few hours later, special delivery.

We moved through an industrial area and then an unpretentious mix of commercial and residential, all pretty sleepy on an early Sunday afternoon. In the plush Country Club District, broad, winding boulevards followed the contours of the terrain, interrupted by public areas overseen by sculptures and fountains; a classy retail plaza ran to Spanish-style stucco and cream-color brick. The homes themselves were near mansions—not just "near," really—with impeccably landscaped, evergreen-garnished yards that in warmer weather were likely trimmed as often as their owners saw their barbers.

"We in Kansas now, Mr. Heller."

We'd only been traveling fifteen minutes. "Over the state line already?"

"Yessir. This is Mission Hills. Lots of rich folks. You a golfer, sir?"

"I am." I disliked the sport, but sometimes it was the best way to keep clients happy.

"Well, they's three golf courses to choose from. They keep 'em open till the first snow."

Autumn had turned the plentiful trees into a riot of color, orange, yellow, red, green, even purple, that last desperate burst of life before winter delivered death. But the grass was still green, brown barely intruding, with a scattering of those vivid colors making a patchwork quilt of lawns. Fathers were tossing footballs to sons while littler kids leapt into heaping piles of leaves with a fearlessness they'd yet to outgrow, their mothers leaning on rakes and looking on in worried surrender.

The cab was about to turn onto Verona Road from West 63rd

when a figure in a fedora and raincoat ambled out from around the corner and planted himself before us with his arms outstretched. The cabbie hadn't been traveling fast in this residential area, but it was startling enough to make him hit the brakes with a squeal.

Tall, his long, narrow oval face home to a prominent nose and jutting chin, eyebrows heavy on a high forehead, the interloper came over to the window the cabbie was rolling down and leaned in like an officious carhop.

"Local traffic only," he said, polite but with an edge.

I leaned up and said to the cabbie, "I'll handle this."

I got out and said, "Nathan Heller. They're expecting me at the Greenlease home."

"Special Agent Wesley Grapp," he said, stepping away from the cab, holding up ID with his left hand and offering his right with the slightest of smiles. His grip was firm but not showy. "You're on our list."

I gave him about half a grin. "I've been on the FBI's list a long time."

That got a chuckle out of him. "Yes, I've seen the file. It's thicker than *Forever Amber* and about as juicy. What did you do to get on the Chief's bad side? It's not included."

The Chief, of course, was J. Edgar Hoover.

"Oh," I said casually, "a long time ago I told him to go fuck himself."

This chuckle came from somewhere deep. "That'll do it. Call me Wes."

"And I'm Nate. So you've set up a checkpoint."

"We have. We'll take you from here."

My overnight bag was in the trunk and the cabbie got it out for me. I gave him a sawbuck and made a friend for life.

Grapp walked me around the corner to his ride, a dark blue

Ford Crestliner. I tossed the bag in front where a younger agent in suit and fedora sat behind the wheel—slender in horn-rimmed glasses—and Grapp and I got in back.

I said, "I guess you know Bob Greenlease called me in personally. You have no objection?"

"None. I'm all for it, actually."

That surprised me; the FBI didn't usually welcome private detectives to the party. "Why's that?"

"We've been pretty well frozen out of this so far. Helping as much as we're allowed. Mr. Greenlease has kept us pretty much at arm's length. The guy's got a lot of clout. He's working strictly through the K.C. chief of police."

Greenlease, a major stockholder in General Motors, was one of the wealthiest men in the Midwest. A self-made man from farming stock, he'd started out around the turn of the century making handmade cars and running a repair garage, then landed a franchise to sell Cadillacs; now he was the largest distributor of Caddies in the Southwest. His founding dealership, the Greenlease Motor Car Company, was where I first met him in 1937, when I was brought in to deal with auto parts pilfering by employees. And since just after the war, the A-1 had arranged security for the Annual Chicago Automobile Show, of which Greenlease was always a big part.

"Of course FBI policy in kidnapping cases," Grapp was saying, "means doing nothing that might jeopardize the victim's safe return. And Mr. Greenlease insists on no surveillance of any ransom drop...or at least he has so far."

"So far?"

"Well, Mr. Heller...Nate...he's called *you* in. Might mean a change of tactics."

"Yeah, but it's taken almost a week." I'd half expected a call; the case had made the papers and even CBS-TV by way of

Edward R. Murrow's fifteen-minute national evening news. But that had amounted to little more than descriptions of the boy and the fake aunt. And expressions of ongoing sympathy for the parents.

"We don't have a man on the inside," Grapp said. "So your cooperation could prove key."

"What *have* you been able to do?"

He offered me a smoke and I declined. He lit up and said, "With Kansas and Missouri butting up against each other, chances are good this thing has crossed state lines, which'll give us jurisdiction. Already we've been able to intercept Greenlease's mail at the K.C. Post Office and record incoming phone calls."

"So there's been contact. Were you able to trace the calls?"

He sighed smoke. "We probably could have, and possibly closed in on the people responsible, but the family's wish was that we do nothing that might hinder the boy's return."

I frowned, shook my hand. "That's crazy."

"I agree. Perhaps you can reason with Mr. Greenlease. After all, he's taken a big step, bringing you in...considering your reputation."

"Somehow I don't think you mean to flatter me."

A thick eyebrow went up. "Nate. Mr. Heller. You're well-known for your underworld connections. And you've been in a number of well-publicized situations where you have, let's say, taken matters effectively into hand."

"Gee whiz, thanks. But let me remind you, Wes, Special Agent Grapp, that J. Edgar Hoover assures us that there is no such thing as organized crime."

The young agent at the wheel frowned at me in the rearview mirror, but Grapp only smiled a little.

He gestured with the cigarette-in-hand. "Nate, let's just say anything you can do to help this situation would be appreciated.

Whoever did this goddamn thing must be aware that, even if state lines *haven't* been crossed, the kidnapping law in Missouri means a death sentence."

"Understood. Since there's effectively been a press blackout, what can you tell me? What don't I know?"

The FBI man's laugh was raspy and wry. "You have been spared experiencing one of the most sadistic, heartless series of letters and messages and phone calls any of us has ever seen. Six ransom notes, over a dozen phone calls. One wild goose chase after another." His eyes, a dark brown and almost black, narrowed. "We do know they have the boy, or at least *had* him—a medal he'd worn to school that day was sent along with the second note."

"When you say 'they'…?"

"It's at least two people. The woman who picked the boy up at school, and a man who's been making the phone calls. He insists Bobby's still alive. Talks about him being a handful and mentions a pet the child misses, how homesick he is. But, uh… they aren't the smartest pair, these two."

"Why do you say that?"

"Well, they were lucky they snagged the kid at all. The nun who answered the door was new, very young, an import from France who spoke little English, and if the mother superior— away on an errand—had been there to go to the door that morning? That damn woman would *never* have pulled off her impersonation."

"Think so, huh?"

He nodded curtly. "When the nun offered to show her the way to the chapel, to pray for her sick sibling? The dumbo dame said, 'No thanks, I'm not a Catholic.' Any other nun in that facility would've known that Mrs. Greenlease was a Catholic, meaning her sister would be, too!"

I let some air out. "That makes the woman a dope. But maybe the guy's got more on the ball."

"You think so, Heller? His first ransom note? He got the address wrong."

They drove me down Verona Road, past a trio of cars with PRESS cards in the rear windows; a TV camera truck was pulled over there, too. A female reporter was using a phone in a box strapped to a tree, a little stool next to it for her purse and whatnot. United Press International had installed the phone, Grapp said.

The press had a good view of the house from there. Of course, "house" didn't cover it. An imposing two-story multi-gabled structure with slate roofs and a cream-and-brown fieldstone facade awaited us when we pulled in the half-circle drive; it was almost a castle and not quite a church, and wide enough to be a hotel.

The FBI dropped me off and I toted my overnight bag to the gabled entrance. I must have been watched from a window, because the door opened after I'd barely rung the bell. In his mid-thirties, my host was of average height and weight with a squared-off head and a rounded jaw, his forehead so high it was like his features had slipped down too far on his oval face. His hair was dark and short, his eyes dark and bloodshot, his dark suit and tie unusual for a Sunday afternoon, unless an evening church service was in the mix. Yet somehow he still seemed disheveled.

"You must be Mr. Heller," he said, and stepped aside and gestured me in. He took my coat, hat and bag and set them on a chair by a mirror.

Then I was in a world of big rooms with dark woodwork, pale plaster walls, dark wood floors, tall leaded-glass windows; along the left wall, a stairway rose with a carved lion for a newel post. The interior seemed oddly at war with itself—everything Prairie-style and spare but for carved touches, as if the house couldn't decide if it was a mission or a manor.

Few lights were on. This was a somber place—not necessarily always so, but right now the inhabitants could not quite acknowledge light, which even the tall windows seemed reluctant to admit.

He was about to lead me deeper into the house when he froze, remembering himself, and turned and said, with a stiff nod, "Paul Greenlease."

This was the adopted son of Bob Greenlease's first marriage; Greenlease's second wife, Virginia, had presented her husband with two late-in-life children, a daughter whose name I didn't recall and of course the missing Bobby.

"I've been serving as the family's spokesman," Paul said, offering a listless handshake. "Dad has taken this awfully hard."

We were standing in an entryway larger than most living rooms.

"I'm sure," I said. "How's your mother doing?"

"It kind of varies, day to day. She's been sedated a lot, frankly. Sometimes things seem to be looking up, then…"

"Then they're down. I understand these creatures have you folks jumping through hoops—one message, one call, one snipe hunt after another."

He nodded, swallowed. "They've left us notes under crayon-marked rocks. They've taped letters underneath mailboxes. One note sent us to another note with instructions too confusing to follow."

"Sounds like you're dealing with dolts."

He had an ashen look. "They want a lot of money. That's not a problem, understand, but it took a while to get together."

"How much?"

He paused, not sure he should share this, then did: "Six hundred thousand. Dollars."

"Good God. That must be a record."

"I wouldn't know. Is that a lot for this kind of thing?"

Lindbergh had been asked for $50,000. Of course that was a while ago. Inflation had hit every business.

"The very first letter specified federal reserve notes," Paul said, "in tens and twenties. Mr. Eisenhower at Commerce Trust is helping. He's the president's brother."

"Of the bank?"

"No, of America. You know—Ike?"

"Yeah." I didn't mention I hadn't voted for him. "And Ike's brother got the money together?"

"Yes. And we tried to deliver it but it was raining and these letters have been kind of illiterate and…well, we left the money but the kidnapper called us later and said he couldn't find it."

Jesus.

"We went back and picked the money up," Paul said, escorting me down a hallway. "We tried another time, but…. You should really talk to my father."

We stopped at a doorless archway. Very softly, he said, "Sue's become a sort of appendage to Dad. She's eleven. They're sort of…helping each other through this."

"I understand."

"But it might hamper what gets said. Just so you know."

"Got it."

We moved through the archway into a big living room. Again, the room was fighting itself, stark Arts and Crafts furnishings, walls of square-panel mahogany, but a ceiling of ornate plaster work with a chandelier; a grand piano lurked in one corner, the fireplace going, dispensing warmth out of a coldly elaborate decorative mantel over which hung a gilt-framed painting, a family portrait of Robert Greenlease and his wife Virginia with a much younger Paul at his side and a toddler Sue by her mother's. Bobby Greenlease, not yet born, was already absent.

A dark leather-cushioned Stickley sofa faced the fire and the back of Robert Greenlease's head and his broad shoulders—he was in a blue satin dressing gown—were to me.

"Dad," Paul said quietly from where we stood just inside the room, "Mr. Heller from Chicago is here."

Greenlease's hand raised slowly, like a slow child risking an answer in class, and he gently motioned me forward. He did not turn.

Paul nodded to me and disappeared and I went around to face Greenlease, who wore a white shirt and tie under the dressing gown, its lapels so dark blue they were almost black. His eleven-year-old daughter, blonde and cute in a plaid jumper, was curled up sleeping next to him on a brown leather sofa cushion, her head on his knee; his hand was on her shoulder.

In his early seventies, Bob Greenlease was a big man with a rectangular head and white hair, wispy on top. His eyes were wide-set and light blue behind browline glasses, nose hawkish, mouth a thin line, a face that could have been severe but wasn't, because he so frequently smiled.

Of course he wasn't smiling now.

Seated or not, he had an off-balance look, as if he'd just realized he stood at the edge of a cliff.

He whispered, "Thank you for coming, Nate. We'll keep our voices down. Don't want to disturb the girl."

He extended his left hand—his right remaining on his daughter's shoulder—and we awkwardly but warmly shook.

I drew up a wood-and-leather-cushion chair, careful not to let it screech on the hardwood floor. "I'm so sorry about this terrible thing," I said, sotto voce.

"Your son is well? Sam, isn't it?"

"Yes. With his mother in California. He's six. Like your boy."

The tight mouth flinched. "Wish I'd called you in sooner. Should have been smart enough to take advantage of your prior experience with Lindbergh and all."

I knew what he meant. But I wondered how it made me an expert, considering how that had come out.

I said, "You don't have to fill me in. I spoke to Agent Grapp and your son and heard all about this damn nonsense you've had to endure."

He nodded, just barely. "We seem to finally be on the verge of arranging the ransom drop. It's been like something out of the Marx Brothers. But we're to get a phone call at eight P.M. with the instructions."

The fire snapped at us and was almost too warm as it cast an orange glow.

"What do you want me to do, Bob?"

"Join the team. Two old friends of mine, valued business associates, have been helping out on this thing—Will Letterman, who runs my Tulsa dealership, and from my K.C. operation here, Stew O'Neill. You'll meet them. Fine fellas."

"I'm sure they are. But you're obviously dealing with dangerous, unscrupulous criminals. You need someone who can handle that breed."

His smile was barely discernible. "Which is why I wish I'd called you sooner. Are you too old and successful, Nate, to still carry that Browning semiautomatic pistol?"

I nodded toward the outer area. "It's in my bag. Holster, too."

"Good. Afraid we don't have room for you here, between the help and my support crew. I've had arrangements made for you at the Hotel President, just fifteen minutes away. I've got a new Cadillac waiting for your use, here in the garage—Paul has keys for you. Go get settled at the hotel and be back at seven-thirty. I'll introduce you to Will and Stew."

"Fine." I got to my feet. "How are you holding up?"

"A lot of support here. Good people. My son and Will have been handling the press. My daughter sticks right by me, and my wife…well, Virginia has occasional rough moments, but she's smart and strong. She took the call that came in today, herself, and let this 'M'…that's what he calls himself…have it."

"Really."

"Yes. Told the bastard there'd been enough runaround. But afterward…" He swallowed thickly and the blue eyes behind the glasses were glittering. "…she rather…came apart. You see, she had specific questions that M couldn't, or anyway didn't, answer. Name of our driver on the latest European trip…what Bobby was building with his monkey blocks in his room. The caller skated over those, just said what a handful Bobby was being. I think for the first time, Virginia…well. You know."

I did know. She had realized how possible it was that her boy might already be dead.

The little girl stirred. She looked up at me with big eyes, as blue as her father's, and grabbed his arm, startled, afraid. "Is he one of them, Daddy?"

"No, darling. This is Mr. Heller. He's on our side."

CHAPTER TWO

The fifteen-story Hotel President in the Power and Light District—Kansas City's business and entertainment section—was unquestionably elegant, even if it was best known for a mysterious murder that happened in Room 1046 in 1935. Nobody asked me to solve it then and I wasn't interested in doing so now.

But Bob Greenlease had always known how to treat the help. The lobby—quiet on a Sunday afternoon but for my echoing footsteps—put any Chicago hotel to shame, what with the golden two-story columns, chandeliers, marble floors, wrought-iron second-floor balcony, green palms and over-stuffed furnishings.

My room on the eighth floor was larger than need be, but who was complaining? The hotel had been around since the late twenties, but a recent remodel had led to modern, spindly furnishings, abstract wall art, and a red coverlet to make up for gray walls and curtains; there was even a small TV by the mirror on the dresser opposite the bed.

I unpacked my bag and retrieved the second suit I'd brought along—a gray twill woolen number from Richard Bennett in the Loop, cut to conceal a holstered accessory. I hung the Botany 500 in the closet and the tailored suit on the hook inside the bathroom door and took a shower, providing steam for the suit to hang out and for me to loosen up. The meeting with Greenlease had left me tight as a drum.

Speaking of which, the hotel's Drum Room—a big circular restaurant with a snare-shaped red-and-yellow bar at its center—

was my destination for an early supper. Sunday was the only night they didn't offer live music—everybody from Frank Sinatra and Benny Goodman to Glenn Miller and Dean Martin had played here. Right now, at six o'clock, one of a handful of diners, I had to settle for mellow Muzak.

I had the filet medium rare, hash browns, buttered lima beans and salad, and a rum and Coke. But I only ate half of everything and limited myself to the one drink. I would be working tonight and even now I was in the tailored Richard Bennett with the nine millimeter under my arm. Maybe I shouldn't have gone over the photostats of the ransom notes before I came down to eat.

You'd have lost your appetite, too.

If do exactly as we say an try no tricks, advised the first missive in what looked to be a feminine hand, *your boy will be back safe withen 24 hrs after we check money.* The second said, *Don't try to stop us on pick-up or boy dies you will hear from us later.* More notes followed, with instructions like: *Tie a white rag on your radio aerial. Proceed north on highway No. 169 past the junction with highway No. 69 about there miles where you will come to Henry's place.* And: *Go west to first rd heading south across from lum reek farm sign.* None of this gibberish had panned out, of course. Phone call instructions had been even worse.

These were people who thought stealing a six-year-old boy was a good way to get ahead—stupid people who'd spent almost a week botching their ransom delivery instructions. When I asked myself if this boy could still be alive, the food I'd eaten roiled in my belly like storm clouds.

Back in my hotel room I put a long-distance call in to my ex-wife in Beverly Hills. Peggy was married to a film director who'd had his ups and downs, currently up. We maintained a truce for Sam's sake, but she not surprisingly never seemed glad to hear from me when I phoned.

"Sam's at a pool party at the Lewises," she said.

He and Jerry's son Gary were longtime pals, longtime for six-year-olds anyway.

"And you're not with him?"

"I think he'll be safe with a dozen other kids and more than enough parents. What did you want with him?"

"Just to see how he's doing. I'm his father, or did that slip your mind?"

A tense truce, admittedly.

"Well," Peg said, "he's fine. You'll see him soon enough."

I got him during his Christmas vacation. He was in the first grade.

"Would you tell him…"

"What?"

Tell him his daddy loves him.

"Nothing," I said.

At seven on this chilly but not quite cold night, I left the loaner Caddy in the driveway outside the four-car garage and walked around to the front door, where I was let in by a tall, white-haired, bald-on-top Sunday school teacher type in a tie under a sweater vest. Somewhat hunch-shouldered, probably nearly as old as Greenlease, he introduced himself as Will Letterman from the Tulsa branch. I had missed Stew O'Neill, the local Greenlease Motors crony who'd been released to spend the evening with his family.

Anyway, that was the story. The real reason for O'Neill's night off, I figured, was my arrival on the scene. For a lot of good reasons—including staying close to his wife and not making a second kidnap target out of himself—Greenlease would likely maintain his executive position here and send his people to make the ransom drop. In this case, that was Letterman and me.

A colored maid in her twenties, shy with a friendly smile but a beleaguered demeanor, collected my hat and Burberry— working in a place under siege was not an easy job. Within moments the missing boy's father—no dressing gown now, rather shirt sleeves and tie—joined us in the expansive entryway and took me aside. No sign of the clinging young daughter now, or the adopted son.

Greenlease's smile was a ghastly thing. "Nate, if you have the opportunity to...*do* something, I know you will. But I must insist you honor Will's lead, if this ransom drop finally happens tonight. He'll be representing me."

"No offense, Bob, but then...why bring *me* in?"

"Because these people are unpredictable and matters could get out of hand. That's where I'm counting on you—the unexpected. You're going to be compensated, of course."

"I didn't ask for—"

He pressed something that crinkled into my hand. "If this isn't sufficient, let me know. And your expenses'll be on top of it, of course."

Then he started down the hall and Letterman trailed after him. I'm human—before I fell in line, I had a glimpse at the check before tucking it away. Five thousand dollars with "Retainer" in the memo line. Well, sure—we would do things his way.

Our little party wound up in a rectangular study with a wall of leather-bound books at right and at left a mural of hunting dogs and their shotgun-wielding masters heading after game in the trees. Leaded windows behind a big mahogany desk at the far end looked out at real trees and leaded-window double doors adjacent surveyed a dark night not helped much by a crescent moon over which clouds drifted like the black smoke of a distant fire.

Down by the mural a well-stocked liquor cart awaited with a leather-cushioned chair arranged in front of a low-slung coffee table with a matching sofa running along the wall under the hunters and dogs and trees. The coffee table had two phones on it, one on a wire from nearby, the other stretched on its cord from another room.

Greenlease poured himself some bourbon while both Letterman and I declined. Our host gestured to the chair and I took it, while Letterman sat on the couch, the twin phones in front of us. Behind me Greenlease began pacing; he might have been walking guard duty.

"I've already told Will," Greenlease said, his words coming in a rush that undermined his controlled businessman manner, "that you'll be handling the call when it comes in."

"Mr. Heller…" Letterman began.

I said, "Please, Will. Nate."

Letterman leaned forward. His features seemed to be hanging off his already long face; his eyes were light blue peering from slitted pouches. "Nate. I've told Bob I think putting you on the phone is a mistake. I have a pretty good rapport going with this 'M' character. He's talked to Stew, as well, and a couple of times to Virginia."

"Where *is* Mrs. Greenlease?"

Pausing his pacing, her husband said, "Still sedated. Our family doctor has been quite good about all this. Ginny was upset earlier today, after taking that call. Paul is at her bedside. This…ordeal simply has to stop, Nate." Some rage broke through the calm: "Has to *stop*."

I caught Greenlease's eyes and nodded to the couch. He

sighed and went over to join his associate; but he took the glass of bourbon along.

"I'm just afraid," Letterman said, "a new voice might raise a warning bell with our 'friend.'"

I said, "Will may be right."

Greenlease's palms came up. "Who the hell knows at this point? But you may be able to get more out of this son of a bitch than we have, Nate. You can size him from your perspective and experience. May be able to get him to, hell, clarify these jumbled instructions he keeps giving us."

I frowned. "Is it a stall, you think?"

Letterman said, "I don't take it that way. He seems...I hate to say this, but I'd swear this M has been drunk every time I've talked to him."

"And you're convinced this isn't an impostor?"

Greenlease said, "He knows about the Jerusalem Cross Bobby was wearing—the medal with ribbons on it that was sent back with the second letter. Which we kept from the press." His eyes went to his crony. "Will, Nate is an old hand at this. He's dealt with this kind of thing before."

The damn Lindbergh case again. Didn't anybody remember how badly that had gone, right down to frying the wrong man?

"And I've told Nate," Greenlease continued, "that if we're able to make the exchange tonight, your word *goes*. You can overrule him, Will....Right, Nate?"

Not to be crass, but the five-grand check in my pocket said yes, and so did I.

I asked, "Are the feds or police in on this?"

Greenlease shook his head. "No. I've requested the call not be traced. They're not to follow us on the drop. I don't want to come this far and have it compromised. The important thing is Bobby making it home safe and sound."

I didn't look at Letterman—I was afraid we'd both give away our doubt that the boy's safety remained an issue. But Bobby could still be alive. He could. Right?

The call was due at eight, which was coming up soon. I asked a few questions and heard some detailed stories from Letterman about the insanely frustrating runaround they'd been getting. Eight came and went. I allowed myself a rum and Coke. Greenlease had a second bourbon. Letterman continued to abstain, his eyes on those phones. We'd agreed that he and I would pick up on the count of three, and Greenlease would join him on the couch to listen in.

At 8:28, the phones rang. Frankly, we all jumped a little— the watched pot had seemed like it would never fucking boil. I counted to three silently with Letterman's eyes on me, and picked up. Greenlease had already made his way over to the couch beside his associate, who held the receiver sideways so both could listen. Hand covering the mouthpiece.

I held the receiver to my ear. Silence.

I said, "Is this 'M'?"

"...Speaking."

"Let's get this thing over with."

"I don't recognize your voice."

"There are several of us who work for Mr. Greenlease helping him out. You and I haven't spoken before."

"If you're police—"

"I'm not police. By the way, did the boy answer those questions his mother gave you this morning?"

That was my way of making him think I'd been part of this for a while.

"No, I, uh...I couldn't....We couldn't get anything out of him."

The voice was tenor and thick, unsure and slurring. As

Letterman said, almost certainly drunk. And his words had been less than encouraging.

I said, "You couldn't get anything from him?"

"He wouldn't talk."

"Are we going to see the boy tonight?"

"No, you can't, because they want to check the money. Anyway, the kid is raising so much hell they don't want to have to deal with him on the pickup. You'll get him back tomorrow, in Pittsburg, Kansas."

The caller, I'd been told, had been portraying himself as an intermediary—hence, "they." As for Pittsburg, Kansas, that was a new wrinkle—I would learn later that it was a town of twenty thousand, one hundred miles south near the Oklahoma border.

I asked, "Is that the straight goods?"

"It's gospel."

"And somebody will contact us there?"

"Someone will contact you. By telegram."

"Where do we wait?"

"The telegraph office."

"Listen, I want that kid tonight. No waiting till morning."

The two men on the couch were frowning at me—they probably thought I was playing it too tough. But I could read this guy. He was soft if you weren't six.

"You'll get him tomorrow," the slurry voice said, "but first I'll call you tonight at Valentine 9279. At 11:30 P.M. exactly."

Letterman was writing that down on a pad.

I said, "Valentine 9279? Where is that?"

"Phone booth in a hotel."

"Here in town?"

"Yes."

"Kansas City? Where in Kansas City?"

"Near the LaSalle Hotel."

"*In* the LaSalle Hotel?"

"Near it. The Something-shire Hotel. Right across from the LaSalle."

"Why didn't you tell me that in the first place? And we'll get instructions for the drop then?"

"Yes."

"Is this another drive in the country? This crap about climbing trees and crawling around on the ground looking for the right rock is getting old. Let's deal man-to-man. Middle of Main Street. Anywhere."

More frowns.

"I would like that too, but I don't have anything to say about it."

"I thought *you* were running the show."

"I'm just 'M'—the middleman. But I'll see to it things go perfectly tonight—no mix-ups. And you'll be contacted about the boy in Pittsburg, Kansas, in the morning."

A click announced the end of the call.

The hotel across from the LaSalle was the Berkshire. Linwood Boulevard at 11:15 P.M. on a Sunday night in downtown Kansas City was underpopulated to say the least and traffic was minimal; tall buildings bore so few lighted windows the effect was black dominos with only occasional white dots.

We pulled in at the entry's drop-off area. Letterman was at the wheel in topcoat and fedora, I was riding with my Burberry unbelted, and the passenger in back was a zippered olive-colored canvas duffel bag with $600,000 dollars of cash stacked within.

This, at least, Greenlease had allowed to be the handiwork of the FBI—the duffel bag had been marked in some undis-closed manner for easy identification. $400,000 was in twenties, $200,000 was in tens, as requested by M days before my arrival (this duffel had gone on several wild goose chases already, due to the incompetent directions of the kidnappers). Seventy employees of President Eisenhower's brother Arthur at Commerce Trust had recorded the serial numbers, all forty-thousand bills were photographed, and FBI agent Wes Grapp had pressed his thumb print to the wrapper of each packet of bills.

The bag of money weighed eighty-five pounds.

This represented the biggest kidnap ransom to date in the United States. Maybe the world, but nobody had seemed to have checked on that. And my presence here was in part connected to that money.

While we'd waited the couple of hours between the last call and the next one, Bob Greenlease in his study had said, "Nate, with no police or FBI tailing us, the possibility some interloper might be watching can't be discounted."

The press hadn't been told the exact amount of the ransom, but it was generally known to be a substantial sum—rumor had it a little low ($500,000) but that was high enough.

"We'll park the car right in front of the hotel," I said, "where it's well-lighted. I'll stay with the money and Will can take M's next call. A Kansas City boy like Will can do better with the instructions than I would."

"I haven't done great so far," Letterman said glumly.

"You'll do fine. But I'm the one who needs to guard that money." I opened my suitcoat and shared the holstered Browning with them. "There's the possibility that M or others he's working with are waiting to snatch this from us right then and there."

Particularly if the boy is already dead—a thought I did not share with Greenlease, though I could sense Letterman was thinking along similar lines.

No doorman was on duty at the Berkshire but the entry with canopy was, as expected, well-lighted. Letterman went in at 11:20. With the motor running, I stayed behind in the loaner Caddy, sliding over behind the wheel, sitting there with my

nine mil in my lap like a getaway man waiting for the bank robbery to wrap up. Twenty minutes or so later, Letterman came
quickly out. I unlocked the driver's-side door and slid back into
the passenger seat.

Greenlease's man got behind the wheel and into gear and
swung out. He filled me in as we went.

"Our 11:30 call came in at 11:31," Letterman said. "The
longest minute of my life."

"Tell me about it." I holstered the nine mil. "Get anywhere?"

"I think so. We're to head east on Highway 40 until it intersects
with County Highway Road 10E—which used to be called Lee's
Summit Road. Turn right at something called Stephenson's
Restaurant and go for about a mile to a covered wooden bridge.
There we throw the bag out on the left side of the road at the
north end of the bridge. M told me they wouldn't be far behind
us."

"This is an area you know?"

"Well enough. The restaurant doesn't ring a bell, but I think
I've been over that bridge before."

"How did he sound?"

"Drunk."

It wasn't much of a drive—southeast of the city about five
miles from Swope Park into a rural area where the only hitch
was the dark night making us miss the junction of 40 and 10E;
we had to backtrack and try again—no sign of anyone following,
at least not yet. This time we turned south on the county road
and soon came to a covered wooden bridge. Midnight now...
midnight on a lonely country road....

I told Letterman to pull over.

He did, then nodded toward the bridge. "Should I leave the
headlights on?"

"No. It'd just make a target of me."

He shut off the beams and the bridge's mouth turned black

and unwelcoming. I got the nine millimeter out again and slipped from the car into the night.

I entered the sheltered structure slowly, cautiously, wood groaning under my feet, sparse moonlight filtering in between slats, my back to a creaky wall, edging along like I was expecting the Headless Horseman at any moment. But no ghost on horse-back came charging and no one was lying in wait—there was really nowhere to do that. I went all the way to the north end and stayed low, gun ready, as I came out. I looked around the low brush on either side of the road, going down the slope on both sides to the narrow gurgling stream.

Nobody.

I climbed back up. There were trees on both sides but anyone who emerged would have shown himself even under that stingy slice of moon.

I returned to the car and got in. "No sign of a soul," I said. "Not L, M, N or P. But go slow."

We rumbled through the rickety bridge and then pulled off to the left as we exited the north end. From the back seat I yanked out the duffel and then the two of us, like gangsters in fedoras and topcoats dragging a dead body, lugged the eighty-five pounds of money—thirty pounds heavier than Bobby Greenlease—to the underbrush just past the north end of the bridge, concealing the duffel just a little, not wanting to attract anyone's attention but M's.

"All right," I said. "Now you head back."

He blinked at me. "You mean *we* head back."

"No. I'm waiting for these bastards." I lifted the nine mil and lowered it, to make a point.

He shook his head—really shook it. "No. We're not taking that kind of chance."

"I'm not asking you to. Don't worry about me getting back, Will. They'll have a car."

He pointed to the Caddy, which sat purring. "Get in, Heller. You heard what Bob said. This is *my* call."

I thought about my options. What could I do, slug him? He was twenty years older than me, and if I knocked him out, who'd drive the car back? It might even kill him, and that only complicated matters.

Well, shit.

We headed back to the Greenlease place.

We were again in the study with the dogs and hunters looking on from their mural. Back in our same seats with the two phones staring at us and us staring at them. Letterman didn't mention our little confrontation to Greenlease and neither did I. We drank a while. I was on my second rum and Coke since our return and Greenlease was behind me, pacing again, but more like trudging now, bourbon sloshing in his glass, when the phones came alive, their doubled ring alarmingly loud.

I'd been appointed phone man again. After the third ring, as arranged, Greenlease was back on the couch next to Letterman, who picked up as I did.

As before, silence.

"You there, M?" I asked.

"Speaking."

"Everything all right with the money?"

The response came in a rush of words: "We haven't had time to count it yet. But I'm sure it's all there. Rest assured the kid will be back with his mother as promised within twenty-four hours."

M didn't sound drunk to me now—more like high....

"How long are we going to have to wait down there before we pick him up?"

By "down there" I meant Pittsburg, Kansas.

M said, "You'll hear in the morning and be told where and when."

"We'll have him tomorrow?"

"Definitely."

"He's alive and well?"

"Yeah, and as full of piss and vinegar as any kid I've ever seen."

This seemed to try a little too hard to make the boy sound... alive. "I can quote you on that, can I?"

"You can quote me."

The phone clicked dead.

I hung up. I looked at Greenlease. I looked at Letterman.

"Well," Letterman said to me, poised to stand, "you and I need to head to Pittsburg."

I shook my head. "No."

Greenlease frowned at me. "No?"

I said to Letterman, "Collect your pal, what's his name? Stew O'Neill? He's had enough time with his family. You two go down to Kansas and have an adventure. You don't need me for that."

Besides, it sounded like a dodge to me. Another snipe hunt.

I rose. "I'll stick around on this end a while in case I'm needed, if you like, Bob. Should our buddy M throw us a curve."

"Well," Letterman said, vaguely offended, "I'm going to head out as soon as I can round up Stew."

"Do that," I said. "I'm going back to my hotel, gentlemen— I'm beat. See you in the morning, Bob. Good luck, Will."

I almost returned Greenlease's check, but something told me I might still earn it.

CHAPTER THREE

I got pulled over briefly at the FBI checkpoint, where Agent Grapp asked me to fill him in, which I did. It was a little after two A.M.

"This little trip Letterman and O'Neill are taking to south Missouri," I said from behind the wheel, "means a state line's been crossed. Surely you can wade in now."

He was leaning in my window like a carhop again; it was cold enough for his breath to smoke and he peered at me above fogged hornrims. "Not unless the kidnappers actually take the kid there. It sounds like the runaround to me."

"No argument. You don't think that boy's still alive, do you?" That forced-sounding remark about piss and vinegar was lingering.

The FBI man's long face got longer. "We have to assume so. And I've been told to follow Mr. Greenlease's lead."

"Because he's a worried father or a big General Motors stockholder?"

The only answer he'd had for that was a smirk as he backed away and waved me on.

Now I was in my hotel room, sitting up in bed with a slit of sun peeking between the closed curtains and the nightstand clock saying it was already after ten A.M. I had left no wake-up call, expecting to hear from Greenlease if anything had broken. Apparently nothing had, except maybe my head. While I hadn't been drunk last night by any means, over the course of a long evening enough rum had been involved to give me a dull headache.

My stomach was in no mood for anything but the cup of

black coffee I grabbed in the President's coffee shop. Then I drove to the Greenlease place in Mission Hills. A different Fed stopped me at the checkpoint, but when I proved who I was passed me on.

Paul Greenlease greeted me again. His suit-and-tie seemed to be standard, for the duration of the kidnapping anyway, and the shyly smiling maid was there to collect my hat and coat. But before escorting me deeper into the big somber house, the older Greenlease son lingered with me in the high-ceilinged, expansive entryway like the only couple on a ballroom dance floor.

"Mr. Heller," he said, and this adopted son looked enough like Greenlease to make a private detective suspicious, "may I ask you something?"

"Of course, Paul. And make it Nate. I'm a friend of the family in this." With a check for five thousand dollars from his father in my billfold, admittedly.

"Now that the ransom has been delivered," he said, stroking his rounded jaw nervously, "will you stay involved?"

"Is there news of your brother?"

"No. Nothing from Pittsburg yet."

I offered a sigh. "It's probably time to let the FBI take over, frankly. That's what I'll be advising your father."

The dark eyes were still bloodshot. "I had the idea that… well, that Dad might want you out there trying to find the people who did this."

"Again, that's probably better handled by the federal investigators, at this point." I shrugged. "I do have means and methods not open to them. Uh, admittedly there are certain…niceties I don't have to respect. So I may be discussing that with your father. Why, son?"

The word "son" had come automatically. For a man in his mid-thirties, he seemed young to me. His high forehead tensed. "Mr. Heller, there's something bothering me that I haven't shared with anyone. Can I trust you not to take this to Dad and Mother?"

The formality of "Mother" next to "Dad" struck me as interesting. Not sure I could tell you why.

"You can trust me to keep your confidence, Paul, unless I think it might bear on bringing your brother home or finding those responsible."

He tried to shrug it off. "It's nothing, really. I shouldn't bother you or…or anybody with it."

"No. Please. Go ahead."

He drew in enough air to make his chest grow; when he let it out, words came along: "I took two of the phone calls. Mostly it's been Mr. Letterman and a few times Mother. But I spoke briefly to this…individual."

"M?"

"M." He lowered his voice to a near whisper. "And this is what I want to share with you. His voice sounded…familiar."

I frowned; put a hand on his shoulder. "You think you may *know* this person?"

"I might. I can't give you a name or anything. I don't think it's one of my friends. I mean, frankly, all of my circle are well-off. Not as well-off as *we* are, but…nobody I know needs money. Nobody needs to do something like, *anything* like…this."

"The voice doesn't remind you of anyone in particular?"

"No. It's almost…eerie. Something, someone, from the past."

"Paul, you aren't old enough to have much of a past."

"I know. Jesus, I know! I've been racking my brain. When I was in military school, and later college, some of us would go out drinking. Could it have been somebody from those days?"

"Could it?"

His eyebrows went up and came down. "The voice on the phone sounded drunk to me."

"And to me. Letterman commented on it, too."

"If I come up with something, can I bring it to you?"

"Of course."

"If I did get a hunch about who this might be, maybe you could look into it without getting some innocent guy in trouble."

Did he already have a hunch? I really didn't think so. But he was right—it might come to him.

I said, "Be glad to." I gave him an A-1 business card. "If I wind up going back to Chicago, call me there."

His eyes widened. "Are you planning to go back to Chicago?"

"No, but I might. If the FBI steps in and your father doesn't have any further need of me." I offered him my hand. "Thank you, Paul. Thank you for coming to me with this."

We shook. Firmly, this time. He smiled a little and nodded, then led me to the library where his father and the hunting wall mural awaited, then quietly slipped away.

Greenlease was sitting on the couch with his little blonde daughter, who wore a green corduroy jumper and was reading a Nancy Drew book, *The Ringmaster's Secret*. She looked up at me, but didn't smile, still wary of me. The kid was a good judge of character.

"Darling," Greenlease told the girl, getting to his feet, "I need to talk to Mr. Heller."

She nodded and returned her eyes to the page while her father escorted me through the double doors onto a patio that looked onto fiery-topped trees and a browning golf course. The sun was out and the chill of the night before had backed off some. We sat at a wrought-iron table on wrought-iron chairs.

"I'm afraid we've heard nothing," he said solemnly.

"Paul told me. He's a nice young man."

"He is. I'm going to set him up in a dealership of his own one of these days." He shifted on the metal chair. "Will and Stew got to Pittsburg around 5:30 this morning. Checked into the

Hotel Besse, caught a little sleep—Will had been up forty hours. They were at the Western Union office at seven when it opened. They took along fresh clothes for Bobby, including a topcoat."

I didn't know what to say to that. It was just so goddamned sad.

"They're maintaining a sort of vigil," he said. "We talk on the hour. Do you have any suggestions?"

I told him it was time to let Agent Grapp take over. "Bob, the FBI have cracked hundreds of kidnapping cases over the last several decades, almost always with a successful outcome. Sometimes kidnapped parties stay in their captors' hands for weeks before their return. So this is far from over."

He nodded, his expression dazed; his dark blue eyes rarely blinked behind the browline glasses. "We'll let the Pittsburg thing play out," he said. A light wind was turning the wispy white hair atop the rounded square of his head into dead-dandelion tufts that refused to fly away.

"Bob, is there anything more I can do for you on this end?"

His head shake was understandably weary. "I don't believe so, Nate."

I got out my billfold and removed the check. As I handed it his way, the light wind whipping it a little, he raised two palms.

"That's not necessary, Nate. You've earned it."

"No. I'll send you an invoice for five hundred dollars—that'll cover my time and any expenses. Hotel and airfare were pre-paid, so this isn't generous of me in the least."

I kept the check held out and it flapped like the golf course flag on a nearby hole. Finally he took the thing before the wind did.

The thin line of his mouth said, "But if I need you..."

"You'll have me. I'm opening a New York office next month,

so you may have to get in touch there. My people in Chicago will help you on that score."

"You sound busy."

I leaned an elbow on a glass tabletop. "Listen. I have a six-year-old myself, remember. You need me, I'm here. In the meantime—and you've probably thought of this—I'd get a priest in to talk to the family. Maybe a nurse for your wife."

He looked alarmed. "Nate, do you anticipate bad news?"

"Let me ask you. Is Bobby high-strung?"

A rare blink came. "No. I suppose it's fair to say he's been sheltered. Pampered, perhaps. We love him very much. Such a good boy."

Which was why he'd been trusting enough to go with a strange woman when she came for him at his school. To a child, the world of adults is unknowable—you did what they told you to.

"That 'piss and vinegar' remark," I said. "Did that ring true to you?"

Greenlease said nothing. He looked toward the golf course. Some fools were playing. Hadn't snowed yet.

Finally, he said, "No." Then his eyes came to mine. "You think he's dead. That's why you're talking about priests and nurses."

"I think you need to prepare yourself for the possibility. Your wife, too. In the meantime, get the FBI on this full-throttle. If the worst happens, I can ask people I know in my world and see if we can find the bitch who took your boy and this bastard M, too. The feds can trace serial numbers. But I know how to trace lowlife scum."

I got to my feet and so did he. We shook hands and went back inside, where he returned to his daughter's side. Finally she smiled at me, just a little. But it was enough.

I was on my way out, back in my Burberry with my hat in

hand, when an unfamiliar female voice called out to me, although I immediately knew just who it was.

"Oh, Mr. Heller?" The voice was a sweet, soft second soprano. "Would you wait a moment?"

I turned and a tall nicely built woman in her mid-forties approached from down the hall; her hair dark and short and well-coiffed, she was attractive in a dignified manner, reminiscent of Irene Dunne in some late '30s tearjerker. She wore a navy suit, white silk blouse and low heels, as if ready for church on this Monday. Of course Catholics went to church all sorts of times we heathens couldn't keep track of.

"We may have met years ago," she said. "I know you've done a number of jobs for Bob." She seemed utterly composed, but her dark eyes screamed red like her husband's.

She had offered her hand for me to take—not a handshake, but for me to hold, which I did in both of mine. "No, Mrs. Greenlease, I would have remembered. I can't tell you how sorry I am about all this."

"You were very kind to come from Chicago to help us," she said. "I understand you played a crucial role last night."

I wished I'd played a more crucial role, like grabbing that M by the goddamn throat when he picked the money up and squeezed out of him what he'd done with her son.

I said, "I have a boy Bobby's age. Glad to do anything to help. I'm heading back to Chicago for now, but I'll be on call."

Her smile was a lightly lipsticked wound. "You were on the Lindbergh case, I understand."

Oh, Christ—not that again.

I risked the smallest smile. "Yes, I was a liaison between the authorities there and the Chicago police department—I didn't have my own agency then."

"Why a liaison?"

"Well, Al Capone was claiming he could get the child back through his underworld connections if we'd just let him out. All kinds of crazy things were going on back then."

Her hand was still in mine. "Are things really any different now?"

"Yes, and for the better. Out of that tragedy came the FBI's ability to look into this kind of crime. I've advised Bob to let them take over. People like me, and family friends like Will Letterman, can only do so much."

Her smile widened enough to reveal perfect white teeth. "That sounds like good advice. But we've had wonderful help. Paul has been just a dear. I don't know what…" The tears she was holding back were pooling, threatening to overflow, and the smile was crinkling.

She hugged me. Cried into my shoulder, quietly, softly, but she cried. That was what this had come to: a mother needing a stranger's shoulder to cry on.

She drew away, leaned in and kissed me on the cheek, and nodded, slightly, embarrassed now, and turned away and started up the stairs. But then she paused two steps up, at the first landing, and leaned a hand on the newel-post lion.

"You know, Mr. Heller…Bob and I would be lost without our faith in God's constant and abiding love. Even in our darkest hours, we know God is holding each one of us in this family very close. Bobby included."

As if ascending into heaven, she went slowly up.

Me, I had my doubts. If God was in this, He might have whispered in the ear of the young nun who was so quick to hand over their kid.

And that was it.

I booked a late afternoon flight back by phone, then made a call to my partner Lou Sapperstein at the A-1 in Chicago, letting him know I'd be in tomorrow. Lou had a few things that couldn't wait and we took care of those over the phone. I hadn't bothered with a shower before going out to the Greenleases', so I took one now. Then my minor hangover was dogging me enough to encourage lying down and I fell asleep for a while.

The two o'clock check-out time had come and gone when I awoke. Brushed my teeth, packed hurriedly and went down to the palatial lobby, which was pretty dead again. I was waiting for a salesman from somewhere to settle up his bill when a voice called out to me. This one was male and I didn't recognize it—a husky baritone.

"Nate! Nate Heller!"

I turned and a big man—and I mean *big*, six-four and pushing four hundred pounds—came trundling toward me like a runaway circus elephant. Appropriately, he was in a tent of a brown suit with a yellow and red tie adding a clownish splash of color. His oblong head was too small for his massive body, eyes close-set and an unexpectedly pretty light blue, eyebrows perpetually high, hair curly black and pomaded, mouth small and thick-lipped, a little chin enveloped by a thick neck rising from the preposterous torso.

Distinctive as this individual was, I didn't recognize him at first.

"Nate, I heard you were in town!"

"...Barney Baker?"

"In the flesh," he said in a surprisingly mellow, mellifluous baritone. "What, have I changed so much? Okay, so maybe I put a few pounds on in the interim."

He'd been big when I knew him before, but another hundred or so had been added.

We shook hands. That fat paw of his could generate real power.

Barney Baker, who looked fifty and was probably forty, had

been one of Ben Siegel's bouncers at the Flamingo in Las Vegas back in '46. Siegel (Don't Call Him Bugsy) had hired me to train security personnel at his new casino with an emphasis on spotting pickpockets—I'd been on the Pickpocket Detail of the Chicago PD a thousand years ago.

Even back at the Flamingo, Barney had been such a hulking presence he merely had to tap the shoulder of a troublemaker, who would turn and get a gander of the looming bouncer and look for the nearest exit with no further inducement. Not that Barney couldn't do damage if need be. He had come with an impressive résumé—a waterfront collector in his teens who did a prison stretch in New York for throwing stink bombs in theaters during a union drive.

"You had lunch, Nate?"

He was the sort of guy who kept track of such things.

"No," I said. "I thought I'd catch something at the airport."

He settled a catcher's mitt hand on my shoulder. "Listen, let me buy you lunch. We got things to talk about."

We do?

"All right," I said, "just let me check out."

Which I did, leaving my overnight bag at the desk, and Barney slipped an overwhelming arm around my shoulder and walked me across the lobby to the coffee shop like a parent escorting an apprehensive child to the doctor's office.

We took a table—Barney couldn't fit into a booth—and I asserted myself. "Who told you I was in Kansas City?"

He was looking at the menu. "That colored cab driver who drove you to the Greenlease place in Mission Hills."

"Why would he confide that to anybody?"

"The cab company keeps track of public-figure types who come to town. Can be valuable information. You should feel complimented."

I smirked. "Why would you be privy to such valuable information?"

His big shoulders shrugged. "I'm their union representative. Ace Cabs are run out of St. Louis, which is where I'm out of, too, these days. I was in K.C. on union business and got the call about this just, oh, half an hour ago."

"What call?"

"The call pertaining to you."

I squinted at him. "When did you get so goddamn eloquent, Barney? I recall you being a dese, dem and doser."

He waved a plump thing with fingers. "A union organizer has to be both a man of the people and a decent public speaker. I give a hell of a speech, Nate. You should hear me on Civil Rights. Nobody stirs up the colored vote like yours truly. I'm a good Democrat, you know."

So was I, but that was enough to make me question my party affiliation.

"Ah," he said, and his eyes glittered, "here's the waitress. Pretty little babe, don't you think?"

She was indeed, a pretty blonde and pretty bored, weighing about a hundred pounds, a considerably better-looking hundred than the one Barney had added on. I ordered the clubhouse sandwich with potato chips and cole slaw. Barney had a triple order of the boneless butt steak with mushroom sauce and triple french fries; it came with three salads too, but he passed on those. Cutting down, I guess.

I figured he would get around to what this was about soon enough. Till then, I thought we could stand some catching up.

"So after they bumped Ben," I said, "you went back into union work, huh?"

"Yeah, the Teamsters. I was president of local 730 in D.C. for a while. Then opportunity knocked here in the Midwest.

You done all right for yourself, Nate. L.A. office and every-thing. You get around. I mean, here you are in Kansas City."

"Here I am. And what's that to a union organizer who spe-cializes in cab companies?"

Our drinks came—Coca-Cola for me, coffee with cream and sugar for Barney. The disturbingly nice blue eyes looked rather fondly at me.

"What I always liked about you, Nate, is your attitude toward money. There were lines you wouldn't cross. But also, there were lines you didn't mind crossing. Or are you too respectable now to turn your nose up at a good opportunity? Let me give you a hypothetical."

"A what? When did you drop out of school, Barney?"

"After the third grade."

"Ah."

"But I learned to read by then. So. If we can get hypothetical and all? Suppose there was a despicable fucking crime like a kid getting snatched."

I can't say I didn't see this coming, but it rocked me a little just the same.

Very quietly I said, "If you were involved in such a thing, Barney, I would gladly kill your un-hypothetical ass. I assume there are *some* vital organs still lurking under all of that blubber."

His frown looked hurt, not mad. "Unkind, Nate. You ever know me taking part in an act of such a lowdown nature? You recall me ever doing something so criminal I'd go straight to Hell and take it up the ass from the Devil himself for all eternity?"

"Hey, you brought it up, Barney, and frankly? I never knew you all that well. Here's the food."

It came and we ate. Conversation ceased. He frowned throughout the meal, annoyed when he would rather just be savoring the enjoyment of shoveling butt steak between his thick lips. Somewhat surprisingly, he finished his three orders about the time I finished mine. He had tapioca coming with his meal. That came, was gone in seconds, and then he had another cup of coffee and I sprang for a second Coke, though I pretty much let it sit. I leaned back with my arms folded, kind of wishing the nine millimeter weren't in my overnight bag at the desk.

"Hypothetically," he said, very quietly, "we may have a line on the snatch."

"No participation."

"No."

I unfolded my arms, sat forward, folded my hands prayerfully on the table as if tacking grace on after the meal. "Let's skip the phony hypothetical bullshit, Barney. What's this about?"

He took a couple of moments before answering, patting his mouth with a napkin almost daintily. "You know Joe Costello?"

"I don't know him. I know *of* him. He and that Vitale character are the top rackets guys in St. Louis, they say."

Barney nodded. " 'They' are well-informed. Anyway. There's a guy calls himself Steve who approaches an Ace cabbie this very morning looking for a hooker, but he doesn't want to go to a house—he wants a 'real nice girl.' The guy is loaded with dough, a regular angel first-class."

An angel, as cabbies and pimps called them, was a big spender, usually from out of town.

"Steve, in addition to throwing money around like it's going out of style," Barney said, "is also going from bar to bar in the daylight hours with the kind of thirst you can't quench. As he gets deeper in his cups, he starts talking."

"About the kidnapping?"

A stop palm came up fast. "No, no, no. Steve is some kind of insurance guy, he says, who has come into dough and not in a legal way. Steve says he has a bundle, and he wants it washed. Afraid the bills might be marked."

What kind of insurance man had access to cash that might be marked bills? This sounded a lot more like a kidnapper than an embezzler.

Barney was saying, "One of our Ace guys got our buddy Steve a hooker, who can be trusted or at least for a hooker can be, and at some point our guy got a glimpse at stacks and stacks of green in a footlocker."

Not a duffel bag.

"Maybe," Barney went on, "our insurance guy really is somebody in insurance or at a bank who's helped himself, and is worried about serial numbers. In which case, Joe is not concerned."

"Joe Costello."

"Joe Costello, who owns the Ace Cab Company. He has no moral compunctions about washing money from a bank or insurance company, either. But a kidnapping would be immoral. Joe has kids. I got kids. Who doesn't have kids?"

Also, a racketeer who got dirtied by a notorious in-the-headlines kidnapping would not be looked upon kindly by public officials who might otherwise turn a blind eye in return for a filled palm.

I was at a stage of my professional life where normally I would not want anything to do with embezzlers whether the take was insurance or bank money. Hell, I had clients in both lines of business. But this sounded like it might be the path to the Greenlease kidnappers—the kind of path I could follow more effectively than the by-the-book likes of Wes Grapp.

"Look, Nate," Barney said. Usually loud, the union goon was almost whispering now. "Joe wants to bring you in. What exactly he has in mind, I don't know. You *sure* you don't know him? 'Cause it sure seems like he knows you."

"What if this bundle is the kidnap ransom?"

He swiped the air with a sideways hand. "If Steve is the kidnapper, we finger the fucker. Call in the cops. We got plenty of 'em in our pocket." He had something else in his pocket, too, and he shoved it toward me: an engraving in green of Grover Cleveland.

In other words, a thousand-dollar bill. With a business card attached: *Joseph G. Costello, President, Ace Cab Company, Taylor Avenue and Forest Park Boulevard.*

"That's just to come to St. Louis and talk to Joe," Barney said. "You don't even have to tell the tax boys about it. That's between you and your conscience."

I got my wallet out and slid the bill in. Barney apparently didn't know my conscience was packed away in my overnight bag.

"You got wheels?" he asked.

"Yeah."

"You go on ahead and see Joe. I got business here. You may not see me in St. Louis."

Was I supposed to be disappointed?

I got to my feet and put my wallet away. "Despite this windfall, Barney, I'll let you get lunch. I don't buy anybody three meals in one sitting."

He tossed a fat hand. "Fair enough."

The waitress was back and he asked her what kind of pie they had.

CHAPTER FOUR

The front desk traded me a roll of quarters for a ten-dollar bill and, just off the lobby, I selected a phone booth from a row and settled in. An operator gave me the numbers I needed and the first call I made was to the airline at the Kansas City Municipal Airport, cancelling my reservation for a flight back to Chicago.

The second call was a quick one to Lou Sapperstein at the A-1 telling him I might not be back for a few days. The third was to the Pittsburg, Missouri, Western Union office; I was told that the two gentlemen waiting for an important wire had gone back to their hotel, but that if it came in, a runner would take it over. The fourth was to Pittsburg's Hotel Besse, where the hotel switchboard connected me to the room shared by William Letterman and Stewart O'Neill.

"I thought," Letterman's voice said, "you'd be on a plane by now back to Chicago."

He and Greenlease were talking "on the hour," so his knowing that was no surprise.

"I just cancelled that," I said.

"We've had no word."

"I gathered. How long are you going to wait for M to get in touch?"

"Another day at least."

"That kid isn't coming home, you know."

"…I have to keep a good thought, Nate. What can I do for you?"

"I need to get word to Bob and I don't dare call him. The feds will be listening in."

"They've been listening in all along."

I knew that. But they'd been sitting on their hands, so what good had it done? That they hadn't traced M's calls was damn near as criminal as the kidnapping itself. I didn't blame Wes Grapp for that—complying with Greenlease's wishes was a directive that came from the top.

I said, "I need you to tell Bob I have a possible lead in St. Louis on the kidnappers. It may be nothing, but there are promising aspects."

"Can you be specific, Nate?"

"No. Just remind Bob what I told him about my ability to track down lowlife scum. Tell him this may be a long shot, but I'm going to play it out. I won't do anything to endanger his boy. Tell him I'll report in when or if I have anything."

"All right. You're sure this is wise?"

"Of course not." What would have been wise was Letterman letting me grab M at the ransom drop, but that hadn't happened. I referred to that only indirectly: "We're past playing it safe being a good plan. Tell Bob I'll be holding onto the loaner Caddy. In a day or two, I'll return it and, with luck, have something to report."

"Maybe you'll be bringing Bobby back, too."

Letterman had to know he was kidding himself.

"Yeah," I said. "Go with that."

They called Highway 40 the Main Street of America, and one reason might be that driving from Kansas City to St. Louis made you slow down for half a dozen bump-in-the-road Main Streets and a major one through Columbia. The trip took better than four hours, and though the slice of moon was even smaller tonight, the sky was clear, the traffic light and the sailing smooth, some of it four-lane. Fighting boredom, I tried the big car's fancy radio but the result went a little too well with the farm country I was cruising through—I heard more fiddle playing than in a Hungarian restaurant.

Finally St. Louis showed itself, its light hovering as if promising a carnival. I followed 40 into the city through an industrial area, turning onto Nineteenth cutting through a nest of apartment buildings before factories and warehouses took over. Ace Cab Company, at 1835 Washington Avenue, shared its downtown intersection with an Esso Station, a Katz Drug and a busy White Castle. I parked on the street in front of a Swiss Chalet-style shopping arcade.

Ruling over a modest parking lot with two rows of varicolored and varied-make taxis, the dingy white-brick building's mechanics in dingy white uniforms were at work under vehicles on lifts in the two-bay garage. On the far end, a picture window an-nounced the place in big red letters as, not surprisingly, ACE CAB COMPANY, with a couple of phone numbers not much smaller.

I pushed through a door that said, in the same red lettering, EMPLOYEES ONLY. At left, a blond male dispatcher in khaki hunkered over a microphone in front of a metal city map dotted by magnetic pins; at right, a henna-dyed looker in a white blouse, black slacks and a headset sat at a switchboard. Both were shouting numbers and locations.

Covering his mike, the dispatcher—a burly guy of maybe thirty who glared at me like I'd interrupted him in the middle of a song—said, "You Heller?"

I resisted the impulse to say, "Me Jane," and just nodded.

Half a dozen cabbies were seated in wooden schoolhouse chairs with their backs to the big window on the street, a rough-looking bunch who made the Bowery Boys look like actual boys. All but one wore matching caps with triangular

ACE CAB patches but otherwise—like the cars in the lot—they were a mixed bunch, in jackets of leather, corduroy, gabardine, several in neckties, one in a bow tie. Their shirts ranged from white to pale blue to pale what-have-you. Two of the cabbies were colored; they were the only ones with white shirts.

"Go on in," the dispatcher said in a grudging, we-don't-cotton-to-strangers-in-this-here-town way. Probably an in-law. The switchboard redhead glanced at me with a little smile and shrug. Probably a mistress.

There was only one door, so I didn't have any questions. In I went.

The scarred-up wooden desk was older than I was, the top empty of anything but a cup of coffee and a butt-filled glass ashtray, in a small office as dingy as the outer building and the mechanics in the two-bay garage. But the man at the desk—slender, mid-forties, with sandy, curly hair—was if anything spiffy. He wore a gray suit and a white shirt buttoned at the neck, no tie; a snap-brim fedora sat back rather jauntily, its indoor use suggesting he might be bald.

"Nate Heller!" He vaguely resembled Bing Crosby. He stood and shoved his hand across the desk at me like a spear. I shook it. You'd think we were old pals.

"Mr. Costello?" I said tentatively.

"Joe. Why would we stand on formality?"

He seemed to know me, and by more than just reputation. But if we'd met, I didn't recall. He told me to make myself comfortable—"Take off your coat and stay a while!"—and I hung the Burberry and Dobbs on a corner coat tree with his own topcoat. I was in the Richard Bennett, by the way, cut for the holstered nine mil.

That precaution had to do with the type of cab company Ace almost certainly was—not that it was an unusual type for a city the size of St. Louis, or a lot of cities either, of any size. Certain cabbies all across America were rolling pimps, ready to fix up a visitor to their fair communities with female companionship, games of chance, and assorted other illegal recreational activities.

Beyond that, this cab company was run by a top Gateway City mob guy, said to be a front for fencing stolen goods, smuggled firearms and burgled jewels. I didn't know Joe Costello personally, but I knew he'd done time on robbery raps in his salad days, and in his main-course years had made a rep setting up heists for others to pull off.

Looking like Bob Hope's co-star in *Road to Alcatraz*, Costello folded his hands on the desk—whether he was intentionally showing off that big gold-set diamond ring, I couldn't tell you. On the wall behind him were framed photos, all hanging crooked, of Joe and a narrow-faced, hooded-eye guy who looked vaguely familiar, taken over a period of time—shaking hands, smiling, laughing, sometimes with a cab in the background, other times in a barroom.

I pulled another of those wooden schoolhouse chairs over and sat down. "You paid well for the right to see me here in St. Louis. What can I do for you?"

"Maybe it's what I can do for you." Like Bing, he was a baritone, though not melodic. "You still working for the Greenlease family?"

"I was about to head back to Chicago when your friend Barney Baker caught up with me. I'm on call if Bob Greenlease needs me. Uh, Mr. Costello—"

"Joe. Please. I mean, Nate, I feel like I *know* you."

I eyed him. "Why do you feel like you know me, Joe?"

He jerked a thumb over his shoulder. "Are you kidding? I *owe* you, friend."

Was he pointing at those pictures?

I asked, "Who is that anyway?"

"You really don't recognize him? My late partner. We ran the

Clover Club on Delmar together. Then we opened up Ace— he's the one came up with the slogan, 'Call an Ace cab for ace service.' He never spoke ill of you, Nate. And him and me, we was like brothers."

And then I finally recognized that narrow, jug-eared face: Leo Brothers! In June 1930, Jake Lingle, a mobbed-up Tribune leg man who phoned scoops in to rewrite men, was in the pedestrian walkway beneath Michigan Avenue, about to catch the 1:30 p.m. to Washington Park racetrack, when someone shot him in the head. Leo Brothers took the fall for it, identified on the witness stand by a uniformed cop who'd been paid off by the Capone mob. Brothers, also paid off, did eight years of a fourteen-year sentence, and the cop got promoted to plainclothes. His name was Nathan Heller.

"Your buddies in Chicago," Costello said pleasantly, "set Leo up here with me in the Clover Club after he got out. Piece of luck for yours truly. I knew Leo from the old days when I was driving cab and he was union organizing. This is all news to you?"

"I heard the Outfit took care of him," I admitted.

"Took care of him in a *good* way," Costello clarified with a grin. "Nate, I never heard him say a bad word about you. Matter of fact, when you turned up in the papers or the true detective magazines, he always laughed and said, 'My old pal Nate Heller—the man who made me!' "

Made him was right—made him in court as a man running away from the scene of the Lingle murder. And yet I'd never spoken to Brothers in my life. But I wasn't surprised I'd made an impression.

I asked, "What's become of my...old pal?"

Costello made a sad click in a cheek. "Booze and gambling and babes caught up with him, couple years ago."

"How so?"

"Ah, well, when he drank he got hotheaded, and he was known to slap a mouthy broad now and again. He made his share of enemies here, too, frankly, getting tough with help who was holding out. Not every driver we hire is a fuckin' boy scout. Somebody shot him through his screen door in the kitchen grabbing a beer from the fridge. Three times. And it took him three months to go. Tough man, my partner."

"My condolences," I said. "But you didn't send Barney Baker to flag me down with a grand because it's Old Home Week."

"No. But before I make my pitch, I want you to get the low-down on this Good-time Charley my boys have been driving around town all day."

Then began a parade of the mostly questionable-looking cabbies I'd seen lined up in the outer area. Each came in and stood with cap in hand like this was the office at school and Costello was the principal.

It's about eight o'clock, the first cabbie said, a flat-nosed character who referred to his logbook, *when I get called to the Sportsman's Bar at 3500 South Jefferson. This guy who needs a shave is with a blowsy blonde who must have drunk her breakfast. Guy says he's Steve Strand and this is his wife Bonnie, and somebody broke into their car and stole their luggage. He wants me to take them to the nearest pawnshop so he can buy replacements. I don't know of any pawnshops around there, but we get in the cab and drive around.*

Nothing.

I even pull over and ask a couple of times.

Nothing.

Finally I head downtown and find a pawnshop but it's closed. Slay's Bar at 114 Broadway is open. We go in and Steve has a shot of Walker's Deluxe whiskey and so does Bonnie, twice. They buy me a drink...just a Coke, Mr. Costello, just a Coke...while we wait for the Army Store at 17 North Broadway to open at nine.

Nine comes, and Steve goes off to buy luggage and comes back with a green footlocker and a black suitcase. Both metal. Both empty. I load 'em in the trunk. They have me take 'em back to the Sportsman's Bar and unload the footlocker and suitcase onto the sidewalk. They pay me. I go.

I find their behavior peculiar and take a spin around the block. On the return trip, I see 'em loading the luggage in the blue Ford's trunk. I look to see if any windows in the car look busted, because of what they said about it being broken into. All the windows was rolled up and looked fine.

I get called to the Hi-Nabor Buffet at 2801 Wyoming Street, said the second cabbie, mustached, fifty, *which sounds like a restaurant but is mostly a bar. It's just after ten a.m. and they're drinking bourbon.*

They have some metal luggage, a footlocker and a suitcase. I go out and put them in the trunk but they are so heavy I can hardly lift them. Steve asks me to take him to buy a used car. But the woman, who is drunker than he is, says, 'No, take us to the bus station downtown.'

I take them to the Greyhound Bus Depot at Broadway and Delmar. Help them unload the luggage. The fare is a buck twenty-five. He pays with two one-dollar bills and lets me keep half a dollar. This is around 10:35 a.m.

I picked them up outside the bus station at 10:45, a round-faced young colored cabbie said, no more than twenty-five, *and they were arguing but I can't tell you about what. I had to load a couple of heavy pieces of luggage in my trunk, a footlocker and a metal suitcase.*

The guy had me drop them at Columbo's Bar at 3132 South Kingshighway. They paused and seemed about to cross the street where there are a couple of used car lots. Then they made like a bee to honey into that bar, guy dragging the footlocker and the blonde lugging the suitcase. They could hardly manage it, heavy as that stuff was and drunk as skunks as they was.

Maybe two o'clock in the afternoon, the middle-aged heavyset cabbie said, *I was in the Old Shillelagh Bar at 3157 Morganford Road, catching a few innings of the World Series—sixth and deciding game! Yankees beat the Dodgers four to three.*

Guy sat down next to me...Huh? No, he didn't have a woman with him. Watched a while, had a drink or two; said his name was Steve Strand, like that was a big deal. Musta noticed my cap, because he said, 'You on duty? I can use a ride to Hampton Village.' You know, the shopping center? He was looking for an appliance store, but neglected to say so. They don't got one at Hampton Village, and Jesus, there's one right across from where we was before at the Shillelagh!

I take him to Petruso Electrical Appliance and he buys a radio for twenty-eight bucks. Says he likes to keep track of the news. I say, yeah, I like to be up on things, too. He wanted a box for it but the clerk only had a box that was too big. That only made the guy happy. He said, 'It swims in this one!' A nut, this guy. And drunk, though not falling-down drunk. Just loosey goosey.

I drop him and his big box with the little radio on Arsenal Street, and good riddance.

No, I'm not with Ace Cabs—I'm with the Laclede Company, the driver said, Negro and older than the others, hair and mustache salt-and-pepper. *But Mr. Costello here called my supervisor and I'm glad to help out.*

I picked this Steve Strand fare up at the Squeeze Box tavern at 3225 Morganford Road. He was drunk. I would say very drunk. And he was free with his money in a way that could get him in trouble....How so? He got in, handed me a twenty-dollar bill, and said, 'Just drive. Just drive around.' Then, as I did that, he dozed off.

He woke up after five, perhaps ten, minutes. Said, 'I'd like to have a girl. I don't want to go to a whorehouse, understand! I want a nice girl.'

I told him I didn't provide that kind of service. He handed me up a second twenty-dollar bill and...well, that's a lot of money. I told him I could drive him downtown to a driver I knew who might help him. That pleased him.

On the way, he asked to stop at Arsenal Street. He said he had an apartment there. He had some sample cases he wanted to pick up—he was, he said, a salesman of some kind. Then he spotted a tavern, Brownie's just east of Gravois Avenue on Arsenal, and told me to pull over. He wanted a quick drink. I waited for him. Then he went inside his apartment house and I again waited outside. He returned twice, first with a metal suitcase, then with a footlocker. Struggling with them.

We loaded up my trunk with them, or I should say I loaded them up—he was bent over catching his breath. How much did they weigh? The suitcase, thirty to thirty-five pounds. The foot-locker, forty to fifty pounds. He seemed very concerned about them, making sure they were locked.

We set out again, and I took him to the Jefferson Hotel, where I thought I might find Johnny Hagan. I knew that Johnny had several girls he, uh, worked with. He was happy to take Steve off my hands, and helped me load that heavy luggage in his own trunk.

❖

Next in was a broad-shouldered, black-haired lady-killer about five ten, his handsome, five o'clock-shadowed features compromised only by a scar through his upper lip. He wore the cap of his trade with triangular ACE CAB patch, a black leather zippered jacket, a yellow shirt with a red tie, pleated wide leg pants, and black-and-white wingtips.

Costello said, "This is Johnny Hagan, Nate."

Hagan came over, took his cap off with his left hand and offered his right. Without getting up, I shook it and nodded. He pulled up another wooden chair and angled it toward me. While Hagan spoke, Costello made a muffled phone call, keeping his voice down, but I caught it: "Yeah, he's here....Filling him in...Yeah....Yeah."

There's a few girls I work with, Hagan said, *but the best of 'em is Sandy O'Day. Smart and good-looking and honest for, you know, a doxy. Perfect for a big spender like this Steve character.*

I pick her up at her apartment over on North Ninth Street, and she gets in back with Steve and they hit it off fine. I take 'em to McNamee's Bar at 2500 St. Louis Avenue for a couple of drinks, beer for Steve and me, highball for Sandy. The only thing that gives me, you know, pause was he had a bulge in his right-hand coat pocket. Might be a gun, so suddenly I think maybe my fare's a vice cop.

I follow him to the can and at the urinals, I say, 'Steve, I'm only fixing you up with Sandy as a favor. You wouldn't return a favor by busting me, would you? I mean, you aren't a cop, are you?'

'Johnny boy,' he says, 'if you knew the truth, you'd know just how wrong you are.'

Back at the bar, he pays for the drinks with a twenty and pushes the change across the table to me, and says, 'Here, it's all yours.' Which is when I realize I better not let this angel fly away.

I decide to take Steve and Sandy to the Coral Court Motel, where a lot of us hackies got an arrangement. We make a couple of stops—a drugstore for Steve to buy some shaving gear, then a liquor store for some bourbon and cigarettes. After that Steve gives me five twenties, saying, 'Here's some money on account.'

I get them checked in at the Coral Court around five. Registered as Mr. and Mrs. Robert White of Chicago. I help them haul that damn footlocker and suitcase up to room 49-A on the second floor. I hang around a while. We have some drinks, some laughs. Steve talks about how he likes to go on benders for three or four days at a crack. How it's nothing to him to spend two or three G's on a good time.

That footlocker and suitcase are just sitting on the floor by the wall. Steve goes over and cracks open the suitcase and pulls out a fistful of bills. Sandy and me can see in for a second and it looks like the damn suitcase is jammed with money. Steve goes over to the bed and starts counting what he grabbed, but is too drunk to make a go of it. He has me do it and it's $2,480. He takes a twenty from his pocket and makes it an even $2,500, and says, 'Johnny, hold onto this for me.'

He says he wants to go nightclubbing and needs some fresh clothes and I should use part of the twenty-five hundred to buy him a nice white silk shirt, some underwear, some socks. Sandy says she is not dressed for an evening out and asks me to go to her place and get her some things.

Which is how I got away from there for a while.

But before I go Steve grabs my arm and says, 'Johnny, you seem like you know people. You cabbies always do.' And I say I suppose I do. And he asks if I know anybody who would buy marked money off him. Money where the serial numbers have been recorded.

And I say I might.

So I come here, fill in Mr. Costello, who already seems to know about this Steve spreading money around town while he drinks like a fish. For now Sandy's keeping him busy.

That's about it.

Costello said, "Thanks, Johnny. Wait outside a minute. Nate will be joining you, I think."

Hagan got up, gave me a little grin and a nod and went out, cap still in hand.

I said, "The woman with this Strand character could be the one who picked Bobby Greenlease up at that Catholic school. And Strand himself could be 'M,' the guy making phone calls and writing letters who got the ransom payoff last night."

"Could be," Costello said. "But if he's the insurance man he claims, and it's money he embezzled, or otherwise stolen…and needs laundering…that's *my* business and not the FBI or cops or nobody's."

Leo Brothers was looking at me over his partner's shoulder. That was why I was here: my host didn't know my relationship with the Outfit had been largely reluctant and had mostly faded away when my patron, Frank Nitti, died ten years ago. But to Joe Costello I was still just another crooked cop. Ex-cop, at that.

"But I want nothing to do with kidnapping," Costello said. "Particularly not a child. I'm a fucking father, five times over! If it's just garden-variety dirty money, we'll wash it. But if this Strand pulled the Greenlease snatch, then we turn him in and get credit from the cops and all of St. Louis for doing a public service."

And maybe, I thought, *if this is M, I could find out if that kid was alive and, if so, where he's being held.*

Or was *I* kidding myself now?

"Either way," Costello said, "there's another four grand in it for you, Nate."

Looked like I was getting my five thousand after all. "How do you propose we go about this, Joe?"

He flipped a hand. "We'll have Johnny Hagan introduce you as a mobbed-up PI from Chicago who has to approve laundering the insurance cash."

A knock came at the door. "Joe—it's me!"

Costello gave me a conspiratorial smile, whispering, "That's Lt. Lou Shoulders. Rugged copper, handy with a pistol—three kills on duty.... Come in, Lou!"

A big bucket-headed guy in a baggy black suit burst in like an undertaker late for the embalming. Maybe fifty-five, he had features as baggy as the suit, his Vitalis-heavy hair black, white at the temples, eyebrows bushy.

"Nate Heller, this is Lt. Louis Shoulders."

Shoulders, who lived up to his name, was a little taller than me and I had no urge to look up at him, so I stood and we shook hands in a half-hearted, perfunctory way.

"My contact at the PD, and now yours," Costello said. "Lou and me been pals for years. We both started out driving cabs. You run into trouble, he's your man."

"Mr. Heller," Shoulders said amiably, dark eyes cold, "here's my card. Home number on the back. Joe here's explained the situation. I'll be right behind you."

If he racked up his fourth on-duty kill, I'd prefer it was the other way around.

CHAPTER FIVE

My headlights careened off the golden glazed ceramic-brick walls and glass-block windows of the array of Streamline Moderne bungalows that lurked on a slight slope among towering pin oaks like invaders from another planet getting ready to make their move.

I pulled the Caddy into the motor court drive at 7755 Watson Road in the St. Louis suburb of Marlborough, following Johnny Hagan in his '49 Chevy taxicab. Each of over thirty two-unit, brown-trimmed, round-cornered structures on the winding drive through the well-manicured several acres had a room on either side of paired white-door garages providing unusual privacy for motel guests.

The pink-and-black neon sign told much of the story—

Coral Court
MOTEL
MODERATE RATES

—and the marquee below gave some particulars:

Room Phones

Free Television

Air Conditioning

The rest had been filled in on a St. Louis job of mine just after the war when I stopped by the Coral Court office looking for a client's wandering wife. I found her in what I was told then was one of the new "Mae West" bungalows, so-called because of their rounded bays. I'd got a real eyeful, not just of my rich old client's pretty young wife, but the double life of the Coral Court.

That it was the ultimate No-Tell Motel with hourly as well as nightly rates—the hourly (minimum four hours) were ostensibly to allow truckers to come in off Route 66 for a few hours of Z's—did not stop families from making annual trips or honeymooners making legal whoopee. Some World War II newlywed brides, who never saw their husbands again, would remember their night at Coral Court forever.

Despite my previous visit, I had never stayed here. I pulled up at the office near the highway, joining Hagan, who was already out of his cab.

Hagan sent me in and I paid a reasonable $5.50, single occupancy, for the room reserved next to the one Steve Strand had booked earlier today as Mr. and Mrs. Robert White. The desk clerk was an almost good-looking red-lipstick brunette about forty in pink angora, her sultry friendliness suggesting a secondary business transaction was a possibility.

"Beds are comfy," she said with a Groucho lift of the eyebrows. "We're strictly Beautyrest mattresses at the Coral Court."

"Good to know," I said, and took my fifty cents in change.

That seemed to disappoint her a little. Still, there was promise or maybe hope in her voice as she said, "50-A's next to 49-A—upper floor in the middle one of the new buildings."

These proved to be a trio at the rear of the property, more conventional two-stories that hadn't been here on my previous stop, but the same brick-and-brown-trim minus the bungalows' rounded curves—two rooms above, two below. Paired garages were on the first floor in front with two more in back, where Hagan stowed his cab in Strand's. I slid the Caddy into 50-A's adjacent garage. You accessed the upper floor by an outer staircase snugged along the building's side and leading to a little hallway off of which were, as promised, 50-A and 49-A.

I stowed my overnight bag in my room, which had none of the moderne motel's exterior style but did maintain yellow walls and brown trim with serviceable modern furniture and a double bed, presumably with the promised Beautyrest. And that bed looked good to me. It had been a long day with a long drive, and of course yesterday with that ransom drop had taken its toll.

Nathan Heller was not as young as he used to be.

In a personality-free hallway, Hagan—some clothes draped over his arm and a bottle of I.W. Harper in one hand—knocked at 49-A.

"It's Johnny!" he said.

The door opened on a tall, surprisingly good-looking chippie in low heels. She wore a white blouse and brown skirt and there was nothing sexy about that wardrobe except the voluptuous body it hugged. Her hair was big and blonde and phony, but who cared? Her eyes were big, too, and gray-blue, her nose pert and her mouth too wide and too red and too full and still nobody cared. She looked like Cleo Moore in the B-movies, only tall—five ten easy.

"Sandy, this is Nate Heller," Johnny said. We were out in the hall. "He's from Chicago."

"Remind me to be impressed," she said. "Here, give me those clothes. You pick out something good? Hope you didn't ask my aunt's help. Her taste is in her fucking ass."

We went in.

Sandy stepped aside, examining her share of the clothes— Hagan had provided several options. A guy only in his white-and-black polka-dot boxer shorts, a sleeveless sweaty white undershirt, and the black socks/shoes combo you see in stag films rolled off the bed and came over in a clumsy, hurried stagger. He was maybe five nine and not fat exactly, more a fruit-gone-bad softness, his legs short and stocky and nearly hairless.

He had dark thinning hair swept back, a receding hairline that emphasized a widow's peak, and a short, wide nose and dull light blue eyes, like somebody who couldn't remember where he put his car keys. No, his car. His mouth was a rosebud thing, and he had the kind of five o'clock shadow that just makes a face look dirty. A cigarette with an ash about to fall off drooped from the small, plump lips.

Like a greedy kid, he grabbed from Hagan the bottle of Harper's and the remainder of the clothing—a silk shirt and fresh boxers—then beamed at him. "You are really on the ball, Johnny!"

"Aim to please, Steve."

Steve put the shirt on over the grubby t-shirt and turned his back to us as he dropped his drawers and got into the new ones, giving us a look at a flabby ass that made Hagan and me share a cringe. Sandy was off to one side paying no attention to anything but the selection of clothes, which seemed to satisfy but not thrill her. Like her life. She took her fresh things into the bathroom and shut herself in. Nice to know she had a sense of decorum.

Then Steve turned and his face went as blank as a baby's. He pointed at me. "Who's this? Chicago?"

Steve's voice was husky, low, smarter than the face.

I offered my hand. "Nate Heller. You must be Steve Strand."

He stuck something out that proved to be a clammy excuse for an appendage.

Just looking at him, I knew he'd done this evil thing. Over against the wall was the metal luggage from the pawnshop—a green footlocker and black suitcase, likely filled with the money Letterman and I had dropped off by that covered bridge last night.

"That's who I am, I'm Steve Strand," he said, as if reminding himself, and went over and sat on the edge of the bed as he stuck his stubby legs into some trousers he'd plucked off a chair. "Thanks for making time. It'll be worth your while, I promise."

The voice *might* have been M's. It seemed lower here, but a phone voice can sound higher. And he could have been disguising it on the calls.

Or wasn't M.

I sat next to Steve. On the Beautyrest. "Well, I promise you I'll be fair. We want you to feel like you can do business with us the next time you have a windfall."

The dull eyes tightened. "We ever met?"

I shook my head. "I'd remember."

Maybe he recognized my *voice.*

"Well, we'll get to know each other," he said with a shrug. He looked at me the way a dog does a hydrant. "We're just gettin' ready to go out on the town. You're coming along, right? What's your name again?"

"Nate."

"Nate, you won't be sorry you met me."

"I'm damn near giddy already."

Steve laughed at that. So did I. Neither of us meant it.

Sandy came out in a four-alarm fire of a red pencil cocktail dress with a square-neck that showed off at least a third of her breasts. Once a man got past thinking contemptuously, "She's for sale," his next thought was, "How much?"

"Take me to the Hill," she said to nobody in particular. That was the Italian-American enclave of St. Louis famed for toasted ravioli and roasted gangsters. "Ruggieri's."

"No," Steve said, getting into a new-looking houndstooth sport coat that had been slung over a chair. "We'll just get sandwiches somewhere."

She gestured to herself and her screaming red sexuality. "You're not gonna buy *this* a goddamn sandwich."

He waved her off like they were married. "Okay, okay. But it's getting late. Not everything's open. I'll take you for a nice dinner, but someplace near here." He looked at Hagan, who was leaning against the wall near the door. "Know anyplace?"

"Harbor Inn is close," he said with a shrug. "It's all right. You can get a full meal, if the kitchen's still open."

"Harbor Inn it is," Steve said, and Sandy rolled her eyes, hands on hips.

I said, "I'm not that hungry. I'll wait for you folks to get back." I was thinking about that footlocker and suitcase against the wall; I still carried lock picks.

Steve came over and put a pudgy hand on my sleeve; he smelled like Old Spice and desperation. "No, you come along, Nate. We'll have a chance to talk. Get to know each other. Can you hold onto this for me?"

He reached in his pocket and got out a .38 revolver. He held it in his hand like this was a stick-up. For a moment I weighed diving for him, as death seemed a possibility and I'd rather it be his; but he shifted it to his palm and held it out like a gift.

"Ain't it a little beaut?" he asked.

"I'm not licensed in this state," I said, which was a lie. The nine mil was under my left arm. Thank you, Richard Bennett.

Steve swung toward Hagan. "How about you, Johnny?"

"No can do, buddy," handsome Johnny said through a stiff smile. "I'm on parole."

Sandy came over in a lightning flash of red and plucked the

gun from Steve's palm, startling him. "Cute," she said. "Just what we need, going out to dinner, case the waitress is a bitch." Efficiently she emptied the bullets into her hand. "What's an insurance agent doing with a gun?"

"Protection," Steve said defensively, "what do you think? I carry around considerable sums of money, you know."

She closed her fingers around the cartridges and swayed back to her purse, a black leather clutch, and dumped the slugs into it. Then she sashayed back and returned the gun.

Under the five o'clock shadow, Steve's cheeks were as red as Sandy's dress. "You think I don't have more slugs?" Proving his point, he dipped a hand into a sport coat pocket and showed off his own handful of bullets.

But they were .25 caliber. Whose gun did they belong to? A female partner, maybe? That blowsy dame he seemed to have ditched?

Steve left the .38 under a pillow and we set out for the Harbor Inn. I did not suggest using my car, tucked away in one of the garages below, because Steve—if he was M—might recognize the Caddy from the ransom drop last night; Letterman and I had not been sure we hadn't been watched.

We went in Hagan's taxi and I sat in front with him, keeping an eye on the couple in the backseat. Looking out opposite windows, they had less chemistry than oil and water. Steve was smoking again, and it soon became clear he was a chain-smoker. Hagan had a cigarette going, too, and so did Sandy, and a nicotine cloud formed inside the cab.

"Not a smoker, Nate?" Steve asked with his sphincter of a smile. He was fidgety back there. The woman might have been waxworks but for her occasional blink.

"I smoked overseas during the war," I said. "Gave it up when I got home."

I'd smoked in combat but dropped the habit when I was

recuperating at St. Elizabeth's. The only time I got the urge in peacetime was when I found myself in a combat-tense situation. That was rare. Even last night, on that wooden bridge, hadn't qualified.

The Harbor Inn did not have so much as a small body of water to cozy up to, and the only "seafood" served was catfish; it was just a small roadside joint with table and booth seating, a horse-shoe-shaped bar, and—for a touch of class—linen tablecloths and bentwood café chairs. For a Monday night, the place was hopping, jukebox blaring and couples dancing. Hagan ordered fried chicken and the rest of us went for the open-face steak sandwich—the menu was limited after nine. Sandy seemed annoyed or maybe frustrated with her sweaty john, who seemed to sense that, sensitive individual he so clearly was.

"Did you say you got a daughter?" Steve asked her. Beer had come for everybody while we waited for the food.

"Yeah. Michelle. We call her Mickey. She's smart as a whip and cute as hell. Lives with my aunt and me. I'm a good mom."

"I'm sure you are," Steve said, nodding, though the only thing about her that suggested motherhood was her neckline. "I hope you're putting your money away."

That actually seemed to hurt her feelings a little. "Don't take me for just another party girl. I already own a farm."

If this doll owned a farm, bodies were buried on the back forty.

Steve said, "Oh, that's great. Everybody needs a dream."

"It's not a dream! It's real. Maybe you'd like to go in on it with me. You have a lot of money in that footlocker and suit-case, don't you?"

Hagan and I exchanged quick looks: *here it comes.*

"Those are sample cases," Steve said. "I'm a pharmaceutical salesman. Those are serum samples."

Nobody brought up that earlier he'd been an insurance agent. Maybe because Sandy had glommed the greenback "serum" in the footlocker.

"Veterinary medicine," Steve went on. "Animals and humans, what's the difference?"

She smoothed some edges off herself. "Well, I want to buy a big Guernsey bull. To raise prize show cattle. If you'd buy me a bull, I would be the happiest woman on earth."

If he bought her bull, Steve would be the biggest jackass on the imaginary farm.

"Maybe I can arrange that," he said, with a wave of a plump-fingered paw. "Ah. Speaking of cattle."

The steak sandwiches arrived; so did the fried chicken. The conversation slowed, most of what ensued coming from Steve, who had talked about how he was starving but only ate a few bites. What he had to say, however, was interesting.

"Johnny," he said to the matinee-idol cabbie, "you seem like a right kind of guy."

"Well, thanks, Steve."

"You taxi drivers know a lot of people."

Which was how Hagan had been able to add me to this little party.

"I know a few," Hagan admitted.

Very quietly, Steve asked, "Can you score me some morphine?"

Like, *Pass the salt.*

Hagan was chewing, and obviously wondering how to respond, when Steve said, "My car was stolen, and along with it, my medicine, and all the paraphernalia that goes with it."

And yet his "sample cases" were still in his possession.

"Look, I'm no damn lowlife junkie," he said, with a sickly smile. "I just got hooked on the stuff when I was in the Pacific.

During the war. When I was wounded. And they gave me more in the hospital, so till I can catch a breath and get some proper medical treatment...."

"I don't really know of any place where I can get the stuff," Hagan said with a noncommittal shrug, "but I can ask around."

"Good! Good. Pick up a number 25 or 26 needle, while you're at it. You can drop us off after dinner at the Coral Court and go on home. Your missus is probably wondering about you by now."

"I gave her a call, but yeah. I should get home."

Steve leaned in and put a hand on Hagan's. "One more thing. Before you come by the motor court tomorrow morning, rent me a car and buy me a nice leather suitcase and a briefcase."

That sounded like two things. Or three.

"All right," Hagan said.

"Dig into that dough I gave you."

"Sure."

Sandy, sitting next to Steve between him and Hagan, perked up. "Oh! I *love* that song. Johnny, come dance with me."

"Vaya Con Dios" by Les Paul and Mary Ford had started up on the jukebox.

They went off to dance.

A waitress brought another round of beers. The third.

Steve said, "So, Nate—you were in the war, too?"

"I was."

"What branch?"

"Marines."

The dull eyes got a little lively. "You're shittin' me! Same here! Well, Semper Fi, Mac! Where did you serve?"

"Guadalcanal. Second Marines. I was wounded and sent home. My war lasted less than a year."

His chest puffed up. "Oh, I was in for the duration....First

Marine Division—New Britain, Peleliu, Okinawa campaigns. Made sergeant."

"What did you do over there?"

"…Oh, whatever they asked me to."

"What was your job? Mine was trying not to get my ass shot off in a foxhole."

"Uh….telephone equipment repairman."

I managed not to laugh. Deadpan, I said, "Where the hell would we have been without communications? Listen, while we have a moment alone…" Sandy and Hagan were dancing to "Crying in the Chapel" by June Valli now. "…we can talk money."

He folded his hands and tried to look calm, but the eyes were lively again. "Why don't we?"

"Depends on the nature of the currency," I said. "Bank money could have some marked bills mixed in, so maybe fifty cents on the dollar. If it's insurance money, why is it in cash? What's the story there?"

He merely shrugged. No answer beyond that.

"If it's out of a company safe and you don't figure the serial numbers are recorded," I said, "you can get an even higher return. Much as seventy-five, eighty cents on the dollar. But if it's something like this kidnapping that's in the papers, well, that could mean twenty, even fifteen cents on the dollar. Money doesn't get much hotter."

Steve's laugh seemed forced. "You don't think *that's* what this is? Do I look like that kind of guy?"

You do, Steve. You really, really do.

"It's insurance money, okay?" he blurted. "Everything would have gone fine if this one guy hadn't made a mistake."

If Steve was trying to wash the ransom money, did this remark indicate three accomplices? Steve, the blowsy broad he maybe already dumped, and…*who?*

"Get in touch with your people in Chicago," he said. "Tell 'em you got a line on a big bundle. Say I want seventy-five cents on the dollar, no questions asked."

Sandy and Hagan joined us—apparently they didn't care to dance to the "Theme from *Dragnet*" by Ray Anthony—and we gathered our things. Hagan used Steve's money to pay the check and we headed out.

Hagan dropped us off at the Coral Court and Sandy went up the exterior staircase first followed by Steve and then me. I stopped at my door and said good night to them and Steve, who was stumbling drunk now, threw me a wave and Sandy winked at me before they disappeared into 49-A.

I paused, then moved down to the door they'd gone through and listened. I could probably have accomplished the same thing in 50-A with a drinking glass to the wall, but their conversation bled out just fine right here. The rooms at the Coral Court, unlike the glazed-brick-and-glass-block exteriors, were fashioned of flimsy stuff.

Sandy, in a sultry, slutty way that tried a little too hard, said, "*Come on, honey, let's go to bed....*"

"*Don't worry,*" Steve said, "*you'll get your money.*"

"*What the hell kind of deal is this?*"

"*I got you here for one reason and I'll tell you what it is later.*"

Sandy's voice spiked. "*What's* wrong *with you, anyway? You got physical problems or something? Shit, I don't understand this at all!*"

Steve yelled back: "*Listen, goddamnit! I haven't slept for five days. I'm half-gone on nerves, whiskey, and dope. The last thing I wanna do right now is fuck! So sit down and shut up!*"

"*Oh? Well, fuck you, buddy!*"

"*Fuck you too, you goddamn tramp!*"

Sandy shrieked and must have been hitting him, because he said, *"Stop it! Stop it! Goddamnit, all I want from you is to run a goddamn errand for me tomorrow."*

"What?"

"You do a simple fucking favor for me and I'll buy you the biggest fucking bull I can find for that fucking farm of yours."

Then she was cooing at him and when I heard the Beautyrest starting to sing, I guessed Sandy was plying her trade. I went to my room, got into my pajamas, slipped under the covers, and switched off the bedside lamp. Went over everything I'd heard and seen tonight, feeling more and more convinced that metal luggage held the ransom money.

I mulled calling my wife's number out in California and talking to my son, but even with the time difference it was too late for that.

Considering what I had on my mind, I fell asleep fast. The knock at my door came so soft, it worked its way into my dream. But it grew louder enough to wake me. I crawled out of bed and cracked the door open.

Sandy O'Day looked at me. For a moment I didn't recognize her—her hair was short and black now, carelessly bobby-pinned up. Seemed all that blondeness had been a wig. Her too-wide, very red, generously lipped mouth came up with a hell of a smirk.

She said, "That limp-dick jerk-off fell asleep on me. I think I had too much coffee at that dump we ate at. Can I come in?"

I opened the door for her and she swept in, a pink night-gown trailing after like a cape. She let it drop to the floor and unleashed her long-legged body, slightly plump in the best ways, displayed in a Frederick's of Hollywood-style purple bra and panties. Her hair might have been tousled, but her make-up was working overtime.

"You got anything to drink?" she asked.

"A couple bottles of 7-Up I got from a machine at check-in. A bucket of ice from down the hall. A couple of water glasses."

"Sounds like a party."

I poured us glasses with ice and we sat on top of the unmade bed with pillows propped behind us.

"I must be losing my charm," she said. "When nothing developed in bed, Steve-a-rino took a bath to relax and I crawled in with him and got nothing but the wrong kind of wet. I'm starting to think he has eyes for Johnny or maybe you."

I shook my head. "He's just a lush. But he may be a rich one."

She frowned curiously at me. "Where do you think he got that dough?"

I gave her back a question of my own. "How good a look did you get at it?"

She shrugged. "Just a flash. But, man, it looked stuffed in there like a Thanksgiving turkey." She showed me small feral white teeth and her eyebrows went up and down and up and down. "You and me could grab those babies and South America here we come. You're right, he's a lush. You probably won't even have to kill him."

"That's a relief. South America, huh? Wouldn't you rather plow your share into your farm?"

Her head went back and she horse-laughed. "Ha! You didn't buy that load of bullshit, did you, Nate?"

"No. I think you fooled Steve, though. He's not very bright. Did he ever tell you what errand he wanted you to run?"

She sipped 7-Up, ice clinking, nodded. "Yeah. He's gonna give me a thousand dollars to fly to Los Angeles and mail a letter."

"What the hell?"

She repeated that word for word.

But by now I got it: "It's a letter from him to somebody."

"Yeah. A lawyer in St. Joe."

"He thinks the postmark will give him an alibi. Make it appear he's in L.A."

"I guess."

"You have the letter?"

"No. I saw it. He says I can keep anything left from the thousand after air fare and hotel and incidental shit. And he'll give me enough to buy that Guernsey bull." She giggled, then got serious and conspiratorial. "Which is all well and good, Heller, but I say take the money and run."

"He has a gun."

She glanced at the nightstand, where my nine millimeter was resting. "Looks like you do, too." She worked her hand in my hair. "I think we'd make a good team. We both been to the rodeo before...."

Hard as it may be to believe, she smelled good. Arpège by Lanvin—a showgirl I dated a while back wore it. And the truth is, over the years, I have dated (to put it euphemistically) all kinds of females—from rich to poor, from brilliant to dumb, and a good number have been strippers and showgirls. Now that I was respectable, with a L.A. office and all, you can add starlets to the list. How can I put it politely? I'd screwed sleazier.

She turned the lamp to a low setting—that was one of Coral Court's trademarks, although the ceiling mirrors proved to be a rumor, at least in 49-A and 50-A—and the room fell into a kind of dusk. She glided off the bed and slowly stripped off the bra—her breasts full and high and beautifully shaped—then turned her back to me and slid off the panties, revealing a dimpled bounteous ass as smooth as a marble statue. She turned to reveal a plush dark pubic bush and kicked off the heels and climbed back onto the bed and onto me. She slipped a hand inside the pajama trousers' fly and fished me out and worked me to attention.

She was about to mount me when I took her by the arms and said no.

"It's all right," she said. "I have a rubber." She revealed the coil in her left palm; hadn't seen that. She was good. Or shall we say, practiced.

"No," I said. "I'm just not in the mood."

"You *look* like you're in the mood!"

"No. No offense, but…no. I don't want to give you the wrong idea."

"The wrong idea?"

"Call me old-fashioned, but I draw the line at murder."

"I said you probably wouldn't *have* to!" She huffed a sigh and scrambled off the bed. She got into the panties and bra in an irritated, unsexy way, stepped into her shoes, and stalked to the door, where she stopped and, clearly frustrated, looked at me as I reached to switch off the lamp.

"Jesus," she said as she went out. "Doesn't *anybody* wanna fuck me tonight?"

CHAPTER SIX

This time the knock at the door woke me at once. Insistent, the pounding was accompanied by Steve's husky voice saying, "Nate! Are you up? *Nate!*"

The urgency put a frown on my face and the nine mil in my hand. But by the time I was on my feet, the sunlight peeking through the Venetian blinds said it was morning. I went over where the ruckus was, put the gun behind my back in one hand, and edged the door open a ways with the other.

Steve looked sweaty and upset, in desperate need of a shave, his dull blue eyes wide; he was in his houndstooth sport coat, brown trousers and bare feet. "Oh, good, you're awake. I just don't wanna leave my things unattended."

He apparently meant the footlocker and suitcase, though he'd never admitted they were full of money.

"Okay," I said. "You want me to watch 'em while you, uh... what?"

"Come see me when you're dressed," Steve said hurriedly, and was gone.

Everything's a crisis with this guy, I thought, *except things that should be.*

I'd just closed the door when I heard Sandy's voice and for a moment thought I was imagining it. Or worse, that I'd relented in the night and let her back in. Then I realized it was coming from outside, and went over and peered between blinds at the drive curving around past the small rear parking lot bordered by pin oaks.

Nobody.

But I could still hear her. In my pajamas, leaving the gun behind, I exited the room as barefoot as Steve had been, the door ajar, and stepped out onto the white metal landing at the top of the exterior stairs; it was crisp and chilly outside.

Sandy was on the far end of the landing in her purple dressing gown, leaning over the rail and yelling at a young colored maid poised by a housekeeping cart.

"What do you mean," my unlikely Juliet was indignantly asking, "you can't bring us some breakfast? We'll pay for the privilege!"

The maid, in a green and white uniform, looked up and said, "We ain't allowed to do that, lady. And I ain't asking the manager a question when I know the answer, because he's not in a good mood mornings. Actually, he ain't in a good mood, period."

And the maid and her cart rumbled on.

Sandy hadn't noticed me, so I spoke. "Good morning."

She gave me barely a glance. "Go fuck yourself."

"Why, aren't *you* available?"

That got a throaty laugh out of her. "Well, breakfast isn't. I'm not hungry, but Steve's having a cow."

"That'll save him buying you a Guernsey."

She laughed again, just something short from her belly. Now she looked at me—surprisingly pretty, make-up free, though the hardness of her life lingered. "You always this funny in the morning?"

"Keep trying. Maybe you'll find out."

She grinned and gave me a middle finger. We were finally getting along.

"I'll handle Steve," I told her, as she slid past me into the hall and we slipped into our respective quarters.

Bathed and shaved and back in the Richard Bennett with the holstered nine mil accouterment, I knocked at the 49-A door and Sandy answered, back in her big blonde wig and in a pink knit sweater and black pencil skirt and low black heels. She rolled her eyes at me. Beyond, Steve was pacing like an expectant father.

I stepped past her. "What's the problem?"

"I'm gonna talk to that fucking manager," he said, still pacing. "Johnny told them, when we checked in, we were to get the first-class treatment."

"First-class treatment in this kind of place," I said, "does not include breakfast. They don't have a restaurant, much less room service."

"I'm gonna let that manager know who he's dealing with."

Sandy took my arm, sending her words back and forth between me and Steve. "I *know* the manager. Jack Carr. He's tight with Buster Wortman and an ex-con himself. Not a good idea getting his attention."

Wortman was known as the rackets boss of East St. Louis, Illinois.

She gave me a little nod toward the footlocker and suitcase against the wall. The likes of Carr and Wortman would just love to know about those…if they didn't already.

I said, "I'll go out and get us some breakfast."

Steve froze but his expression melted. "Would you, Nate? That'd be mighty white of you."

"Anything else you need?"

He put his hand on top of his head like an ice pack. "Aspirin."

So I would play delivery boy. I only hoped this errand wasn't meant to get rid of me just long enough for Steve and his money to move on without me. If Sandy had told him about the nine millimeter on my nightstand, he might think I wasn't here for the advertised purpose. Which I wasn't.

Of course, that would require Sandy telling Steve she'd been in my room, which would not thrill him, since he was the one paying for the pleasure of her company; and anyway, I was representing the Chicago Outfit, wasn't I? Why wouldn't I travel heavy?

I returned in forty minutes or so with three fried-egg sandwiches and paper cups of coffee from a diner up the road and Bayer aspirin from a Katz Drug. When Steve sat on the edge of the bed, to eat his sandwich, setting his coffee on the bedside stand, I picked up his hat to make room for myself, tossing it onto a chair.

"Don't you know it's unlucky," I said, "to leave your hat on the bed?"

Through a mouthful of white bread and fried egg, Steve said, "Do I look like some superstitious chump?"

Well, he didn't look superstitious. A glimpse at the fedora's sweatband had revealed "CAH" and "LEVINE HAT COMPANY, ST. LOUIS, MISSOURI." Not being a chump myself, I knew at once Steve Strand's initials were not CAH.

Nobody had much to say. Sandy turned on the TV while she ate and a sickeningly folksy Arthur Godfrey kept us company by way of a bunch of blather and Julius LaRosa singing "Eh, Cumpari!" When "Strike It Rich" came on, it was a relief.

Meanwhile, Steve prowled and paced, pausing on occasion to peek through the Venetian blinds at the rear parking lot. Finally I stepped up next to him. "Checking for cops?"

"No, no—insurance investigators, maybe."

About a quarter after eleven, Johnny Hagan arrived, wearing the same working man's clothes as last night but minus his ACE cap. He had a tan leather two-suit bag over one arm, a matching briefcase in one hand, and a brown-paper-bagged bottle in the other. Still barefoot, Steve strode over, annoyed.

"Where the hell have you been?" he blurted. "We been sitting around all morning with our thumbs up our asses!"

The big good-looking cabbie cowered, as if this pudgy punk was a threat; of course Steve did have a gun in his sport coat pocket.

"I'm sorry, pal," Hagan said. "That was some laundry list of errands you gave me. I got that luggage you wanted. Hey, and I rented you a swell ride—a '52 Plymouth sedan, two-tone green." He held out a handful of pills. "Plus I got you Bennies off a bellboy."

"Gimme!" Steve said. He snatched the pills from the cabbie's palm and stuffed them in a pocket. At least he didn't just toss them down his throat like Vitamin Flintheart in the funnies.

Hagan shook the paper bag off the bottle—I.W. Harper again—and handed it toward Steve, who grinned like a ventriloquist's dummy. "Johnny, I won't soon forget you!"

Then Steve was passing around drinking glasses in which he'd poured several fingers of amber liquid, like the pacing father's baby had finally been delivered. Crossing her nice long legs, Sandy replaced me in the seat of honor next to Steve on the edge of the Beautyrest while Johnny and I found chairs.

"Stick by me a few days," Steve said to the cabbie, between generous gulps, "and see me through this rough patch, you can be damn sure I'll take care of you."

What rough patch exactly?

Steve went on: "Sandy here wants a bull to hey-diddle-diddle the cows on her farm. What's *your* dream, Johnny?"

The cabbie gestured around him, sloshing the whiskey in hand; his eyes traveled to where the walls met the ceiling as if that were where heaven began.

"Place of my own like this would be just about goddamn perfect," Hagan mused. "Can you picture it? Motel down in Florida, beach for a back yard, away from the Saint fuckin' Looie snow." He snorted in self-contempt. "Rolling drunks in your cab only takes a guy so far. Why hustle johns for whores out of a Chevy…

no offense, Sandy…when you can run a ring of 'em right out of your own clean and comfy motel? Drivin' cab is no kind of life for a real man. A place like the Coral Court—hell, *half* as nice —would cover what it takes for a guy to make his support payments *and* make a bet when he feels like it, maybe buy a new suit of clothes now and again, and never feel the pinch."

"Everybody needs a dream," I agreed.

"Well, yours is gonna come true, Johnny," Steve said, saluting him with an already empty whiskey glass. "Like Sandy and her farm and that male nympho bull I'm gonna buy her… I'm gonna set you up for life, kid. And Nate, you are not forgotten in this—I'm gonna kick back ten percent of whatever you arrange for me with the Chicago boys. Consider that a *promise.*"

Sandy, not too subtly, said to Steve, "That new bag you had Johnny buy? You need help shifting the money into it from that footlocker and suitcase?"

Steve took no offense at this breach of etiquette. He just shook his head gently and said, "No, suit bag's for clothes we're gonna buy this afternoon, me and Johnny. Now, Johnny boy, first you should drop Sandy off at a cab stand, where she can get a ride to the airport for her L.A. trip. Use the car you rented and come back here after. Sandy, I got a couple more letters for you to mail from out there. Then, Johnny, rent me a nice apartment in a quiet, refined neighborhood where I can lay low for a while. If it hadn't been for one man's slip-up, none of this would be necessary. But it is. Pay a month's rent if you have to."

"Okey-doke," the cabbie said.

"And can you score me some fake I.D.? Know anybody can provide that?"

"There's a guy."

Sandy was listening intently. I could hear her wheels turning: the last thing she wanted was to get on an airplane to the West Coast and leave the fortune in those metal suitcases behind.

"I need the rest of that twenty-five hundred back," Steve said to Hagan, "but keep five C's—a man without money is nothing. Use what's left after buying my new I.D. to fix yourself up with some classy new threads."

Hagan complied. At her host's prompting, Sandy gathered her extra things and got ready to leave. Then she gave me a wry look that said, *Maybe next time*, and thanked Steve for the grand. He said no thanks were necessary and she could get in touch with him about that Guernsey bull through Hagan, on her return from the Coast.

Before following the cabbie into the hall, Sandy gave the footlocker and suitcase a longing look—the kind a man wishes a woman might give him before parting.

When they'd left, Steve poured himself a fresh glass of whiskey and gave me one I hadn't asked for. He went to the window and parted blades of the blinds to watch the Plymouth go, then returned to his spot on the edge of the bed.

"Nate, I wanted to talk to you alone."

As if sending Sandy to L.A. to mail letters had been all about giving us a little privacy.

I sipped whiskey. I've never cared for the way it burns when it hits bottom. "What's on your mind, Steve?"

His unblinking gaze was unsettling. "I want to play it straight with your friends in Chicago. I got no desire to have the Outfit unhappy with me."

"Sound thinking."

"So I'm not going to lie to you." He pointed to the footlocker and black suitcase. "That's not insurance money or from a bank vault, either. That's ransom dough. The Greenlease kid."

I'd been pretty much convinced of that since the moment I first saw Steve's sweaty smear of a face. But hearing it still landed hard.

"I'm no fool," he said. "That money is bound to be marked. Means I have to settle for whatever I can get. But you can help."

"How?"

He shrugged. "You *know* these Chicago people. They're your business associates. Maybe even your friends. And the more they give me, the more I can give you, right?"

"How many others are in this with you, Steve?"

"I got a girl named Bonnie. I stowed her in an apartment because she came a little unglued after we took the boy. She drinks too much."

"Does she."

He nodded, looked into his own glass, finding no irony there. "I said somebody slipped up, remember? And I guess you could say somebody was me."

"How so, Steve?"

He jerked a thumb at himself, defensively. "I thought up the plan. The whole thing was mine. I have a real mind for this kind of thing—in my time, I robbed stores, and stuck up a whole string of taxi cabs…ha, don't tell Johnny! Never a hitch, except maybe that bank job…just bad luck, after I case the place and plan so perfectly, it turns out to be closed on Saturdays. But when I was doing time, I got *really* good at planning."

I had a regular criminal mastermind here.

"You see, I come from a wealthy family, but I had a bad run of luck with some businesses, legit ones that chewed up my inheritance. In stir, I got to thinking about the rich kids I grew up around…and a kidnapping seemed like a safe, easy way to get rich again. If only…if only I hadn't got mixed up with that crazy bastard."

"What crazy bastard, Steve?"

"Tom Marsh."

Marsh? *M?*

He sighed, shook his head. "He was just somebody I ran into in the Netherlands Hotel bar, in Kansas City. We hit if off right away—talked the same language. You know, words and expressions only ex-cons use. He had charm and he was tough. But he had bad qualities I didn't pick up on."

"Such as?"

"Well, he was low-class. Had tattoos on his arms and chest. And he was a perverted son of a bitch. You think I woulda snatched a kid if I knew I'd thrown in with a short eyes?"

The flesh on my arms goose-pimpled and the hair on the back of my neck bristled.

"Short eyes" was prison slang for child molester.

"And," Steve continued, "Marsh has been looking after the Greenlease boy ever since Bonnie picked him up at that school. In a nice quiet house in a nice quiet neighborhood, never mind where. Marsh swears he's leaving the kid alone—that he knows if he touches him, in *that* way, it could sink the whole damn deal. But how can I trust a goddamn kiddie-diddling drug addict?"

Good point. "He still has the boy?"

Steve nodded. "He was supposed to deliver the kid to a hotel in Pittsburg, Missouri. But he hasn't yet. He thinks we can squeeze another round of money out of Greenlease. Greedy, grasping prick! When I found that out, I grabbed the money, and Bonnie and me took off."

"Then it's Marsh you've been on the lookout for," I said, nodding toward the blinds.

"Yes! Yes." He sat forward, the dull eyes getting some real life in them now. "I want to do the deal with your Outfit boys, score some real money for me and Bonnie, and *you*, of course…then I'll call the cops and tell them where to find Marsh and the boy."

"If he hasn't killed him."

Steve waved that off. "Oh, no, the boy is fine. Marsh is nuts but not stupid. Then Bonnie and me will lie low in an apartment till the cops take Marsh in and the boy back to Mommy and Daddy." He slapped his knees. "So. Everything hunky-dory now?"

Yeah. Fucking swell. Bobby Greenlease's babysitter was a drug-addicted pedophile. Steve and Bonnie were drunk and on the lam. What could go wrong?

And yet the kid seemed to be alive. I'd been ready to write Bobby off in this thing. Now here was a ray of hope in this nightmare tragicomedy.

A car motor outside announced itself. Steve went to the window and peeked out. "Johnny's back! Help me take the luggage down and load it in the Plymouth."

As if carrying a coffin, him in front, me in back, I helped him down with the footlocker. Hagan went up and got the black metal suitcase. We loaded the Plymouth trunk and the cabbie pulled the vehicle into the first-floor garage marked 49-A, got out and shut it inside.

"Catch yourself a cab," Steve told Hagan, an arm around him. "I have some things to do this afternoon. Three of us'll meet at the Pink House bar-and-grill up the street for a drink and a bite at four o'clock. Don't forget my fake I.D. Okay?"

Hagan said, "Covered," and the cabbie walked off to catch a cab.

Steve locked the garage and I followed him back up to his room. He poured himself some whiskey, then asked me if I wanted a "snort" and I declined. He resumed his favorite seat on the bed's edge.

"Nate, can you get your Chicago friends to give me a figure for the money? Like I said, it's a hell of a big bundle—around six hundred grand."

I whistled, like I didn't already know. "See what I can do. But I don't know about trusting the phones here. They could be tapped by the cops or even the management."

He nodded. "Maybe you could walk to a booth and call from there. Or use a pay phone in a restaurant."

"You could drive me."

He shook his head. "No, I got things to do."

"Why not take me along?"

"No. Things I need to do on my own."

"You're not meeting up with Bonnie, are you? Or maybe Marsh?"

"No! Why are you pushing me, Nate?"

I got up and sat beside him. Put a hand on his shoulder. "Steve, you gotta be straight with me. If I tell the boys back home you can be trusted, and something goes off the rails, it'll come back and hit both of us. Hard."

He thought about that. Then had some whiskey and asked, "What if the kid was dead?"

"What? You mean, what if Marsh kills the boy?"

"I mean, what if he already *has.*" His eyes were looking right at me but registering nothing. "I mean…Nate. It's better you hear this. He already has. Killed the kid."

I didn't say anything.

"If your Outfit pals knew the kid had been killed, would it mean less money? I mean, can we keep that from them? Make 'em believe we didn't know ourselves?"

I stood. "Excuse me."

I got up fast and shut myself in the bathroom. I raised the toilet seat and knelt before the porcelain altar on the ceramic tile floor as if in prayer and threw up. Well, first I retched a while, then everything flew out—the fried eggs, the bread, the coffee, the whiskey, and considerable bile.

It took a while.

I got uneasily to my feet and ran cold water in the sink. I looked at myself in the mirror and my reflection looked ghostly white. My features, which were so like my son's, stared accusingly at me. I splashed cold water on my face and then I toweled off. Thoughts were careening in my brain, but one was that I didn't dare kill Steve until he'd led me to Tom Marsh. And the child's body.

When I came out, Steve was gone.

A car motor roared outside and I ran to the window, fingered open blind blades and saw a two-tone green Plymouth taking off, fast.

"Shit," I said.

I sat on the edge of the Beautyrest where Steve had perched minutes ago. I breathed hard. I clenched my fists. Tried not to trash the room. Then, slowly—and it took a good two minutes—I came to my senses. Steve had left things here. Extra clothes, toiletries, an unfinished bottle of I.W. Harper. This last alone meant he had not checked out of the Coral Court.

He would be back. He would likely still make that meeting at the Pink House at four P.M. He may have heard me puking but that didn't mean he was on the run from me. Quite the opposite—he likely wanted me to settle down, after my unexpectedly human reaction to hearing that a little boy had been murdered. We needed a time out, before we completed our hot money transaction. Or perhaps he had things to do, unaccompanied.

So I was breathing normally as I poked around the room, a detective again. Steve hadn't brought much with him, but I did find in the wastebasket yesterday's morning edition of the *Post-Dispatch*. I lay it open on the bed and paged through. An ad in the classifieds was circled in pen—for a two-room furnished apartment at 4504 Arsenal Street.

From the Coral Court to the apartment house on Arsenal took only fifteen minutes, even for a non-native. The area was somewhat schizophrenic, scenic Tower Grove Park with its sassafras trees, manicured grounds, and gazebos facing a row of once-proud brick residences now given over to apartments—4504 somewhat larger than most buildings here, probably home to seven or eight flats on its two floors.

The middle-aged, well-preserved landlady on the ground floor accepted unquestioningly the badge I flashed, though a closer look would have revealed it to designate a State of Illinois Licensed Private Investigator. The salt-and-pepper-haired, blue-eyed Mrs. Webb seemed to like me—I was well-preserved, too—and answered all of my questions unhesitatingly.

About noon yesterday, John Grant of Elgin, Illinois (maybe she *had* read my badge) rented for twenty dollars and a five-dollar key deposit her only available apartment. He and his wife Esther were staying in St. Louis while Mrs. Grant recovered from a serious illness.

"Don't know what her problem is," Mrs. Webb said. "But she seemed very weak. She was leaning on her husband."

"What did he look like?"

The description of John Grant was Steve Strand right down to the five o'clock shadow and oily complexion. He had dragged in and up the stairs, one at a time, two very heavy pieces of luggage. Later in the day he had carried them back out, one at a time.

Mrs. Webb took me upstairs and knocked, said, "Mrs. Grant?" a few times, before unlocking the door for me and smiling and nodding and leaving me to it.

I went in and the place was two rooms that I would describe more as under-furnished; still, pleasant enough with its floral wallpaper and fleur-de-lis rugs. The lumpy double bed had a lumpy woman in it. In a slip, she was walking the line between deep sleep and out cold. The nightstand bore two whiskey bottles (one empty, one two-thirds empty), a water glass and the small radio Steve bought yesterday.

And one other thing: an envelope addressed with "Mrs. Esther Grant" scrawled on it. Inside was a note, similarly hasty: "Had to move bags in a hurry as report came in on radio—Girl next door looked funny—Couldn't wake you—Stay here and I'll call you when I can."

On a bureau was a brown cloth purse and in it was $2,500 in twenties and tens, and another note, folded in half: "Stay where you are baby. I will see you in short order. Tell them you are not well and they will bring you food. Just say your husband was called away unexpectedly."

I got a pad from my sport coat and jotted down a dozen of the serial numbers, then returned the money to the purse.

Mrs. Grant seemed to be rousing a little. I went over and sat on the bed by her. She groaned and so did the mattress—not a Beautyrest. Nor was Steve's "Bonnie" a beauty at rest. She had a contusion over her left eye and a red streak across the bridge of her nose. Her dark hair medium length and unkempt, she reminded me of a dissipated version of Patsy Kelly, the movie comedienne you used to see in the thirties and early forties with Thelma Todd or maybe the Ritz Brothers.

Round-faced with a weak chin, narrow wide-set eyes and, spookily, the same kind of cupid lips as Steve, she had probably been good-looking once or nearly so. Her nose was red and it didn't take my detective skills to figure why, though the stench of booze aided and abetted.

I helped her sit up in bed and her eyes tried to focus and her busty, not quite fat frame worked to right itself.

"You're Bonnie?"

She frowned at me, as if to say, *Am I?*

"Tell me about the boy. The little boy."

She seemed like she might cry but never got there. "It's…it's all hazy." Words were hard for her. Her lips, tongue and teeth just weren't working in tandem. "I'm so hazy on things…I don't remember."

"Try, Bonnie."

Her voice had traces of emotion, but her face was a putty mask. "If you'd been drunk as long as me, you'd understand."

"Understand what?"

"It does something to your brain. I travel around in a haze most of the time."

"Did Steve give you those marks? Did he hit you?"

"Steve…you mean…Carl?"

CAH.

"Yeah, Bonnie. I mean Carl."

Her shrug was in slow motion. "We fight sometimes. I didn't like this place. I said it was a dump. He didn't like that."

"Tell me about the little boy."

"I picked him up at school. Carl told me he was the boy's father, custody thing. He took the boy off somewhere. Then I saw in the paper it was a kidnapping and thought maybe Carl wasn't really his father. I asked him what he did with the boy and he told me to mind my own business."

"And he hit you then?"

She swallowed, nodded. "Yeah…I been looking like hell ever since. I…I don't remember how I got here. We were in K.C. and this is…St. Louis, right? Look, I started drinking after I saw the papers. So it's hazy, like I said."

"Did you see the ransom money?"

"Carl has a lot of money in his luggage."

"If you knew Carl kidnapped the boy, why didn't you call the police?"

The putty face managed a frown. "If I did that, they'd come

take Carl away. And I love him very much." She clutched my lapel. Something human entered her eyes. "You know, that boy just put his little hand in mine…he was just so trusting."

Then her eyes rolled back in her head and she was snoring again.

From a phone booth down the street, I called Lt. Lou Shoulders, getting him at the Newstead Avenue Police Station, his work number.

I brought him up to date, then said, "You need to put some men on the apartment house. This woman Bonnie is the accomplice, and Steve or Carl or whoever the fuck is going to lead us to Tom Marsh."

Shoulders groaned, "And the kid's body, sounds like."

"Yeah. Look, this is going to break real soon. You should post men at the Coral Court, too. Plenty of rooms to watch from. But don't rush it…and don't rush *him.* He's armed and screwy as hell. I've got his confidence, though, and I'm on top of it."

"Brother, you better be."

CHAPTER SEVEN

The Pink House was indeed pink, a dirty coral, but not what you'd call a house—just a dive with a red overhang roof that bore its name. Though typical bar food was on offer, its rationale for existence was clearly stated by the vertical sign near the front door, red letters on pink:

D

R

I

N

K

The cigarette smoke within was no thicker than carbon monoxide fumes in a suicide garage, the grizzled regulars at the U-shaped bar consisting of that breed of working men who never seemed to be working. The dark-wood interior had half a dozen dark-wood tables and dark-wood chairs, on loan from the kind of jury room where guilty verdicts are frequent and deserved.

Only a couple of the tables for four were taken, and the one I chose was away from those patrons, a bald guy negotiating with a redheaded hooker at one table, and at another two guys laughing too loud as they drank too much. Maybe they were trying to be heard over the jukebox—Tony Bennett, "Rags to Riches." After I collected a bottle of Schlitz from the bar, I made sure to sit on the opposite side of the room from the corner where a currently not-in-use dart board dwelled, in case some barroom athlete got ambitious.

I'd been right on time but my cabbie pal Hagan was five minutes late. I almost didn't recognize him, and he sure was in the wrong bar for his new duds—navy felt hat and blue gabardine suit, blue-and-white tie on a crisp white shirt, wing-tip Oxford shoes. Florsheim, probably.

He got himself a bottle of beer and joined me. "Any sign of Steve?"

"No. But that gives us a chance to talk. We'll start with his name isn't Steve. It's Carl."

A puzzled look. "He tell you that?"

"No, his forty-year-old 'girl' did. She's Bonnie. And Bonnie and Carl make Bonnie and Clyde look like geniuses."

I filled him in on what little I'd managed to get out of our friend's drunk-out-of-her-mind accomplice, and how Lt. Shoulders had the Arsenal Street apartment house under watch.

"When I get Steve alone," I said, "I intend to squeeze it all out of him. But I did get the gist from Bonnie."

His dark eyebrows flicked up, then down. "Oh, Christ. This *is* the Greenlease thing?"

"Yes. It is. Is the Greenlease boy alive? No."

A loud sigh followed. "How fucked in the ass are we?"

"Let's put it this way, Johnny—get sticky fingers around that ransom dough? Even a snazzy new outfit won't make you feel good in the electric chair."

Hagan shook his head glumly. "It's the gas chamber in Missouri."

"Sorry. Hard for an out-of-stater to keep track. But they let you sit down for that, too."

He scowled. "Come on, man. You *know* Costello was only interested in that bundle if it came from some righteous source like embezzlement or robbery."

I let him get away with that—bigger fish to fry.

"If Joe's to be believed," I said, "he wants nothing to do with the Greenlease kidnap except getting credit for helping nab the snatchers. Okay, then, fine. With luck and a little sweat, I can shake the whereabouts of this Marsh character out of 'Steve.' And what became of the boy...of his body."

I gulped air, then gulped beer.

Hagan was nodding. "Give 'em Steve and Bonnie and Marsh, it'll make the cops look good, and take some of the smell off Costello's reputation."

"He'll be content with that? You got any idea how much money six hundred grand is?"

"I know it's heavy carrying it up and down those damn stairs at the Coral Court." He sat forward. "Look, I wouldn't worry about Costello. He's no saint, but the one to watch is Shoulders."

"You're saying a crooked cop who killed three times in the line of duty might be a threat?"

He missed the sarcasm or anyway ignored it. "Shoulders is a shakedown artist from way back. He'll give a free pass to any thief who'll cut him in for half. He's nightwatch commander at the Newstead Avenue Station—perfect spot to not be seen doing what you shouldn't be seen doing."

I was glad I didn't have to diagram that sentence.

I said, "You think Sandy got herself off to the airport?"

He shook his head. "No, she's headed to St. Joe."

"What?"

Flipping a palm, he said, "She told me she got a real good look at that money in Steve's, or Carl's, luggage. She said he's from St. Joe."

"Keep thinking of him as Steve for now," I advised. "How did Sandy figure that?"

"Saw it in his hatband."

So much for me being a great detective.

"I put her with another cabbie I know," Hagan said, after a gulp of beer, "who said he was willing to make a meter-off trip out of town, if the two of 'em could come to terms. She has that grand from Steve, y'know. I wonder what terms Sandy and him will come to."

"I don't."

Finally Steve/Carl rolled in, a cigarette drooping from his cupid's bow mouth. He looked sloppy, the houndstooth jacket rumpled. His baggy brown slacks bore dirt stains. What had he been up to?

But his manner was upbeat and his eyes had more life than I'd seen before. He came over, grinning, and gestured with open arms like a ringmaster. "Gents, you are looking at an idiot!"

Tell me something I don't know, I thought.

"I was sitting at the bar across the street," Steve said, still grinning, jerking a thumb in that direction, "at Angelo's. Waiting for you fellas! Thought that was the Pink House! They both got a red roof, y'know? Anyway, I was grousing to the bartender, a gal, about people who can't keep their appointments on time, and then I went outa there to go back to the motel and, bingo, I see this place across the street! What a dummy!"

His words were flying.

"Johnny boy!" he said. "Man, you really look sharp. That a Hickey–Freeman suit?"

"Yup."

Steve laughed twice. "We're gonna both of us buy a whole *closet* of new clothes. Two closets, each! Nate here already knows how to dress, but you and me, Johnny Boy, we gotta spruce up our style!"

Bennies.

"You guys want sandwiches? I could eat. I'll get us sandwiches. Burgers okay? Cheeseburgers with everything, onions too? French fries?"

"Sure," I said, and Hagan nodded.

Steve got up and went to the bar, fast.

"He's sure in a good mood," Hagan observed.

"He's high as a fucking kite. You see his pupils? They look like black polka dots."

Steve came back, informed us we'd be having chips not fries because "this fine establishment doesn't seem to have a frier," and leaned in, settling a hand on Hagan's shoulder. I was starting to suspect this guy's gate swung both ways. He was an ex-con, after all, and being inside could expand a man's horizons.

"You got that I.D. for me?" Steve asked the cabbie, thinking he was whispering but wasn't. Booze and bennies are a tricky combo.

Hagan said he did and got from his suitcoat pocket an Army discharge photostat, a Social Security card and a medical record, all in the name John Byrne of Kirkwood, Missouri.

"Man, you did *fine!*" Steve said, looking the things over, then slapping Hagan on the back and sitting back down. "You find me new digs?"

"Yeah. Two-room suite at the Town House in the Central West End. Apartment annex of the Congress Hotel."

"Nice?"

"Oh, yeah. Living room with a couple of couches, bath, kitchen, bedroom, whatchamacallit French doors out to a balcony. Class all the way."

"Perfect. Perfect. Perfect. Who needs more beer? I need more beer."

He got us more beer.

"You know who I miss?" Steve was drinking Schlitz. All three of us were. It made Milwaukee famous, after all. Of course we were in St. Louis.

"You know who I miss?" Steve repeated. "Sandy. What a great gal."

Yeah, they'd really hit it off.

The cheeseburgers arrived with a basket of greasy potato chips, delivered by the bartender, who looked irritated about it. The burger was almost as thin as the slice of cheap cheese on it, but I started eating the thing anyway—my stomach had been empty since I puked earlier.

Steve took a bite of the burger, chewed, swallowed, then said, "So did she get away all right? To the airport? Sandy?"

"She got in a cab with a guy I know," Hagan said. "Another Ace driver. Dependable. She'll be fine."

That was a fairly skillful lie—Sandy had gotten in a cab with another cabbie, all right; but wasn't going to the airport unless it was the one in St. Joseph, Missouri.

"I miss her," Steve said again. "I was too tired last night to do right by her, but I could use some, you know, companionship of the female variety. You think you could fix me up with another girl tonight, Johnny? I don't wanna spend the night by myself. I get lonesome. Or is the Town House too high class for that?"

"I can find somebody," Hagan said. "I know some girls who work the big hotels. Wised-up broads who know their way around."

"Good. I like *nice* girls, remember."

I knew all about that. I'd met Bonnie.

I ate about half of my burger, and Hagan wolfed his down, although Steve took only that one bite. He finished the second beer before saying, "If I'm gonna have myself a big date tonight, I can't be looking like a bum when a guy like you all spiffed up is making the introductions. You know anyplace around here I can get some decent things myself?"

The cabbie shrugged. "There's a Famous–Barr department store in Clayton."

"Where's Clayton?"

"Just another suburb, not far."

In the small parking lot, dusk now, the green two-tone Plymouth waited; mud was on its tires and fender.

Where had Carl/Steve been this afternoon?

He told Hagan to drive—"I don't have a license, why take chances?"—and I got in the back. Propped against the seat next to me was a shovel. The hair on the back of my neck prickled again.

Steve got in front and Hagan started up the car.

I said, "What's the shovel for, Steve?"

"Oh, sorry. I was gonna bury something and changed my mind. No room in the trunk. My metal suitcases are still in there. Hey! Get a load of that."

He had spotted my loaner Caddy in the lot nearby. He'd not seen me driving it—did he recognize it from the ransom drop two nights ago?

If he did, he made no mention of it. Instead he said, "Johnny boy, we'll all be swimmin' in Cadillacs before long. Drivin' 'em right down the middle of Easy Street."

I said, "That's *my* ride."

He turned and looked at me in the back sitting next to the shovel. "You Outfit guys travel right."

"Well, we don't go Second Class."

The Famous-Barr was closed, but a pedestrian directed us to a Boyd's branch close by. Hagan parked out front and Steve led the way, playing the big shot, striding into the men's department and telling the first salesman he came to, "I need a new suit."

The slender, pomaded salesman, with a superior attitude from home and expensive suit provided at work, said, "I'm afraid we have a considerable backlog of alterations. It will be several days, I'm afraid, before anything can be ready for you."

Steve was already thumbing through hanging Hickey-Freeman suits like they were wallpaper samples. "Are you a gambler?"

"Sir?"

"I will bet you ten dollars you can have a suit ready for me by tomorrow."

And Steve yanked a wad of cash from his dirt-smudged pants and fanned out twenty-dollar bills like he was dealing cards. "Price tag says one-hundred and-twenty-two dollars," he said. "That's one-hundred-and-thirty right there. Put the rest against any alteration charge. That assumes, of course…"

"It will be ready tomorrow, sir."

"Good."

I sat to one side and watched rather numbly while Steve— who introduced himself to the salesman as John Byrne—was measured for his suit, then bought a new pair of shoes, several pair of trousers (one to replace his muddy ones), a Dobbs hat (we were all wearing them that season), an assortment of socks, three sets of cufflinks, a belt and various neckties. Steve turned Hagan loose—"Buy yourself half a dozen shirts"—and, as the store closed around us, settled up with the salesman.

"We'll be doing more business with your fine firm," Steve said, "when we pick up my Hickey–Freeman tomorrow." He had changed trousers and had the rest of his purchases in a big-handled bag. "Shall we say at noon?"

"Noon will be fine, sir."

Back in the Plymouth, with Hagan again at the wheel, Steve said, "Sometimes I think these people don't know who they're dealing with."

I couldn't argue with that.

But Steve was coming down off his high. "I want a nice girl, remember. Some nice, sexy doll, Johnny. Go two hundred. Go three if you have to."

"Okay," Hagan said. "Sure."

He'd been confident minutes ago, but now he was all nerves, lighting up a cigarette clumsily. "I don't think I care to move to the Town House tonight. If it's a nice place like you say, Johnny, the Coral Court's better for a rendezvous."

"Okay," Hagan said.

"We need to get my luggage up to the room again."

Outside the Pink House, they dropped me to pick up the Caddy. I followed them to the motor court, our middle two-story building at the rear, then parked in the 50-A garage and walked around where the Plymouth was backed up to the foot of the exterior stairs, trunk lid up. Hugging the black metal suitcase to him as he went up, Steve looked like he might lose his balance and tumble down onto us any moment. We were following, perhaps too close, the green footlocker in a coffin carry again, the cabbie climbing backward.

A car pulled in behind the Plymouth. In the darkness, I couldn't discern the make or its occupants. Could it be Shoulders and his cops jumping the gun? *Gun* being the operative word— Steve was still armed, and the cabbie and I were between him and the new arrival. This night could easily go Fourth of July on us, exploding into deadly orange muzzle flashes and the sharp firecracker reports of pistols.

Steve, not surprisingly, panicked—somehow, still clutching the heavy suitcase to himself, he made it up those last few steps and got to the landing and through into the hall. Below, a car door opened and shut, but no one in the vehicle called out. Hagan looked startled and seemed about to panic himself when I said, very quietly, "We're working *with* the cops, remember?"

An arguable benefit, but it calmed him.

We finished the last few steps of this latest trip up and rested the footlocker on the landing. We caught our breaths. Then I raised a settling palm and said, "I'll check," and went down. I did not withdraw my nine mil, although I unbuttoned my suit-coat and Burberry.

A man in a topcoat and hat stood next to a late-model Ford sedan. In the rider's seat, looking abashed, was his pretty wife (or possibly "wife").

"Sorry," the man said, embarrassed. "We just need to get in our garage here. You're blocking, I'm afraid."

We exchanged a few additional friendly words and I moved the Plymouth enough to allow these occupants of a first-floor room to pull into their private garage.

Then I rejoined Hagan atop the exterior stairs on the landing, told him the score, and we carted the footlocker of ransom money back into the building. Hagan knocked with his elbow, said, "It's us," and Steve let us in.

He had the .38 revolver in hand, so my instincts were right —if that had been Shoulders down there, the night would have burst into gunfire with Hagan and me right in the middle.

"Just a couple motel guests downstairs," I assured Steve, "wanting to get in their garage. Put that thing away."

I meant the .38. He went over and stowed it in the night-stand drawer. We placed the footlocker in its familiar position along the wall by its black metal mate.

"I got the goddamn shakes," Steve said. "That really fuckin' spooked me! Man, I am jumpy as a damn *cat.* I really thought that was…you know, insurance investigators or something."

"Yeah," I said.

Hagan looked a bit disheveled despite his new wardrobe. He was still over by the door and Steve joined him. "I'm sorry, Johnny boy. That really threw me. Everything's gonna be fine. Let's have a couple of drinks."

The cabbie shook his head. "No, I need to round that girl up for you. If she has a friend or two, maybe we can have a regular orgy. Nate, you up for that?"

"Sure," I said. Who wouldn't want to get naked with Steve and Johnny Boy?

Hagan opened the door and Steve asked him when he'd be back with the girls.

"Oh," the cabbie said, "maybe half an hour."

"Okay. Knock twice fast, once slow, and say, 'Steve, this is Johnny.' Got it?"

"Twice fast, once slow, 'Steve, this is Johnny.' Got it."

And Hagan was gone.

The air seemed to go out of Steve. He'd come down from the Bennies, then got rattled by that car pulling up, which had him going again; but that was over now and he was looking at me with those familiar dead dull eyes. He went over to the nightstand and poured himself a glass of whiskey from the half-empty bottle. Or maybe he was an optimist and it was half-full.

"You want a snort, Nate?" He was pacing as he drank. A slow pace, but pacing.

"No thanks. Sit down, Carl."

He caught it quicker than I figured he would.

He stopped in mid-pace and said, "Carl?"

"That's your name. Your first name. What's the last?"

He trudged over to the bed and sat on the edge like he'd done so often yesterday and today. Sat hunch-shouldered. Defeat settled on him like heavy humidity.

I dragged a chair over and sat facing him, but he was looking past me into nothing.

"Your last name, Carl. What is it?"

"Hall. How did you know my name is Carl?"

"Bonnie told me."

Now he looked at me. "Bonnie!"

"You left a newspaper with the apartment marked on it here in this room. When you slipped out this afternoon, I found it. Went over to Arsenal Street and had a little talk with her."

"What did she tell you?"

"Not much. She was pretty drunk."

"Big surprise."

"Here's the thing. My friends in Chicago don't *like* surprises. If you don't come clean with them, they'll find you and kill you."

"Kill me."

"Right. If they're going to risk fencing that money, they need to know exactly what happened and what your role was in it. If Tom Marsh killed the boy, they will want Marsh in custody or better still dead, but out of the way. That's a must before they can do business with you. A must before they wash that dirty goddamn money of yours."

His laugh was a small thing that happened in his chest and barely got out. A private joke. But then he shared it: "Tom Marsh had nothing to do with this. He wasn't involved. He's a guy I met in a bar once, yeah, and we pulled a small job together, but...I haven't seen him in a couple years. His name just popped in my head when I needed...someone to blame."

"Is the boy dead?"

"Yeah. Since the first day."

That made me squint at him, like I was trying to believe he was really sitting there. "What do you mean...the first day?"

"Bonnie picked the kid up at that school. A cab took her and him. Dropped them at a Katz Drug parking lot where I was waiting with our station wagon. I had her dog along with me— Doc. She raises boxers. She's good with dogs and horses and other dumb animals. We told the kid we were going to get him some ice cream. You know how kids like ice cream. I took

Westport Road into Kansas. Into farmland. The kid enjoyed the ride. I drove us into a field and stopped. Bonnie took Doc out for a walk. I was going to strangle the kid, but I didn't bring enough rope. He fought like a little wildcat."

…as full of piss and vinegar as any kid I've ever seen…

"I shot him in the head. I missed the first time, but the second I did okay. You'd be surprised how much blood there is in a kid."

The nine millimeter under my left arm was talking to me. I could feel it like some part of me that ached.

Somehow I said, "What did you do then?"

"Well, I had this plastic sheeting I brought. Wrapped him up in that and put him in the back of the station wagon. Covered him with a comforter Doc sleeps on. We stopped for a drink. I had to send Bonnie in because I had too much blood on me. We just sat and drank in the car. I got out once and walked around the station wagon to make sure it wasn't leaking blood. It got on the floorboard in front, you see. When we finished our whiskey, I drove us home."

"To St. Joe."

That surprised him. "Yes. Bonnie has a little house there. We buried him near the back porch. She put flowers in on it and it looked nice. Seemed like the right thing to do."

The Browning talked to me. Do it. Do it. Was that my father's voice?

I said, just filling the air, "Must have taken a while to dig that hole."

"Oh, yeah. I'd dig an hour, then go inside and lie down and rest a while…you know, drink a little…then go out and dig some more. Wasn't much of a hole, though. Three feet deep, maybe. Five feet long?"

Was he asking me?

I said, burying the sarcasm deeper than the boy, "You must have been beat after such a busy day."

"Oh, no. I dug the hole in advance."

I backhanded him.

Then I got the nine millimeter out and his little mouth opened big, trailing blood from one corner but not enough blood to suit me, and the dead eyes got wide and afraid.

A bang followed, but it was a fist on the door—it banged three times, twice fast, once slow, and Hagan's voice said, "Steve, this is Johnny."

A key worked in the door and Lt. Lou Shoulders and a young patrolman came in with their guns out and ready. I put mine away. Hagan was out in the hall, glimpsed for a moment, before he slipped away.

Still just sitting there, trickling blood, Carl looked at me in tragic disappointment. "I can't believe Johnny Boy betrayed me…"

"There are worse sins," I said.

CHAPTER EIGHT

Lt. Shoulders kept his revolver trained on a dazed Carl Hall as the young uniformed officer shuttled me into my room next door. Oddly, the patrolman might have been a junior version of Shoulders: dark hair, high forehead, dark bushy eyebrows, prominent nose over a small but full mouth. The difference was Shoulders' fleshy face, which had seen considerable wear and tear, while this crossing guard of a cop seemed like his had barely been used yet.

The young cop followed me inside, shut the door behind him, and gestured with a traffic-cop palm, as if I'd been charging toward him and not just facing him with folded arms.

His voice was high and reedy. "Now, you just stay put, buddy, till Lt. Shoulders tells you otherwise."

"Name's Heller. What's yours, officer?"

He was already halfway out the door; his slim frame didn't resemble Shoulders—his superior had a hulking physique. "Dolan. Patrolman Elmer Dolan."

I gestured to the wall separating 50-A from 49-A. "That creep put a gun in the nightstand drawer. You'll want to collect it."

"Okay. Thanks, Mr. Heller."

I stopped him with one last question before he closed the door on me: "You're a rookie, aren't you?"

"I am, yes, sir."

"Well, keep your wits about you. That dope is *on* dope, boozed-up out of his gourd, and capable of just about any evil shit."

He swallowed, nodded thanks and closed me in.

I looked at the phone by the bed and wondered if I should call Bob Greenlease. But all I had was Carl's confession. And while I believed what that greasy-faced monster had told me, it was just the latest of several versions of the kidnap tale.

On the other hand, it had been chillingly credible, and the one thing I accepted as a certainty was that Bobby Greenlease was dead.

So I stared at the phone and it stared back at me. Was what I'd got out of Carl something appropriately shared long-distance with the father who'd been hoping against hope that $600,000 would bring his boy home alive and well?

A knock was followed by an announcement: "Lou Shoulders, Heller."

I let the big baggy cop in. He had a raincoat on over his black suit, his tie black, too, and a shapeless gray fedora tugged on his skull indifferently—he had a circuit preacher look about him, right down to hard eyes in a soft face.

"He says his name is John Byrne," Shoulders said, in his low, rumbly way. "Insurance agent from Elgin, Illinois. No driver's license, though some other I.D. backs that up. But this is Steve Strand, aka Carl Something, right?"

"Oh yeah. His last name is Hall. Middle initial A, if his hat-band is to be believed. From St. Joseph, Missouri, if *he's* to be believed."

"You smack him? He's bleeding a bit."

"Just once and not hard enough. And it was after he talked. I told him if he wanted the Chicago Outfit to wash his ransom money, he had to be straight with me about his role in the kidnapping. He copped to everything."

I gave Shoulders a quick recap. I won't lie to you: my voice caught a couple times.

The circuit preacher's look turned mournful. "Yeah. I got kids, too. I wouldn't mind shooting him trying to escape."

He didn't know how close I'd come to doing that without an excuse.

"So," I said, "how can I help?"

"You can't. You already done plenty, Heller—tied a red ribbon around this slimy cocksucker. We'll take it from here."

I reached for my wallet and got him out a card. "I should be back in Chicago in a day or so, unless you advise otherwise. You need me for a court appearance or anything, I'll be there with bells on."

He took the card but shook his head. "That's doubtful, Heller. Y'see, you was never here."

"Is that right?"

"Carl is scared as shit of you and the Outfit. And my pal Johnny Hagan and his favorite whore Sandy, they'll stay mum, too."

"Like I said, I'm willing to testify."

He shook the big bucket head. "It'd just open up a whole can of worms. See, we're taking Carl for a ride...no, not the Chicago kind. We're hauling him over to the Town House where Johnny Hagan rented him a suite. That's where the arrest'll be made."

"Why not here?"

Shoulders lit up a cigarette and it bobbled as he talked. "Matter of jurisdiction. Marlborough is well outside the St. Louis city limits. Need to make the bust on home soil, so to speak."

"Ah. You probably want me to clear out of this room and make myself scarce. I'll check out right away."

"You're already checked out. Manager, Jack Carr, is an old pal. He's helping us keep things on the q.t. This isn't the kind of publicity a, uh, respectable little Mom-and-Pop shop like the Coral Court needs."

"You're saying I should fade."

His grin was an unsettling array of big yellow teeth. "Heller, you are so close to gone already I can barely see you."

He gave me a nod and sauntered out, shutting the door soft, like he didn't want to wake the dead.

I drove through the night.

No moon, just blackness, the big Cadillac cutting through nothing, farmland rolling flat and anonymous, with only the occasional small-town Main Street to indicate the world hadn't ended. What seemed a fire in the night was only the lights of Columbia, where a We-Never-Close service station filled the belly of the Caddy. I was hungry too, and had a Baby Ruth bar and a cup of vending machine coffee. The heater put out fine. I found a radio station that wasn't playing Grand Ole Opry, instead putting me in the soothing company of Johnnie Ray, Rosemary Clooney and Eddie Fisher. I turned it off once, when Patti Page started singing "(How Much Is) That Doggie in the Window." The song was worth hating in general, but it reminded me of Carl and Bonnie's dog Doc and the comforter the animal used to sleep on before it became Bobby Greenlease's shroud. I thought the veins on the back of my hands would pop, clutching the steering wheel. After a while I switched the radio back on and Frankie Laine was singing "High Noon," all about killing bastards and that was better.

Then, somehow, it was four hours after I left the Coral Court and I was in Kansas City—or I should say Mission Hills, coming up to the FBI checkpoint at West 53rd and Verona Road, the sleepy affluent neighborhood that at midnight was even sleepier.

I slowed and the passenger door opened on the parked blue Ford and agent Wesley Grapp stepped out. Like me, he was in a raincoat, just not a Burberry—I made more money than FBI agents, which wasn't fair but that was capitalism for you.

I pulled over and, leaving the motor running, met him just outside the driver's door of the Cadillac.

We skipped any greeting.

I went right to: "Has anybody informed Bob Greenlease yet?"

Once again, it was cold enough for our breath to smoke, and his glasses were already fogging. "Informed him of what?"

"That the kidnappers are in the custody of the St. Louis police."

His face was immobile but I could tell he was frowning inside. "What do you know about it, Nate?"

"I asked you first, Wes. I'll remind you that I'm in Mr. Greenlease's employ."

His sigh made a misty cloud. "We don't know much yet. Just that the two suspects keep confessing but never the same way twice. They can't seem to stop gilding the lily. We're looking for a third suspect."

That would be Tom Marsh. I could have told him it was a waste of time, but better to let the feds track the guy down and make sure he really didn't have anything to do with anything.

Now Grapp's frown emerged. "What's your role in this, Nate?"

"I did some poking around in St. Louis. Undercover, essentially. The key cops are in the know, but I'm to stay off the official radar, unless I'm needed."

His jutting chin came up. "You like these suspects?"

"In the 'like' sense of yes, they are the scum responsible. That boy is dead, Wes. His body will turn up tomorrow at the latest. They were thoughtful, though. They planted flowers over him."

"This is our case now," Grapp said. "Lindbergh law kicks in—maybe you've heard of it."

I didn't rise to the bait. "I'm guessing there will be some

jurisdictional squabbling between county and city and federal, but I don't care about that. I might lean toward Missouri because they are more liable to execute this lovely pair. Uncle Sam hasn't killed a woman since Mary Surratt. That's before your time—she conspired to kill Lincoln."

"I know my history. What are you doing here?"

"I want to prepare Bob Greenlease for what's coming. He has a right to know."

He sighed another cloud, then said, "I don't know that that's your call."

"You don't know that it isn't. Let's just say I'm returning the Cadillac he loaned me."

I gave him a smile that barely cracked my face and got back in the Caddy where it was warm. He seemed to be thinking about stopping me, but probably couldn't think of a legitimate reason why.

The Greenlease house, so austerely lovely by day, seemed just a barely defined geometric shape on a night so black it threatened to swallow the structure up. The handful of yellow flickery windows might have represented a fire not quite out of control yet.

Rather than ring the bell, and risk waking more people than necessary, I knocked, gently. I had a hunch someone would be posted near the door. They were still in the mode of getting Bobby back, and time was a precious commodity. Yes it was—but one little boy's had already run out.

The door cracked open. I'd been right—a guardian *was* at the gate, and once again that guardian was the other son, the adopted one, Paul. He was in a suit that looked slept in and lacked a tie—probably camped out on the living room sofa, should the door need him.

"Mr. Heller," he said, blinking, making himself wake up more. He gave his head a shake. "Come in. Please."

He opened the door for me and I stepped into that ballroom of an entryway, the stairs rising to darkness, its lion's-head newel roaring with silence.

I said, "I don't suppose your father is still up."

"No." Quickly he gathered my raincoat and hat, placing them on a chair nearby. "He went upstairs about eleven. Have you heard something?"

"Could we sit down for a moment, Paul? I'll fill you in." I gestured toward the living room, down the hall to the right.

He nodded and led the way. Then we were in the room where just days ago I'd spoken with his father while his young sister slept nestled to Daddy on the sofa that faced the fireplace, which was going now, giving off ironic warmth. A blanket was on the cushions—this was indeed where Paul had been bivouacked—and he picked the thing up quickly, folded it, set it on a chair.

We both sat.

"I do have news," I said. "Most of it very bad."

"Tell me."

"I will, but I need to know whether you think we should wake your father up for it."

"Oh, we should. Whatever it is. But…but not Mother."

I nodded. "Listen first. Your brother is dead. The kidnappers took his life right away the first day."

The blood drained out of his face and made a ghost of him. He swallowed. His lower lip quivered.

"The only good news," I said, "is that the two who did it are in the custody of the St. Louis police."

"What…what kind of people are they?"

"Possibly a married couple. They seem to have lived together, at least. A pair of drunken lowlifes looking to make a bundle."

"They did this…together?"

"The woman picked your brother up at school. The man killed Bobby shortly after. Shot him to death. It was relatively quick. Bobby suffered, I won't lie to you…but not for long."

Tears came from his eyes and then trailed onto his cheeks like rain down a window. His voice wobbled. "What kind of man…."

I shrugged. "You'll know soon enough. He's about your age and from your social class. His name is Carl Hall. From things he said, I'd gather he squandered his own fortune and looked for a way to…replenish it."

Paul's eyes had grown wide. Large. "Carl Hall? Carl *Austin* Hall?"

"His middle initial is 'A,' so it…it could be Austin. Why? Does that sound familiar?"

"Tell me what he looks like."

I did.

"My God," Paul said. His tears had stopped. He dug out a handkerchief and dried his face. "So that's why his voice stirred something. I think I know him. Or, anyway…*knew* him. Carl Austin Hall was at Kemper with me."

"What's Kemper?"

"A military school. 'West Point of the West,' they call it. Boonville, hundred miles from here. It's just high school with gray uniforms and no girls. I hated it. My circle had a good time despite that."

"Was Carl part of your circle?"

"No. He wanted to be. He was a hanger-on. He would get liquor for us and try to…worm his way in. I frankly thought he was a jerk."

Paul hadn't been wrong.

"We weren't close by any means," Paul said. "But I did *know* him. I wonder…my God, did I *cause* this somehow? Was he taking it out on my family because I snubbed him? Or maybe… did he think I flaunted the family wealth?"

"No, no, he was well-off himself at that time. Paul, this is nothing you could have predicted."

His face tightened like a terrible fist. "What if my father… what if he blames *me* for this? What if people think I had something to do with it?"

He began to cry again, but it was a different kind of crying now; he'd gone past sad into despair.

I don't know how long he was in the doorway, listening, but suddenly the figure in the blue satin dressing gown seemed to fly by and gathered into his arms this man in his mid-thirties like a boy of six and held him close. Paul was sobbing into his father's chest and that private detective's mind kicked in again and I suspected this adopted son was in some way of Robert Greenlease's own blood—perhaps the wrong side of the sheets, if not his own sheets then perhaps a relative's. But blood was blood, and when it wasn't being spilled, it was a good thing.

I started to get up.

Greenlease looked at me, his older son still in his arms, standing together like a statue carefully designed not to fall over, and raised a hand as if in benediction, but his tears-slick expression said to wait.

I did so, sitting on the stairs by the carved lion.

Greenlease joined me in perhaps ten minutes and bid me follow him. Soon we were once again in the study where hunters and dogs looked to lush trees for their prey.

"How much did you hear?" I asked.

"Almost all of it," he said.

Somewhere, somehow, he'd had the presence of mind to make me a rum and Coke and pour himself a good slug of bourbon.

"But," he said, "I want to hear everything. All of it."

"Bob…"

"All of it, goddamnit."

I gave him chapter and verse. He didn't need some of the more salacious details, like Sandy O'Day's wee hours visit to my room, or the quiet horror of "Steve" throwing around ransom money on suits, socks and shoes. But I didn't stint on what I knew about Bobby's demise. I kept it understated, but then so had been Carl's telling of it and that didn't help soften the blows any. The boy's father sat expressionless, eyes unblinking and blue, in an eerie reminder of the kidnapper's dull glazed look.

I said, "I have no idea when you'll get an official call. Sometime in the morning, I assume. The questioning of those two will go on through the night. Their stories are shifting in pathetic attempts to lessen their roles."

"This fellow Marsh?" he said, the first he'd spoken in a while.

"Yes. I believe he exists, but doubt he had anything to do with this. Just a name that the real perpetrator pulled out of his past. Be secure in the belief that I got the truth out of Carl Hall—he had the threat of Chicago hanging over him. The police will have to work at him for a while to catch up with me. And the woman was drunk out of her mind through most of it."

His sigh started high and stair-stepped down. "I appreciate what you've done, Nate. It's a great help. I want you to accept that five thousand dollars. I'll write you a new check…"

"No. I'll invoice you for my time and expenses. It won't run anywhere near that."

"If you get pulled back into this—"

"I'll let you know and we'll discuss it. And of course I'll cooperate if either the police or FBI need me. But the details of how I came to identify Carl and Bonnie as the kidnappers, and turn them both over, are unlikely to go on the record."

"Why is that?"

"Frankly, I was working with a cop and a crook—this Lt. Shoulders, a bent copper if I ever saw one, and Joe Costello, a known racketeer. They suspected Hall was the kidnapper but were prepared not to turn him in if he proved instead to be an embezzler or bank robber. In that case they were ready to do business with him."

He shivered though the room was quite warm. "It's appalling. And they thought you'd go along with that?"

"I have a reputation for being, as they say, 'connected' to the Chicago mob…the Outfit. When I started out, frankly, there was some truth to it. Years later, that assumption on the part of some people can come in handy. It was in this instance."

He was shaking his head. "What kind of world are we living in, Nate?"

"A world where men like us can get ahead, Bob. Can make a nice life for ourselves and our families. But it's also one where men of envy and greed and stupidity and flat-out evil are ready and willing to take everything away."

"And now I have to tell Virginia."

"You do. And I have no advice for you but to spare her the details as much as possible. Hitting her with all of it at once… well, the cruelty of that is just too much. She's going to have to take the biggest, worst blow now, and then as the terrible details make themselves manifest, she'll have to suffer again, but at least with that initial impact behind her. Hell, what do I know about it? I know one thing for sure—she needs to hear this from you, before it gets out otherwise."

Sorrow and shock had erased any expression from his features. The only difference between Carl Hall's blankness and Robert Greenlease's was the humanity behind Bob's.

Or was Carl Austin Hall all *too* human? Was he all our

weaknesses wrapped up in one selfish, careless package? Where killing a child was just another get-rich-quick scheme?

Greenlease walked me to the door. I told him I'd be heading back tomorrow. My presence here was no longer needed or desirable—he knew where to find me and so did the authorities. He told me a room would be waiting at the President Hotel and that I could leave the Cadillac there. I should be sure, he said, to include such items as cabs to the airport on my expenses. I said I'd book my own flight. Life goes on. Like death.

When I approached the Verona Road FBI checkpoint, Special Agent Grapp waved me over. I rolled the window down and he leaned in, a federal carhop again, asking, "Did you give Greenlease the news?"

"Yeah."

"How did he take it?"

"Like a guy so far gone he couldn't feel his guts being ripped out. What do you think?"

He shook his head. His glasses were fogging up again. "They've confessed everything, but they're still all over the map. We're gonna have to step in."

"As well you should."

"For one thing, the count is way off."

"What count?"

"The money count. Less than three hundred grand in Hall's luggage. That's not even half the ransom haul."

"Your math skills are impressive."

"You're not surprised?"

"There are crooked cops and racketeers and cabbie pimps and grasping whores and drunken idiots all over this fucking case. What surprises me is there's still almost three hundred grand *to* confiscate."

"You have a cynical outlook, Heller."

"Wow. They must train you FBI guys in psychology and everything. Goodnight, Agent Grapp."

He grunted a tiny laugh and waved me off.

A room was waiting at the President and I fell asleep so fast you would think nothing troubling was on my mental and emotional horizon at all. But I was almost in my fifties and of an age where exhaustion could prevail.

My bedside phone rang and I wondered if I'd been dumb enough last night to put in for a wake-up call; my watch, also on the nightstand, said it was almost ten, so maybe I *should* get up, even if I hadn't got to bed till two A.M.

When I finally answered the insistent ring, it wasn't a wake-up call, but a familiar voice that shook me awake just as effectively.

"They stop serving breakfast at ten-thirty," Barney Baker said. "Shake a leg."

The giant man with the small head—in another tent of a suit, this one charcoal gray with a black-and-white striped tie—was seated at a table in the underpopulated coffee shop eating ham and eggs and hash browns. This might have seemed a relatively restrained breakfast for this particular diner but for the half-eaten side plate of stacked pancakes rising a good five inches. Atop it, three pats of melting butter swam in hot syrup that dripped down like Johnny Weissmuller's hair after a swim.

I sat across from Barney and nodded hello and he smiled and nodded back, too polite to speak with his mouth full. The same pretty waitress from a couple of days ago took my order, after giving me a wide-eyed look behind Barney's back, as if challenging my selection of dining companions. I ordered coffee and a doughnut.

"Everybody's happy with you," Barney said. His potatoes were gone, making room for the transfer of the top three pancakes.

"Not everybody," I said.

"Well, not those two fucking deadbeat lowlifes keeping the St. Louis cops entertained with one self-serving story after another. You're out of this now, understood?"

"Yeah, I got that. Of course, I can't duck a subpoena, if it comes to that."

"No, that'd be un-American. But if you have to go public, we'll help you through it. You been coached on giving evidence before, right?"

That was a low blow.

He ate a while. My coffee came. Too bitter. I added a touch of cream.

Barney delicately dabbed his syrupy puss with a paper napkin. "They picked up Johnny Hagan and his whore."

"Together?"

"No, she was in St. Joe shacked up with another whore. A lot of those dames swing both ways, y'know. I can't blame 'em. Would you wanna fuck a guy?"

The four-hundred-pound slob made his own case. No, that's unfair—for a guy who weighed four hundred pounds, he was the personification of grace and refinement.

"Not that either her or Hagan know anything," Barney said. "To them, Hall was just another big spender. And neither of 'em are gonna mention you, not and risk Joe Costello's enmity."

"Pretty fancy vocabulary on the kid," I said. "Last time it was 'hypothetical,' this time 'enmity.' "

He grinned. To his credit, he had no syrup on his face, though it was dripping off the triple bite of pancake waiting on his fork. "You really oughta come hear me speak some time, Nate. Did I mention Civil Rights is a specialty?"

"You did."

"Oh, and speaking of Joe Costello…that's why I called this meeting."

"Is that what this is?"

He nodded. He got a white letter-size envelope out from inside the tent and handed it to me with no discretion whatsoever. I employed some, though, and peeked in at the stack of twenties.

"That's the four you're owed," Barney said and shoveled the syrupy bite in.

He meant four grand.

I tucked it away. "Thank Joe for me," I said, rising. I'd finished my coffee and half of the doughnut. "But give him a message for me, would you, Barney?"

He swallowed. "Sure, Nate."

"Tell him these better not have Greenlease serial numbers on them, or he'll be back in business with his pal Brothers."

I wasn't there for any of the aftermath.

The same morning I breakfasted with Barney Baker, the FBI found Bobby's body buried beneath the chrysanthemums in the backyard of Bonnie Heady's blue-shuttered white bungalow in St. Joseph, Missouri.

I followed the rest in the press and on the TV news. Information came out about both Bonnie and Carl.

Bonnie had been married to a livestock merchant and dog breeder for twenty respectable years, during which time she had eleven abortions. Never really a fan of kids, Bonnie. Voted "Best Dressed Cowgirl" in 1951, she claimed to have been treated cruelly by her husband, but her post-divorce life had found her turning tricks (and to drink), despite having inherited a family farm and not really needing money. She had decided what she really needed was Carl Austin Hall.

Hall was the son of a respected lawyer and his mother had been daughter of a prominent judge. He got in trouble at military school, dropped out of college, paid for the occasional abortion, went into the Marines for two tours, was court-martialed for going AWOL and drinking on duty. Inherited two hundred thousand dollars, started up various businesses—music shop, two liquor stores, a crop-dusting operation—and went broke. He robbed eight taxi cabs on a spree that netted $33. He went to the Missouri State prison in Jefferson City on a five-year term, worked in the dispensary getting hooked on drugs, bragged to his fellow inmates that he'd commit a perfect crime: "I'll be driving Cadillacs and you'll be carrying a lunch bucket." Paroled after a year and three months, he tried to sell cars (unsuccessfully), then sold insurance, and did make one sale.

To Bonnie Heady.

Bonnie and Carl were indicted by a federal grand jury in late October and went to trial on November 16, fifty days after they killed Bobby Greenlease. Took the jury just under an hour to find them guilty. At midnight, eighty-one days after the kidnapping, Heady and Hall sat side by side in the gas chamber as sodium cyanide powder was dropped into vats of sulfuric acid.

Carl died first, Bonnie two minutes later.

On Death Row, Carl had been no help about the missing half of the ransom money. He thought maybe he'd buried some of it, but couldn't be sure—he'd been too drunk. The FBI targeted Lt. Shoulders and Patrolman Dolan, who were caught in lies and both did time on perjury raps, but no money was recovered. Various St. Louis racketeers, Joe Costello included, came under federal scrutiny. Rumor had it the money never left the Coral Court. Some spoke of a mysterious man on the fringes of things.

Him I can vouch for. He, which is to say me, never got a dime of that blood money.

But who did?

BOOK TWO
St. Louis Blues

August 1958

CHAPTER NINE

On a hot August day, I took my almost eleven-year-old son to Disneyland. He'd spent July with me in Chicago, going to boxing and ball games and museums and street fairs, and now I was returning him to his mother and her husband, the supposed film producer; but first Sam and I were having a father-and-son day in the Magic Kingdom in Anaheim, California.

I looked like any other tourist in my Bermuda shorts and polo shirt with a straw fedora topping it off; my son was dressed similarly, right down to the fedora—Nathan Heller's son being too cool for mouse ears—and we looked enough alike in our Ray-Bans to get amused looks. He was in fact my spitting image, although we both had too much class to spit, with only Sam's lack of a reddish tinge to his brown hair to differentiate us. That and one of us had clearly been through puberty.

This was my first visit to Walt Disney's Magical Money Maw, and I initially had a typically cynical Chicagoan's reaction. This place was an amusement park posing as a Disney movie come to life, with college kids in big-headed cartoon-character costumes mingling like monsters among children whose reactions veered between disappointment and terror. Here, the creator (not God but the beaming mustached one on TV) served up turn-of-the-century childhood memories painted with a pastel brush, inviting visitors into a fanciful American past sprinkled with pixie dust to banish actual memories of an era awash in financial failures, railroad strikes, immigrant tenements, racist lynchings, and social protest, right and left.

What a bunch of bullshit, I thought.

And then my son slipped his hand in mine.

It had been some time since my boy had done that simple thing. At nearly eleven, he was just too old for such sentimental slop. But Disneyland was overwhelming, and for every kid there were four adults, so the view moving through the throng was mostly of grown-up asses.

I'd parked my latest Jag in the vast parking lot for a quarter before paying a buck for myself and a half dollar for Sam at the gates. We'd promptly entered a tunnel taking us under the Santa Fe and Disneyland Railroad tracks into the Town Square and Main Street where awaited gas streetlamps and brightly colored Victorian buildings that housed shops with no resonance for a kid like Sam. That Uncle Walt was playing to grown-ups like himself, as we entered his Kingdom, was obvious—firehouse with horse-drawn wagons, Keystone Kops, general store, apothecary, penny arcade, with only the soda fountain not quite yet a thing of the past. Even the movie marquee would mystify a kid like Sam, ballyhooing a Buster Keaton comedy and a D.W. Griffith cowboy picture.

But then Main Street emptied out into pathways to worlds where Sam could immediately relate—Frontierland (Davy Crockett!), Tomorrowland (moon rocket!), Adventureland (African safari!), and (as Sleeping Beauty's castle in all its looming presence promised) Fantasyland.

That was where we started, going over a drawbridge where finally kids seemed as prevalent as grown-ups, and ($4.25 for fifteen attractions) (never a prosaic "ride"!) into the domains of Alice in Wonderland, Peter Pan, Snow White and especially Mr. Toad and his very wild ride (well, even Disney couldn't deny *that* was a ride).

In Adventureland, a jungle river cruise offered ersatz hippos and real foliage, while in Tomorrowland I jammed into a minisportscar with my son at Autotopia's freeway before trading them in for pack mules in Frontierland. As a parent who could afford it, and a single dad anxious to show up his ex-wife, I was prepared to endure any indignity, up to a cumulative fifty bucks.

The hand-holding had only lasted through the squeeze of Main Street, but Sam's giddy reaction to everything but the long lines was almost as good. And in those lines we took advantage of ice cream and other treats from sunny vendors in straw hats and striped shirts who called themselves hosts, addressing us as "guests," not customers.

On the sky ride, as we sat aloft in a bucket, a wide-eyed Sam asked, "You ever see anything like this in the whole world?"

And I realized something had been tugging at me from the moment we emerged from that tunnel—Disneyland was unique and yet seemed somehow familiar. Not because of any kind of county fair nostalgia, but it stirred memories of the Century of Progress exposition in '33 and '34. That I hadn't made the connection at once seems stupid in retrospect, but the Chicago World's Fair had been futuristic whereas everything in Walt's world spoke either of the past or of fantasy—even Tomorrowland had Jules Verne's Nautilus sub in it, and that dated back to the 1800's.

But the size, the scope, the audaciousness of it all, took me back twenty-five years, to where my business had begun—when my late uncle had hired me at my fledgling one-man agency to handle the pickpocket problem at the fair. They'd had a ride like this, too, in a "rocket" car between tall towers. On the other hand, Disney didn't have Sally Rand. But sexy little Tinkerbell was based on Marilyn Monroe, they say, so maybe he did at that....

And Donald Duck's daddy also had Annette from the Mickey Mouse Club, autographing near an old-fashioned bandshell in a mouse-eared cap and white short-sleeve turtleneck with her name on it, as if any identification were necessary. Watching this little Italian dish asking Sam his name was the first time I ever saw my son blush.

"There's something about her, Pop," he said, walking away, staring at the 8x10 image and glistening signature. "Just can't put my finger on it."

"Someday you'll try," I said.

Looking back at that long, terrible, wonderful day, two things really stand out, and I'm not talking about Miss Funicello. The first is Sam and me lining up along the dock by the Mark Twain Sternwheel Riverboat while Zorro—Guy Williams himself, not some nameless stunt man—engaged in a fierce sword fight on an upper deck. When the evil commandant finally leapt from the boat into the drink to flee Zorro's rapier blade, that small hand slipped into mine again.

That was the other thing—not Sam's hand clutching mine in excitement while a good guy in black dueled a bad guy in red, white and blue; but the thought it prompted: that another boy, who'd also have been almost eleven, would never give his father that simple joy, or himself experience the delight of seeing Zorro in person, triumphing over evil.

I might not have made that connection if Bobby Greenlease had not been on my mind of late—after all, the dead boy had in part prompted this trip to L.A. Maybe I'd have just put Sam on a plane home if the Greenlease kidnapping of five years ago had not cropped up again, in however unlikely a way, a few days before.

It began, as much does, in Washington, D.C.

The town's most despised, fearsome journalist worked and lived (when he wasn't on his farm) in a townhouse tucked away on the corner of the kind of cobblestone Georgetown street where few Americans could afford to reside—not even in reconditioned slave quarters. After dark, in the glow of gas streetlamps, the yellow-brick, Early American-shuttered, brass-trimmed house had an antiquated charm that even Walt Disney would consider a little much.

The blue-eyed blonde of perhaps thirty who answered the bell had assigned her curves to a white silk blouse, a navy blue pencil skirt and bright red heels, a patriotic ensemble indeed, unassuming but for its contents. Her name was Connie and we'd met. She wore horn-rimmed glasses that weren't fooling anybody—this was Drew Pearson's latest "fair-haired girl." Pearson's middle-aged wife, who rarely strayed from the family farm, either did not care or had learned how to pretend she didn't.

"He's expecting me," I said.

"Oh I know," she said. We knew each other fairly well. The last time we'd commiserated about what a cheapskate her boss was had been at the Mayflower, where she'd come over.

I followed her, eyes fixed impolitely exactly where most men would, past a glimpse of a living room and adjacent formal dining room, down a few steps into a bullpen of desks where young men and women sat at machine-gunning typewriters and spat dialogue out of *The Front Page* on telephones between insistent ringing. Smaller offices fed this newsroom-like area, whose walls were hugged by filing cabinets and a brace of news tickers attended by several anxious young men, who had to be wondering how their journalism degrees had led them here.

Connie paused outside the open door of Pearson's office, where her boss sat transfixed as he typed a few million words a minute on his Smith Corona on its stand to one side of his scarred schooner of a wooden desk. He wore a maroon smoking jacket (though he was not a smoker and didn't provide an ashtray for any who were), a big man, burly not fat, who even sitting down looked tall. For such a formidable figure, he had a prissy aspect, his egg-shaped head and waxed mustache reminiscent of Christie's Poirot.

We waited.

Connie whispered, "Overnight visit?"

I nodded.

"Mayflower?"

"Statler."

"Doing anything later?"

"You tell me."

"Ten?"

"Ten."

After a while, he pulled a page from the machine, added it to a small stack and glanced over at us, just outside his sanctum. "Ah! Nathan. Come in, come in."

Connie nodded to both of us and evaporated.

I sat opposite him on a visitor's chair of unforgiving hard wood designed to keep stays short. The office around me was more a study, its chocolate plaster walls awash in framed political cartoons pertaining to Pearson and signed celebrity photos with him in them; a fireplace, cold in summer, had its mantel lined with warm family photos; behind him, a sleeping cat shared a windowsill with stacked books and magazines. The desk had the expected in-and-out box, a single telephone, and a glass jar of Oreos, freshly filled, perhaps by Connie.

"Drew," I said by way of noncommittal greeting.

We'd had something of a contentious relationship over the years, mostly based upon his skinflint ways, which extended especially to paying my legitimate expenses. But having Drew Pearson as a client could lead one into the corridors of power, and that had paid off well over the years, even if Pearson himself hadn't.

He rocked back comfortably in his comfy chair, folded his arms in a loose, easy manner, a small smile making the mustache twitch, a maitre d' pleased with his tip. "I understand you're heading back to Chicago tomorrow."

I didn't bother asking him how he knew that. He had sources all over town, high and low and in between.

"Tomorrow, yes," I said. "This was a short trip. I spent a day with Bob Kennedy going over some things—nothing I can share."

He raised a palm, then returned it to his folded arms. "When Bob has something, he'll let me know. He's good about that. I have a very simple task for you."

I helped myself to an Oreo. Did "simple" mean it didn't pay much? Or anything? Still, I said, "I'm listening."

"I have it on reliable authority," he said, "that you were far more entwined in the Greenlease kidnapping case than is commonly known."

None of that pleased me to hear, but the word "entwined" was especially troubling. I chewed Oreo casually and did my best not to show any reaction at all. I'm pretty good at that.

When I didn't fill the silence, he did: "I notice you're not denying it. You know me well enough by now, Nathan, to understand that I make damned sure my facts are solid before sharing them."

He rarely swore—he was a devout Quaker, despite a long line of "fair-haired girls." So "damned" from him was a big fucking deal.

Chewing, I said, "Who are you sharing this with?"

"You. Just you."

I swallowed Oreo; managed not to choke. "You said you had a task."

He nodded slowly. "I am looking into the possibility that the missing three hundred thousand dollars of ransom money, if I might round off the figure, has long since made its way into the coffers of the Teamsters. Specifically, into that ignoble union's pension fund...the final stop on a money-laundering train. Likely used to cover up embezzlement."

I folded my arms. Tried to do so as casually as had Pearson. "An interesting theory. Or is it more than a theory?"

His shrug was as slow as his nod. "More than a theory, but less than a fact."

"This is a story you're working on."

He nodded.

I got up. "I wish you the best of luck with it. It was a tragic goddamn affair. A little boy died—this isn't petty politics. But my role is covered by client confidentiality and there's nothing I can share with you about it."

His eyes popped. "Sit down, man! I'm not asking you to share anything. Didn't I say this was an errand? A task? Sit down!"

I sat. But I was on the edge of my chair—partly in the way a kid does in a scary movie, partly to enable a hasty exit.

His voice was studiously calm. "You are acquainted with a gentleman...and I use the term loosely...by the name of John Oscar Hagan. A former cab driver from St. Louis, I believe."

Jesus Christ! How much did Pearson know?

I remained on the edge of my seat. Did not say anything, but stayed put.

He sat forward, elbows on his desk now. "My investigation into the unrecovered Greenlease money has hit something of a snag. No, I'm not asking you to re-open the case. Not asking you to personally dig in. But we believe that Hagan holds the answers to questions that will lead to the missing money...or at least where it went. If James Riddle Hoffa knows about this, he is finished. And what a gift to America that would be."

"Have you talked to Bob Kennedy or his brother about this?" Both Bob and Jack were on the Senate Rackets Committee.

"Premature," the journalist said. "If I can get Hagan to talk —after he's given me an exclusive interview, of course—I'll hand him over to that committee of yours with my blessing."

I'd been working for Bob on that committee, on and off, for several years. Mostly on Chicago aspects, but sometimes farther reaching—I had L.A. and New York branches now, after all. Its formal title was the United States Senate Select Committee on Improper Activities in the Labor or Management Field.

You know—rackets.

I asked, "What's the task?"

"I want you to offer Hagan $25,000 for his exclusive, on-the-record story."

Now *my* eyes were popping. "Twenty-five grand? Since when do you pay twenty-five *cents* for a story? First of all, it's against your highfalutin journalistic ethics. Second of all, we both know you're the cheapest goddamn bastard on the face of the earth."

He frowned and he had a lot of forehead to do that with. "Now, that was uncalled for!"

"Hell it was! What is going on, Drew?"

His wave tried to be conciliatory but came off as slapping the air. "All I'm asking you to do is approach Mr. Hagan with the offer. We have his address in Los Angeles—he moved there from St. Louis several years ago. He's living in rather dire circumstances. You have a, shall we say, certain cachet with him that perhaps no one else does. After all, you were in that motel room with Hagan and Carl Hall…Carl Hall, the kidnapper?"

"You don't have to tell me," I snapped, "who the fuck Carl Hall was."

Goddamn. The most dangerous columnist in D.C. knew I'd been in the thick of the events the night "Steve" had been caught and the ransom money reclaimed...short by three hundred grand.

"The job pays two thousand dollars and expenses," Pearson said. "I have the two thousand in cash, in my safe. Right here, right now. Or is the A-1 Agency, with its various branches coast to coast, so successful now that you can sneeze at a mere 'two grand'...hmmm?"

Two thousand in cash. Everything in this damn mess was cash. Even when I was dealing with the most notorious tightwad in the nation's capital.

"When can you work in an L.A. trip, Nathan?"

"Soon," I said.

Bunker Hill had once been home to the wealthy of Los Angeles, but the rich and powerful had long since moved on, leaving it to the poor and helpless, the neighborhood's formerly magnificent Victorian homes subdivided into shabby apartments whose inhabitants clung to the leaning walls like poison ivy on a trellis.

Angel's Flight, the funicular railway carting passengers 315 feet up and down the sheer slope between Hill and Olive Streets, had once been a grand tourist attraction and even now its two orange-trimmed-black cars transported several thousand a day, though their cable screech was like screams of pain.

These days it took a reckless tourist to brave the blighted neighborhood. A slum clearance project had begun several years ago, and now the top of the once fashionable hill had been lopped off, razed of its Gothic two-stories to make way for planned plazas and possibly even skyscrapers that would tower over the hill they crushed along with its ethnic mix of pensioners and poets, dope dealers and drunks.

A street over from where the Angel's Flight would have done me some good, I went up steep cement stairs as cracked as the skin of the old men in rockers on the wide porches of leaning gingerbread houses where even the most foolish Hansel or Gretel would never risk entry. My destination—the Hillcrest Hotel—offered monthly and weekly rates and was not without its luxuries: it boasted hot and cold running water.

The cranky old heavyset gal behind an excuse for a check-in desk pointed up toward the second of the hotel's two floors, where (she said) John Hagan lived in apartment 2B.

"Or not to be," I said to her.

"Huh?" she said.

Even I can't charm *all* the ladies.

"Is he in?" I asked.

"It's not my turn to look after him."

I jerked a thumb at the adjacent open stairway. "You see him go up?"

"No. He drives cab some. Might be in, might not." She leaned on her elbow; fat settled around the bone on the filthy scuffed counter, lending support. "Anything else I can do to make your life any fucking easier?"

Somehow she did not sound sincere. I gave her a "no thanks" anyway and went up creaky stairs whose last shellacking had not bothered with cleaning the dirt off first. Of course I hadn't been dusted off either since the old desk gal's shellacking.

The door to 2B was down a short hall to my left. I knocked, twice, hard. Nothing. But I heard movement within, so I gave the paint-blistered thing another couple knocks. Waited.

I was poised to knock again when the door cracked open.

Not enough was showing of the face to confirm it as Johnny Hagan's, but the eye that was part of that slice of flesh started out narrowed—at first he didn't recognize me—and then widened. Now he did.

"Heller," he said.

"Johnny. I was in the neighborhood so I thought I'd drop by."

"Right. Go away. We got nothing to talk about."

"There's money in it for you."

The eye narrowed again.

The door opened enough for him to step aside and me to enter. He was fleshier than I remembered, or maybe he'd managed to put on some weight, despite his obviously impoverished circumstances. But then starchy food is cheap.

He wore a sweat-soaked athletic t-shirt and baggy brown slacks and was in his socks, one of which was letting his big right toe out for some air. He reeked of beer and body odor with a hint of the hallway's disinfectant.

Oh, and he was holding a .38 revolver in his right hand.

Johnny Hagan bared his teeth at me; he'd lost a couple of them, a canine on one side, an incisor on the other. Whether someone had knocked them out or bad dental hygiene had taken a toll, I never found out. He'd had that scar on his lip when we met. In any case, he certainly wasn't the good-looking cabbie I'd known a few years ago in St. Louis—his five o'clock shadow seemed darker, a dirty effect, and his hairline was retreating, all those little soldiers heading for the hills.

"I'm not carrying," I said, my hands up.

He kicked the door shut and patted me down. I hadn't been lying—I'd seen no reason to come calling with the nine millimeter. But I was starting to question my judgment.

"What do you want, Heller?"

"Just to chat."

The one-room apartment opened onto a kitchen area, where dishes in the sink had long ago given up on being washed; the only way it could have looked dirtier was if cockroaches were up on their back legs dancing on the linoleum counter. The ceiling was rather high, typical of such former mansions, but everything else was dingy—faded, curling wallpaper, a meager array of mismatched furniture, a metal frame single bed, its white paint flaking. The bed was unmade, crumpled pillow, fitted sheet, top sheet so twisted he might have been planning to make a break for it out a window. On top of a dresser, with the framework for a mirror but without one, was a cabbie's cap on a folded jacket. They bore the Ray-D-O Cab designation.

An oscillating electric fan sat purring on a small beat-up table by the center bay window whose pale white curtain hung like a limp ghost, an occasional whisper of wind making it go "boo" half-heartedly.

He gestured me to an easy chair with cracked black faux-leather and sat opposite on the bed, which sagged under his weight like a very old horse. He tossed the .38 on the bed and the weapon bounced a little.

"Sorry about the frisk," he said. "This neighborhood isn't the best."

"According to what I hear, your old boss Joe Costello moved you out here and is sending you two hundred a month. You ought to be able to live better than this."

"Does it look like I got that much coming in?"

I shook my head. "I figure you were on Joe's payroll for a couple of years. When that Grand Jury went after Costello for stealing a little matter of three hundred thousand dollars, you were good enough to plead the Fifth. So you covered for him, though by doing that you indicated you had something to hide. So he set you up out here in a new life. If you call this living."

His eyes were lidded but alert. "You want me to talk, Heller? It'll put you in the Coral Court with Hall and me…and Sandy, for that matter. How does that help you?"

I shrugged. "It doesn't. It'd cause a few headaches. But all I did was what Lt. Shoulders, the officer in charge, told me to. I was gone before he and that kid Dolan hauled Hall's ass out and into their jurisdiction. No one asked me about it then, but if they do now, I'll come clean. I broke no laws."

"Neither did I."

"Then why take the Fifth? You helped those two cops transport that footlocker and metal suitcase and probably the briefcase out of that motel and take it, where? To Joe Costello, to count the dough and figure who got what? In '54, Shoulders and Dolan caught a couple of years on a perjury charge, because they lied about having taken that money straight to the Newstead station, when there's an hour unaccounted for. Eight of their fellow cops testified to that effect. Were you there, at Costello's…his office, the cab company, his nightclub…for the real accounting?"

He said nothing.

I extended an open hand. "My client is a well-known journalist who wants an on-the-record interview with you. If you will tell what you know about where that money went…and you sure as hell didn't get much of it…he will pay for the privilege. And he'll pay well."

"How well?"

"Twenty-five thousand dollars."

His mouth dropped; his eyes all but fell out of his head. "*What?* Jesus, you gotta be…"

I raised a swear-to-God palm. "Not kidding. You'll be able to trade your testimony to the Rackets Committee for immunity." I gestured around his seedy circumstances. "You are obviously a small fish in this."

He got off the bed and it whined like one of the Angel's Flight cable cars. He put his hands in his pockets and he walked to the bay windows and stared out.

I let him stare. Several minutes went by, which is a very long time. But soul-searching can take a while.

Then he turned and looked at me, "It's a lot of money."

"It is."

"But Joe made me a better offer."

"Better than twenty-five G's?"

"Much." Hagan looked out the window again; the fan made a dancing ghost of the curtains. "He said he'd let me breathe."

CHAPTER TEN

In the Caucus Room gallery of the Senate Office Building, known as the S.O.B., several witnesses who might have been similarly characterized waited to present their testimony. Teamsters president James R. Hoffa—the focus of much of what the Rackets Committee was looking into—was one of the three-hundred capacity audience in that vast red-carpeted rectangle. A beautiful August day, warm but not hot, was sneaking in the gilt-ceilinged, cream-marble-walled, black-marble-floored chamber by way of three tall sun-slanting windows that made of the large crystal chandeliers ice sculptures that refused to melt. The same could not be said for the senators, witnesses and audience, who despite the air-conditioning were subject to the punishing heat of the lights required for the TV and movie cameras.

The witness on deck right now was sweating as if subject to the worst Third Degree tactics, but in fact he was smiling and even chortling and doing quite well under the irritated questioning of Robert F. Kennedy.

The young Rackets Committee chief counsel looked trim and composed, his striped tie snugged, his suit crisp, his dark brown hair longish but perfectly barbered. His boyish blue-eyed face seemed perfectly calm. But his voice had an edge that sometimes quavered.

Bob, for whom I'd done considerable work last year for the committee, seemed thrown by the clowning of this current witness, and annoyed by the room's amused response to it.

The big man at the witness table—a distinguished-looking white-haired attorney at his side—weighed less than four hundred pounds but not much. Yet he'd somehow managed to find a sport coat and trousers large enough to swim in, his brick-pattern tie loose, the collar points of his soaked white shirt sticking up like noses waiting to be thumbed. His eyebrows rode high over the close-set light blue eyes, projecting an inaccurate air of stupidity, his small head sitting on the huge six-four frame like the mistake of a careless God.

"Mr. Baker," Bob said into his microphone, "it would seem you've been reluctant to appear before this committee."

Barney Baker sat hunkered over the table, hands flat before him, as if he were waiting for a poker hand to be dealt.

"No, sir," he said. "Here I am, right now."

Barney's baritone was surprisingly rich and expressive; amplification only helped it, whereas Bob's voice seemed thin, reedy, nasal.

"You avoided our subpoenas by twice checking into weight-loss spas."

Barney raised his plump hands as if in brief surrender. "I *am* down twenty pounds, sir."

Howls of laughter.

Not from Bob, though, who next asked the witness about a shooting in Manhattan in 1936, in the parking lot of the Hotel New Yorker.

"All I heard was a lot of noise," Barney said. "I hit the pavement. They shot myself and Mr. Joe Butler."

"And what was the outcome?"

"I survived." Laughter from the gallery. "Mr. Joe Butler passed away." A little more. Gallows humor was going over good this morning.

Bob's eyes tightened. He had clearly hoped to expose a brutal thug. Instead he was providing the audience with a rollicking character out of Damon Runyon.

"You knew several men involved in the killing of Anthony Hintz," Bob said. "I'll remind you that Mr. Hintz's job was to pick which longshoremen would work on a given day."

"That's called the Shape-Up, sir."

"Thank you for the information, Mr. Baker. Perhaps you also know that the hiring practices of New York City piers at that time required kickbacks—money from hardworking men to go into the pockets of gangsters. And when Mr. Hintz would not go along with this practice, it got him killed."

Barney just looked at his interrogator as if about to drop off to sleep.

"Mr. Baker?"

"Oh, was that a question?"

More laughs.

Bob pressed on. "Did you know 'Cockeyed' Dunne, Mr. Baker?"

A shrug rolled across his shoulders like a wave into shore. "I didn't know him as Cockeyed Dunne. I knew him as John Dunne."

"Where is he now?"

"He has met his maker."

"And how did he do that?"

"I believe through electrocution in the City of New York in the State of New York."

That got laughs, too. Electric-chair humor to go along with gallows. And I had to admit, Barney's delivery was good. Jackie Gleason couldn't have done better.

"And what of Andrew Sheridan, sir?"

"He has also met his maker."

"How did *he* 'pass away'?"

"Same as Mr. John Dunne."

"Sheridan also was electrocuted by the state?"

"Yes, sir."

"He was a friend of yours?"

"Yes, sir, he and John both."

Bob was machine-gunning now: "A third man involved in the Hintz killing—a Danny Gentile—where is he now?"

Barney had to think about that, or anyway pretend to. "I believe he's in jail. Implicated in a certain case."

"Yes, this Hintz killing we're discussing. And you were friends with these people, Mr. Baker, two electrocuted and another in prison?"

"Yes, I knew them real well."

Reading off a sheet, Bob said, "I have some names here. Joe Adonis. Meyer Lansky. The late Benjamin 'Bugsy' Siegel. 'Trigger Mike' Coppola. I could go on the rest of the morning. Are these also friends of yours?"

"Some who passed away are fond memories. Those who are still with us, sir…sure. They're friends of mine."

Bob showed his teeth. "You seem to be friends with every big gangster and hoodlum in these United States."

A quick one-shoulder shrug. "I know a lot of people."

"Did you ever try to choke a hotel manager in Chicago in a dispute over a bill?"

"I don't remember nothing in the choking department."

Chuckles came from many of the attendees, including one named Hoffa, waiting his turn, who threw me a quick, discreet wink.

Bob's eyes bore down on the witness. "You're associated with leading gangsters and racketeers all over America, so it's not so shocking to think you might be involved with taking the Greenlease money."

Controlled anger came rumbling out of the witness. "Mr. Kennedy, it's 'shocking' you would even suggest I could be involved with that kind of *blood-taint* money...and I don't *go* for that, Mr. Kennedy! I don't go for that kind of action."

The chief counsel's words continued their rat-a-tat-tat. "You could have avoided that kind of action many years ago by disassociating yourself from Joe Costello, could you not?"

"*Whhhhhhy,* Mr. Kennedy?" Barney seemed to stretch the word "why" out endlessly—and into it he put hurt and disappointment and indignation. "Why would I do that?"

Bob's rage was barely reined in. "Every place you go—we've checked your telephone records—finds you calling known gangsters."

Barney's expression oozed brotherly love. "Mr. Kennedy, what happened in the past lives of people, like Mr. Costello, is no concern of mine. They may be nice people now."

"You arranged for Lt. Shoulders' son to work for the Teamsters Union in St. Louis. Lt. Shoulders who went to prison for perjury over the Greenlease money."

"Maybe so, but his son didn't. Sir, you don't give anyone a chance to prove they're nice. They may be nice people."

"Are you a 'nice person,' Mr. Baker?"

"That's for others to judge."

Bob wore the kind of smile a snarling animal does. "I don't want you to leave the stand leaving the impression of being just the Teamsters' joker. You are associated with the scum of this country. And you are just like them."

I tried not to groan. Bob had stepped over the line—he'd become a bully now, and a self-righteous one.

Barney sensed it and just grinned at the young counsel. He even summoned his own chuckle. "What can I say? I'm just a big ham at heart. I admit it. I talk big. I drop names. Just the way I am."

After the lunch break, accompanied by high-profile defense

attorney Edward Bennett Williams, James R. Hoffa took his position at the witness table. The Teamster president had a broad-shouldered, burly look that his lack of stature—five feet five—didn't quite undermine. As usual, he wore an off-the-rack dark brown suit with highwater trousers exposing his trademark white socks, and a ready (if at times menacing) smile. The famous square face, rounded off by his chin, had a vaguely Asian cast, and his roughneck features were offset by an unlikely twinkle in the light brown eyes, his dark glossy hair brushed back, porcupine quills ready to fly at a moment's notice.

Jimmy Hoffa's father had been a coal miner and his mother had polished radiator caps in an auto plant. His first job had been fifteen bucks a week as a teenager unloading fruits and vegetables; by sixteen he'd organized his first wildcat strike. That had put him on the Teamster payroll. He still was.

Bob had something up his sleeve. I knew he did because an operative in my New York office had developed it. Sol Lippman, general counsel to the Retail Clerks International Association, said Hoffa had threatened to kill him for turning down a Teamsters merger. And complaining to the police or FBI about it would be useless, Hoffa said—"I have a special way with juries."

Out of the gate, Bob blindsided the witness: "What did you say to Sol Lippman about having him killed?"

"Killed?" Hoffa asked. What cookie jar?

"Killed. Did you say that you could have him killed right there in your office and nobody would ever know?"

Hoffa's chin jutted. "I did not."

Bob's words flew. "Did you say that Mr. Lippman could be walking down the street and be shot one day?"

Hoffa leaned against his folded arms on the table, his words as staccato as a telegram. "I...did...not."

"Did you say anything to the effect that juries treated you very well?"

Tiny dismissive smile. "Now, that's pretty ridiculous, isn't it, Mr. Kennedy?"

"Did you say anything generally on the subject of having Mr. Lippman killed, murdered, shot?"

Hoffa took a moment, shifting in his chair. "Mr. Kennedy, I know you want to make this dramatic, but the answer is no."

"*Nothing* along those lines?"

Attorney Bennett cut in: "I don't see that this repetition is doing any good."

"Bring Lippman around here," Hoffa demanded. "Have him say it to my face!"

That was the highlight of the afternoon's sparring. Despite the fireworks, Bob's frustration and even weariness was showing. Hoffa, however, wasn't showing much of anything. But his cool didn't fool me—I knew he was mentally dismembering his tormenter.

I slipped out mid-afternoon before the capacity crowd could turn into a human traffic jam and took a cab to the Mayflower, where in my room I called the A-1 in Chicago, just to check in. I had no further D.C. business with Bob Kennedy or Drew Pearson and was ready to get back. After I hung up, I was about to change my plane reservation from tomorrow morning to a red-eye tonight when the phone rang under my hand.

"Duke Zeibert, Mr. Heller." I recognized the friendly, mid-range voice and its Catskills lilt. "Just confirming you for tonight at five."

All of that was odd. First, Duke Zeibert was the owner of a restaurant called, well, Duke Zeibert's. He seemed always to be in attendance, usually at the door greeting his frequently famous guests—politicians, executives, sports figures, stars of Broadway and/or Hollywood. But even if you were one of those, Duke himself didn't call to confirm your reservation.

Also, I hadn't made one. And while I might be an unrefined Midwestern yokel, I nonetheless did not dine at restaurants at five.

"Don't be late," Duke said, and hung up before I had a chance to ask a question. I might have called the restaurant back, but I felt pretty sure Duke wouldn't be handling reservations.

I took one precaution. I was still getting specially tailored suits from Richard Bennett, and my Browning in its shoulder holster was in my suitcase. So I took a quick shower and headed out, in my sharp suit with its tucked-away nine-millimeter accessory, and caught a cab to Seventeenth and L Street NW.

The restaurant with its looming white-on-black neon sign, fieldstone facade and red-and-white canopy served up Jewish cuisine inside. Nonetheless, Duke Zeibert's was Washington's equivalent of Switzerland—it had been Truman's favorite restaurant and Nixon's; the Kennedy brothers dined here and so did J. Edgar Hoover.

Duke met me just inside the door, and this host of hosts looked uncharacteristically uneasy; stout, bald with a trim mustache, he had been described as looking like a cross between Ben Franklin and a race-track tout. As always, he was in a white dinner jacket and black bow tie.

"He's waiting in the kitchen," Duke said, and I didn't bother asking who. Not that I had any idea, but if Duke had wanted to give me more information than that, he would have.

He stayed behind as I passed by the glass trophy case of Redskins memorabilia and into the blue-and-brown-hued dining room. I headed down an aisle between tables toward the back, just a handful of early diners present, though the bar off to one side was doing the usual good business. No one paid notice—the restrooms were back here, after all.

So was the kitchen, and I went through the double doors into the steaming, clanging world of white-coated minions doing prep. The long-faced head chef, whose tall hat made him Alice-in-Wonderland absurd, directed me to the double wooden doors of their walk-in cooler. I paused and frowned and got an impatient look and a head bob to get in there.

I got in there.

Jimmy Hoffa did not smoke but his breath did—it must have been 35 degrees among the high racks of vegetables and low racks of butchered meat. Didn't take long for my breath to make itself visible, too. He was in the same dark off-the-rack suit as at the Caucus Room.

We shook hands—his usual vise-like grip—and I grunted a laugh. "So you finally wound up in the cooler."

He grinned, but his grins rarely showed many teeth and this was no exception—just a slice of white in that wide unhealed cut that served as a mouth in a well-tanned face. "That's no joke, if those silver-spoon Kennedy pricks get their way."

Right behind him were shelves of the kind of produce he loaded off trucks as a kid. That had been his sole connection to such vehicles—he'd never driven a truck in his life.

"Hope you haven't been waiting long," I said. "Freezer burn's an embarrassing way to go."

"There's worse ways. And you and me, Nate, it's not like we can be seen together. Not without riskin' Booby gettin' wise."

That was how he referred to Robert Kennedy: "Booby." Until fairly recently Hoffa had been paying me two grand a month, starting early last year, when I was working close to full-time as an investigator for Arkansas Senator John McClellan's Rackets Committee.

"Jimmy, you know damn well I'm not on their regular payroll anymore."

His features clenched. "Well, get back on. Just temporary. I got a job for you."

It was cold enough in there that I was already shaking. Or maybe it wasn't the cold. "What kind of job?"

"This kind," Hoffa said, and dug in his pants pocket and came back with a roll of bills. He thumbed off hundreds like a banker, then thrust a stack toward me. "That should be two grand. Like the old days."

The "old days" had not been that long ago, not that I had any desire to reminisce.

I raised my hands, palms out. "No offense, Jim, but I got responsibilities in Chicago."

"Don't we all?" He did the Jimmy Cagney hitch of his shoulders that had become a habit with him. He handed the stack of cash and I took it. "But this'll just be a week or two of your time. I got something specific in mind."

I got my wallet out, slid the twenty C notes inside, my hand quivering a little.

That slit of a grin flashed again. "Cold already, kid?"

He often called me "kid," even though we were about the same age.

I shrugged. "How could I be? It's August."

He put a hand on my shoulder. Even though I towered over him a good seven inches, he could look up at me and still intimidate.

"You was in that room today. You saw what Booby was up to—trying to smear me with all that mob shit. Bringin' in guys like Barney, God bless him, to make him look bad and me in the bargain. That whiny little bastard is trying to link me to every gangster in the goddamn country, and drive me out of the

Teamster presidency, besmirchin' me by the company they say I keep!"

"You do keep that kind of company, Jim."

He glared up at me. "I deal with captains of fuckin' industry every day but that don't mean I run Montgomery Ward! I gotta sit down with all *kinds* of people."

I gestured around at the fruits and vegetables, my breath pluming. "But not always in public. Plus there's no chairs in here."

He grunted a laugh. That was the one good thing about our relationship—he didn't expect me to be a yes man.

"You heard the Kennedy kid in that caucus room, poking around in the St. Louis shit pile," he said. "Bringin' up Joe Costello. Even that bent cop Shoulders. Makes me wonder."

"Makes you wonder what, Jim?"

His eyes disappeared in pouches gone tight. "How deep is he digging? What does he know?"

"*Could* he know something?"

The eyes reappeared, and wide. "Nothing *to* know! But if the rank and file start thinkin' we had anything to do with that Greenlease ransom dough…well, it could turn the members against me. Think of it! That dirty little prick Kennedy stoopin' so low as to splash some poor dead kid's blood on me, *me!* Who has nothing but love for innocent kids. I got a boy of my own! And a girl."

I knew there was no saying no to him.

"What do you want me to do, Jim?"

"Look into it! Go to St. Louis if that's what it takes. I'll cover your expenses, no questions asked. You know that. See what shit Kennedy's got—not that there's anything *to* get."

I cocked my head. "You might not like where it leads, Jim. Three hundred grand is a lot of money, and there are a lot of crooks in St. Louis."

"Tell me about it." He patted himself with crossed arms. "Jesus, it's cold in here. But you go first. I'll wait a minute and go out the back. Oh! One other thing."

"Yeah?"

"How's Sam doin'?"

That was one thing Jimmy Hoffa never failed to do.

He always asked about your kids.

The next morning I caught Bob Kennedy in his cubbyhole in the New Senate Office Building basement. Sitting behind his desk in a short-sleeve white shirt with his tie loosened slightly, he seemed composed and in utter control; but his cluttered desk told another story.

"Hoffa suggested you go to St. Louis?" Bob said, amused though his eyes were alert. He'd been slumped there when I entered, but my report of the cooler conversation with his nemesis had him sitting up straight now.

"He did," I said. "At least, he presented it as a possibility. He probably mostly wanted me to pump you for what you're up to."

Bob tossed a pencil on his desk. "Well, uh, that's ridiculous, it's comical, because he knows *exactly* what we're up to."

So did I. The Rackets Committee was on the same path they'd taken to send Hoffa's predecessor Dave Beck to prison on income tax fraud, an approach that dated back to the days of Al Capone and my late friend Eliot Ness. They were looking into savings accounts, business holdings, real estate, and insurance policies, as well as travel receipts and phone records. This should lead to a credible estimate of Hoffa's net worth—wealth that wages, investments and inheritances couldn't explain.

On the other hand, that wouldn't be easy, and Kennedy damn well knew it—not with Hoffa's fleet of world-class lawyers and accountants…not to mention all those members of Congress and journalists in his off-the-rack pocket. Like the one he took that choke-a-horse wad of cash out of.

The best, perhaps the only, way to topple Hoffa was the approach Bob had been taking in the hearings—linking America's favorite union boss to organized crime. After all, that's what got the Teamsters tossed out of the AFL-CIO—Hoffa's much deserved reputation for being in bed with mob types. And, as Jimmy himself had admitted, if Kennedy linked him to enough corruption and brutality, the union president could well lose the love and support of his membership.

"This Lippman, the Retail Clerks guy," I said. "You bringing him in to testify? Hoffa dared you to. Why not take him up on it? You want to show Hoffa's members what he's capable of? Well, threatening another union leader to his fucking face with killing him ought to do it."

Bob's sigh seemed more than a man his size could muster. "I spoke to Lippman on the phone after the session yesterday. He won't go public. His retail clerks depend on the Teamsters to pitch in on boycotts and picket lines and such."

"Where does that leave you?"

The boyish face looked past me blankly, then blossomed into a smile and his eyes traveled to mine. "Do the job for Hoffa. You took his money, didn't you?"

Part of my original agreement with Bob last year was that I would not turn over Hoffa's payments to the committee for a bribery case to be made against the union leader. My position was that if it ever came out, no client would ever trust me again. Bob had thought I was just trying to find a way to keep the money. I told him that to show how little I cared about money, I would not accept the four hundred dollars a month the committee was offering.

His response had made me wonder what kind of language they were teaching these blue-blood kids these days. But I kept Hoffa's money, and the federal government held onto theirs. A fair arrangement, I thought.

I said, "Bob—what do you know that I don't? Has Drew Pearson been feeding you tidbits from that article he's writing?"

"What article?" His smile was mocking. "Did you have a good time in L.A.?"

"Yeah, I saw Zorro, Annette and a taxicab driver who's scared out of his mind. Answer my question—how much do you have?"

He lifted a shoulder and set it back down. "Not much. We interviewed Barney Baker's ex-wife, who told us that he had something to do with the missing Greenlease ransom money. That, she claims, is all she knows."

"A bitter ex-wife?"

"What other kind is there?"

I studied him. "You were fishing yesterday at the hearing—with Barney."

The grin was boyish, too—much toothier than Hoffa's. "I was. And Baker would be a hell of a big fish to haul to shore. He's working with the Teamsters in St. Louis now, and he's been personally close to Hoffa for years. Has been his bodyguard at times. Good ol' Barney has Chicago ties as well, which you probably know better than I. He's the perfect conduit for that money to go into Teamster pension fund coffers."

"Christ. That would sink Hoffa."

This shrug was more elaborate. "Of course, it could have gone right to Chicago."

I nodded. "And it may never have left St. Louis. It's possible our little-lamented kidnapper Carl Hall buried it before he met his maker, as Barney Baker would say. And you've got taxi czar Joe Costello and crooked-cop-of-the-year Lou Shoulders in the middle of things. The proprietor of that No-tell Motel, the Coral Court, may have got his hands on the missing half of the ransom and used his own resources to launder it. But if that tainted blood money Baker talked about yesterday *could* be tied in any way to Hoffa...."

The grin flashed again; so many teeth. Like a cute shark. "Here's an idea, Nate."

"What?"

"Go to St. Louis and find out."

CHAPTER ELEVEN

Robert F. Kennedy and James R. Hoffa agreed on one thing: they both wanted Nathan Heller to go to St. Louis.

But before I could undertake a mission for two clients whose best interests were clearly contradictory, I first needed to confer with a client whose claim on me preceded theirs.

So, after two days in Chicago catching up at the office, I took a late Wednesday morning flight to Kansas City. I'd arranged to see Robert Greenlease mid-afternoon at his place of business, where the day before I'd reached him by phone.

"Don't come to the house," he'd said, almost whispering. "Make it before five, here at the dealership."

That was where the cab was taking me, to the four-story reddish-brick wedge-shaped building on the triangular corner of 30th and Gillham and McGee Trafficway, just south of downtown. The terra-cotta-trimmed edifice, unlike its Used Car lot cousin across the way, was damn near as grand as the Missions Hills mansion. You could almost see Carl Hall and Bonnie Heady driving by drooling, money-green with envy as they took in the facade's lettering:

GREENLEASE

above the familiar coat-of-arms crest, which loomed over

Cadillac

atop a showroom window displaying a current Coupe De Ville.

The cab dropped me by a garage entry where, on the side of the brick exterior wall, a less grand sign read:

IN MEMORY OF

ROBERT C.

GREENLEASE, JR.

THE GREENLEASE

MOTOR CAR CO.

Will Be Closed

OCT. 9th.

I entered a high-ceilinged showroom whose tile flooring was marble as was the wainscoting. All around me were tail-fin rides as if Martians had landed—rich ones. The subtle rocket-styling that had crept in a year or two ago had taken off now, the colors getting out of hand—not just red but pink, not just blue but turquoise, and all the taillights were big bright red bullets.

To a guy with a '59 Jag Roadster at home, I didn't know whether to feel superior or jealous. I settled for superior.

I didn't recognize Will Letterman at first, but he knew me at once. He intercepted me before a salesman in a suit as well-tailored as mine could get to me. Letterman was in a Brooks Brothers or better himself, yet he still had a Sunday school teacher look with his wire-frame glasses and white Friar Tuck hair.

We shook hands and exchanged the kind of smiles that go with encountering a familiar friendly face tied to bad memories.

I said, "I thought you ran the Tulsa branch."

He had already slipped his hand on my shoulder and was walking me past all the Buck Rogers rides toward the offices at the rear. "The old man is only working half days," he said. "He brought me in. It's an honor. This is the flagship store."

Hearing him call Bob Greenlease "the old man"—Letterman being no spring chicken himself—was a reminder that the father of Bobby Greenlease was now in his late seventies.

"How's he doing?" I asked.

"He does well when he's here," Letterman said. "I think that's why he hasn't retired. And both he and Virginia get a lot of satisfaction from their charity work. With her church, you know."

"I didn't. But that's good."

We were outside a glassed-in office whose drapes were drawn.

His bland face took on a desperate look, his voice a ragged whisper. "Nate…it still keeps me up at night."

"What does?"

"Not every night, but…at least once a month, I find myself waiting for the damn sunrise." He gripped my arm. "You were *right*, back then. I *should* have let you stay behind at that bridge. And let you *grab* that son of a bitch. And…"

Kill him.

"Second guessing at this point," I said, "doesn't do us a damn bit of good. And the boy was already in the ground. And that son of bitch has been dead almost as long." I patted the hand on my arm, and it released. "Take a slug of something, next time, and you'll sleep just fine. You were a great friend to Bob. You and your buddy O'Neill, who, hell, I never even met. I'm surprised you two aren't still waiting in that goddamn hotel in Bum Fuck, Missouri."

That made him laugh. I laughed a little, too.

His smile was wrinkled with age and regret, but at least it was a smile. "Good to see you, Nate."

He knocked.

"Is that Nate Heller?" came a voice from within, loud but creaky, like wind coming through a broken shutter.

Greenlease answered the door, thanked his friend Letterman, who nodded and smiled at me and disappeared into the show-room with its wonderful display of space-age ridiculousness.

When he'd closed the door behind us in this rather small office, Greenlease did something that surprised me. It sur-prises me even telling it: he hugged me. Patted my back. He was a rock-ribbed self-made man, a good God-fearing man and I could see on a wall of photos (Kansas City celebrities, I assumed, which is of course an oxymoron) he was shaking the hand of a beaming President Eisenhower. I suddenly recalled that Ike's brother had assembled the ransom money at Bob Greenlease's behest.

When the embrace ended, he seemed perhaps a little embarrassed, then patted my shoulder and guided me not to a visitor's chair opposite a big mahogany desk notable for its lack of clutter or really any work at all, but to a leather-upholstered sofa under a wall of framed color prints of current model Cadillacs. We sat there, turned slightly toward each other, old friends catching up.

Like his sales force, Greenlease wore a well-tailored suit, gray, and his tie was a silk shantung, striped red, black and gray. His glasses were black hornrims, heavy, masculine. He was working hard at projecting strength and competence. But he seemed so much older five years later—the oblong face longer, nose sharper, chin sharper, sudden harsh angles in a kind face. Age splotches, deep lines, liver spots, provided unwanted deco-ration.

Behind the big empty desk, a shelved wall of sales awards and local honors seemed there to taunt him with their ultimate meaninglessness. Only one shelf counted—the middle one, where family photos were lined up around a central smiling Bobby Greenlease and his papa.

We began with small talk. He wanted to know about my son and I told him, without belaboring it. Mentioned Disneyland but didn't go into it. He was one big wound and I didn't need to go flinging salt.

I asked about his older son.

"It's been rough on Paul," he admitted. "He knew this Hall creature in military school, not well but did know him, and felt guilty over bringing him into our lives. Not his fault, of course. And he's doing very well now. Has his own dealership over at 50th and Main—he sells more Cadillacs at that location than we do here."

"Must make you very proud."

"I am. I am. But it does hang over him…the feeling of guilt. And it's same for Sue."

"Your daughter? Why would she feel guilty?" But then it came back to me, from the press coverage. "Oh, that's right… Hall and Heady originally targeted *her*."

He sighed, nodded. "Yes, they made several attempts to take her that we weren't aware of. Apparently they settled on Bobby because Sue was older—she was eleven—and our boy looked… easier to handle."

I touched his sleeve. "You don't have to go into it."

"The point is, she felt guilty. What do they call it?"

"Survivor's guilt. Soldiers who come back from war have it." I had it. "Is she doing all right now?"

"Yes. She's in high school. And she's had counseling over time. A child psychologist initially, lately a psychiatrist. She and her mother are very close. She and I are very close."

"And Mrs. Greenlease?"

He gazed down at his folded hands. "My wife takes solace in her church work. She's a very devout Catholic—I'm not of that faith, but I support her and the charities she's interested in. She's convinced she'll see Bobby again in Heaven."

He didn't sound quite so convinced.

"Mr. Greenlease…Bob. I wanted to talk to you in person because a telephone just wouldn't do."

His head came up.

I continued: "I've been asked to look into what happened to the missing half of the ransom you paid."

That seemed to confuse him. "What was recovered has already been returned."

"I figured as much. But there's a great interest in what became of the missing three hundred thousand dollars and where exactly it went…and who benefitted from it."

He stood. Sudden enough to surprise me. He walked to the curtained window onto his showroom and stared as if he could see anything but fabric. His posture reminded me of Johnny Hagan at his flophouse window.

"I think you care about that money," I said. "I don't think you care about it *as* money…you obviously have everything you need in life."

"Not," he said quietly, "everything."

"No. Not everything. And who else would put up twenty-five thousand dollars to make that cabbie talk?"

He turned quickly—quicker than a man his age might be expected to. "Is that why you're here, Nate? You figured that out?"

"It wasn't hard. I've worked for Pearson. He wouldn't pay two dollars admission for a last moment with his dying mother. You're the only one in this thing who could have afforded an offer like that. So you *must* want to know where the money went. It *must* mean something to you who ended up with it. I have a couple of clients who would like to know, too. Before I say yes to them, I want your blessing to go on with it."

"You don't need my blessing..."

"Oh, I do. You have that much coming. I'd think you would *want* me to go forward. But I need to hear it from you."

His hands were in his pockets. He looked at me like I was an apparition and he was trying to decide whether to be scared or not.

"I don't give a good goddamn about the money," he said finally. "But I can't stomach the idea that anyone is out there profiting off the murder of my son."

I gestured for him to return to the couch.

He did. Sat. His hands were folded in his lap again. His head was lowered but his shoulders were straight.

"What would you have me do?" I asked.

"If you can get the money back, I'll give it to my wife for her Catholic charities. Maybe somebody will build something in Bobby's honor. But what I really want is...I'm not going to say what it is. I'm not Catholic but I like to think I'm a good Christian. Some of what I've read about you, in the cheap true detective magazines, indicates you are thought to have on occasion employed what some might call...rough justice. It seems bad people who have crossed your path, at times, sometimes ...simply disappear. Or have died under violent circumstances about which opinions vary as to the party responsible."

"Such rumors add color in my profession," I said. "There are clients of mine who appreciate an ability to cut a corner now and then."

"Or a throat?" He gripped my right wrist; it was remarkably firm, coming from a bony hand. "I will not only okay your efforts, Nate, I will take over as your client. And I will pay you well."

I patted his hand on my wrist, gently. He relaxed the grip, withdrew his hand.

I said, "I already have two clients. I don't need another. Anyway, you've already paid me enough on this job."

He accepted that reluctantly, then said, "You must do what you think is...appropriate. I ask only two things."

"Yes?"

"I want a detailed report on what you're able, and not able, to accomplish. Client confidentiality should cover both of us in that regard."

"Of course. What's the other thing?"

"My wife is to know nothing of this. She is a gentle soul and she would not...approve."

"Understood."

I rose and he walked me to the door. "When will you start?"

"I'll rent a car and head to St. Louis tonight or tomorrow."

He shook his head. "No. I'll loan you a Cadillac. And if you're staying overnight, I'll book you at the Hotel President. As my guest."

Like old times, I thought.

"Matter of fact," he said, "there's someone you should talk to before you go to St. Louis. You'll need to make time for that."

On my previous visit to the President Hotel's Drum Room, I had barely eaten half of my evening meal. Now here I was again, the identical menu selections before me, seated at a small table designed mostly for drinking in the snare-shaped bar bordered by red pillars. The bar's garish, dominant red with yellow trim and circus touches would have been perfect for a six-year-old boy, if they let kids in. Any who weren't buried in the back yard anyway.

But that was five years ago and here in the present I was hungry, and the filet, baked potato and even the lima beans went down just fine. I passed on dessert and sat there nursing my second rum and Coke, the bar's after-work crowd having faded away and the weeknight dining crowd scant. After a while a guy wandered in who might have been one of Greenlease's sales staff if his suit had cost a little more.

Special Agent Wesley Grapp of the FBI came over and I rose, shook his hand, and we both sat down. About forty now, he looked noticeably older—his wasn't an easy job, the long face longer now, his hairline going Nixon on him. The nose seemed more pointed, the jutting chin cushioned in a second un-jutting one.

Bob Greenlease had put this meeting together, so I got right to it: "Five years, and you're still on this case?"

"Not on Bonnie and Carl we aren't," he said. "Though that bastard Hall is just as annoying dead as he was alive."

"How does he manage that? No dumber criminal ever fumbled a big score."

He sighed, shook his head, laughed a little. A waitress came over in a white blouse, red string tie and short red skirt; she was blonde and pleasant, trying out her nice smile—on a slow night, a couple of middle-aged guys in business suits meant a potentially good tip.

Grapp ordered a highball. My rum and Coke was holding up. She left, and he said, "Hall may have buried the missing half of that money. He didn't deny doing it—just said he didn't remember, and when a drunk who takes a morphine chaser says he doesn't remember, you tend to listen. But he had a pair of trousers with mud that we were able to trace to the south bank of the Meramec River."

I had seen those muddy pants. Of course, as far as Grapp was concerned, I'd never seen Carl Hall. I changed the subject. "You're working the case from the Kansas City end?"

He shrugged. "I hop back and forth between St. Louis and

Kansas City. I've been looking into the old Binaggio gang here in K.C., who've got ties to John Vitale, as a possible money laundry."

Vitale was among the bigger St. Louis gangsters.

"But," Grapp said, "that's going nowhere. Par for the course on this goddamn thing. You know, this investigation couldn't have started out any bigger, and now couldn't be smaller."

"How's that?"

He leaned on an elbow. "Well, for the first three months we were a 'Bureau Special,' which is—"

"I know," I said. A national investigation, operating out of FBI headquarters in D.C. "How many men were on it at the start?"

"At the start, when Greenlease was dancing to the kid-napper's tune, it was just a handful of us—enough to man that checkpoint near the mansion was about it. When Hall and Heady were caught, and the child turned up dead, we moved to St. Louis. Sixty-five agents. A state line had been crossed, and a prominent citizen's child had been killed."

I smiled just a little. "But, Wes—like you said. Hall and Heady had been caught."

His eyebrows went up. "Sure they had, but we still had to make the case. Greenap, the Special was called. We put the physical evidence together for the trial—the sheet the boy was wrapped in, photographs of the bloodstains in Heady's house, bloodstains in the station wagon that matched the boy's blood type, and bone fragments and lead fragments that were found confirming Bobby Greenlease was shot in that vehicle. And of course we handled the interrogations of the pair."

"Getting what it took to put them in their side-by-side elec-tric chairs shouldn't have taken long."

The waitress, delivering Grapp's highball, widened her eyes, getting in on just the end of that.

"It didn't," he said. "Call it five days." His sigh had frustration hanging on it like wet laundry on a line. "Five days, and then months and years of looking for that missing three hundred thousand. We were up to a hundred agents at that point. We kept Costello, Shoulders and Dolan under surveillance, hounded their friends and relatives too, tapped their phones, went over their finances, got their long-distance call records—anything and everything, before Mr. Ace Cab Company went up on an unrelated gun charge and Shoulders and Dolan went away for perjury."

I frowned at him. "If you couldn't prove those two cops were in on taking the bundle, how could the government make perjury stick?"

He sipped then smirked. "Because eight cops at Newstead Station said Shoulders and Dolan *didn't* bring in the money... the half they *did* turn over...until an hour after hauling Hall in to be booked. Asked by a grand jury about that missing hour, Shoulders and Dolan both pled the Fifth."

He took another taste of highball and I thought about what he'd just told me.

Then I said, "Something happened to that money the night they nabbed Carl and Bonnie. Something happened in that missing hour."

"Clearly."

I squinted at him like he'd gone out of focus. "And you minions of J. Edgar didn't start looking for it until five days had flown. Didn't anybody at the academy tell you G-men that the first few days of an investigation are the most important?"

His eyes flared and his voice turned defensive. "Jesus, Heller, we were busy! We had two murdering kidnappers to put away!"

"Two of the dumbest, sloppiest, smallest-time criminals who ever tried for the big time. Wouldn't you agree? Couldn't the

Bureau have spared a few men from the hundred on the case to
go after that money?"

He was shaking his head again. "At that point it was a St.
Louis police matter. The suspects were two of their own, the
heroic officers who'd brought in the perpetrators the world was
looking for, and—"

"And bullshit." I pointed a forefinger at him, thumb up, like
I was aiming. "We're talking ransom money from a kidnapping.
A federal crime. You should have stepped in."

His palms came up in surrender. "I admit we kept hands off the
two cops, at first." He sat forward, eyes tight, jaw firm. "But we
were looking for that money from the start. The day after Hall's
arrest, we raided the Coral Court, thirty of us, went all through
the building where he'd been holed up with that prostitute."

I was taking a chance, but I had to ask: "Did you fellas go
through all seventy rooms? It's a big facility. And I understand
the owner, that Carr character, has ties to 'Buster' Wortman's
bunch and maybe Chicago."

"We knew Carr was a good suspect for the missing money.
We searched the corridors and the furnace room and the
grounds. We even made that joker dig up some fresh trees he'd
just planted. Nothing. Not practical to tear apart every room,
but we did hit 49-A hard—not that there's much of anywhere to
hide anything in a motel room—just ask a cheater. We gave the
front office and the owner's quarters a thorough shakedown.
Not a damn thing."

I didn't push it further. I wasn't anxious to have my presence
at the Coral Court that evening get in the FBI's crosshairs. As I
told Johnny Hagan in L.A., I hadn't broken any laws and had in
fact been sent home by the cops. Crooked cops, though, I now
knew; and I wasn't anxious to have my own finances and business practices poked around in.

A second highball arrived for Grapp, who said, "Remember Tom Marsh, Carl's supposed mastermind? We had on file a Thomas John Marsh, arrested in St. Louis, who did a stretch for sexually abusing an eight-year-old kid. We thought that would change everything. Then Hall, in his full confession, admitted pulling the name 'Tom Marsh' out of the air. When we tracked down Thomas John Marsh's father, he informed us his son was dead. A literal dead end."

I sipped what was left of my rum and Coke. "In five years, you must have had your share of those."

"Oh, yeah. How about the disgruntled cabbie who claimed he'd overheard Shoulders and Costello scheming at Ace Cab, and saw them stow a big bundle in an employee locker in the basement there."

"Sounds promising."

"We thought so. Then we tossed the place, and you know what we turned up?"

"No. What?"

"No basement. No lockers either."

"So what *has* turned up in five years of 'Greenap'?"

He saluted me with his glass. "A grand total of 115 bills, tens and twenties. We repeatedly put the serial numbers of the missing ransom money in newspapers, distributed booklets to banks and businesses, and out of the missing seventeen thousand or so bills, a whole seventeen *hundred* bucks has shown up. Fifty-eight bills of which come from the Midwest."

I frowned. "Turned up where, exactly?"

His shrug was loose now—thanks to the two highballs. "Well, often they came from a bank in a town where a state or county fair with a carnival had recently been. Easy enough for a carny to pass a hot bill in change. And the Outfit in Chicago runs a good share of those touring shows."

That method of getting ransom dough into circulation would take time, but then the Outfit had plenty.

"Only about half of the recovered bills come from the Chicago area," Grapp was saying, "the rest showing up every which where—but your hometown shows a pattern. One bank in particular pops up frequently—Southmoor Bank and Trust Company."

Grapp didn't have to explain the significance of that. Southmoor was an Outfit bank on the South Side, founded by a bookmaker for bookmakers, going back to Capone days. The bank's co-founder had been taken for a ride just last year—the .45-slug-in-the-head kind.

Southmoor would make the perfect laundry for the ransom money. They'd have paid probably twenty cents on the dollar for a tidy $240,000 profit when they replaced regular funds with hot money for channeling through ordinary bank transactions. They would then pocket those regular funds, minus the $60,000 they'd paid someone for the hot money.

But who was that someone?

"Both Costello and Shoulders are on the streets again," Grapp said, "Costello back at his cab company, Shoulders managing four rooming houses he owns. He's also gone into the dry-cleaning business with the Dolan pup. I think Dolan is just an innocent who got caught up in this, but I've had no luck turning him—he's a clam. Shoulders got religion in stir and weeps at the drop of a hat over the death of Bobby Greenlease, and especially his own travails—the hero cop who got shafted and sent away for no good reason."

"Such a sad story."

"These are men who might open up to you," Grapp said, "where they won't to us. Won't to me. You do have a reputation, Nate. Mr. Greenlease asked me to cooperate. You're going to sniff around, I understand. I'd start with Barney Baker's ex-wife, Mollie, and that prostitute, Sandy O'Day. She's a madam now, running hookers out of the Coral Court for the last couple of years."

Coming up in the world, our Sandy.

"You can try Jack Carr too," he was saying, "but he's one hard apple. You'll need to watch your ass. I doubt you can get to Buster Wortman, who probably knows more than anybody about the Greenlease money, but isn't likely to give you a damn thing. He runs East Saint Louis, which is purgatory by day and Hell at night. You know how they say a man's home is his castle? Well, Buster has a moat around his. You already know Barney Baker, I understand, but he's in Washington, D.C., right now."

"So I hear."

"He may be back before you've wound up your investigation. I have contact info on everybody, and a few notes on some of them." He had a last gulp of highball. Stood. "Well. I better get home to the wife and kids. To my castle."

"You're awfully cooperative."

The long face softened. "I think I'd do about anything for Bob Greenlease, after what he suffered. Including turning you loose. If Bob wants to see what somebody less official can turn up in this thing, I'm all for it."

"That's a little surprising."

"Not really." He threw some money on the table. "I don't have a hundred men anymore."

CHAPTER TWELVE

I set up the meet with Barney Baker's ex-wife Mollie by phone before I left Kansas City.

After I gave her my name, and identified myself as a private investigator, I said, "I'd like to chat with you off the record."

Her voice was husky, sleepy. I was pretty sure I'd woken her, though it was close to ten-thirty A.M.

"What about?" she asked.

"If there's a hundred bucks in it, does it matter?"

"...The D.C. boys weren't paying anything. They appealed to my patriotism. I think they had me confused with Betty Ross."

She meant "Betsy," but that was close enough.

"I'm not from D.C.," I assured her.

"Where are you from?"

"Chicago."

The pause was like that proverbial long drop off a short pier. Then she said, "We'd have to meet in a public place."

"Okay. Where?"

"I work at the Club Cosmopolitan in East St. Louis. I waitress there. I have a fifteen-minute break every two hours. One of those comes at 8:45. Can you find your way?"

"I'll buy a compass. Should I ask for you at the bar?"

"That'll work. Or maybe you'll just spot me. I wear a name tag."

"What do you look like, Mollie?"

"Claudette Colbert, in some movie where she's sunk to working as a waitress."

She hung up.

I timed my drive in the used '56 Series 62 Sedan so I'd hit St. Louis just after dark, having specifically asked Bob Greenlease for an older, pre-tailfin Caddy to avoid undue attention. The still familiar trip with its farm country and little towns hadn't changed any, but some of the radio stations were playing rock 'n' roll now. Which I didn't mind—it wasn't Sinatra or Brubeck, but it was better than country and western. In downtown St. Louis at Washington Avenue, I took the Eads Bridge to the Illinois side of the Mississippi past railroad yards and onto Broadway, cutting through industrial sprawl.

East St. Louis had been named an All-American City, fourth largest in the state, with a prosperous array of stockyards and factories. But the factories were starting to close and meat-packing was moving away, and the only industry still flourishing seemed to be vice. Like Chicago's wide-open suburb, Calumet City, this was where St. Louis cab drivers on commission would steer passengers to gambling houses, brothels, burlesque bars and after-hours saloons.

Inside the story-and-a-half white-awninged brick building on Bond Avenue, I found a nearly packed house of maybe three hundred. A bar stretched along the wall at right and a pool table was in its own little world at left, glass-block windows letting in the vague bright colors of a dying city desperate for nightlife. Red and blue neon beer signs glowed in the smoke like the lights of incoming planes on a foggy night while raucous rock 'n' roll emanated from a small stage at the far end of the big square high-ceilinged room. The back two-thirds was jammed with red-vinyl-and-chrome chairs at black-topped tables where the mostly young crowd drank from bottles of beer—the criteria for alcoholic beverage service here seemed to be a capacity for human speech. Space had been allowed near the stage for a dance floor consumed by wildly gyrating patrons, and I suppose there was nothing special about any of it except the nearly equal mix of colored and white. The Supreme Court had approved desegregation a while back and it had hit this club in East St. Louis in spades. And ofays.

In a black suit and tie and blue suede shoes, a clowning Chuck Berry was on stage doing "Maybelline," a radio hit I'd heard on the trip from K.C.; he and a bass player, drummer and piano man were squeezed onto the small platform with a backdrop that said COSMO in pink sparkle lettering. I'd seen this outstanding showman on the South Side at the 708 Club, where one of my black A-1 operatives had succeeded in making me appreciate Chicago blues. This variant had humor and crisp diction and told kids Negro and white the kind of stories of high school, cars and young love they could all relate to.

Berry, after getting a big round of applause, whistles and whoops, announced a break, and a female voice next to me, a bored alto, said, "He used to get twenty-one bucks a weekend in the house band. Now he gets eight hundred a week."

I glanced at the short, curvy dish beside me, who did nice things to a red-aproned white waitress uniform. As some of the crowd threaded out to smoke in less smoky environs, Mollie Baker directed me to a vacated table in a back corner. Pool balls clacked not far from where we settled.

"How did you know me?" I asked. "I forgot to say I'd wear a white carnation."

"You didn't need one," she said, as we settled into the red vinyl-and-metal chairs. "You're Nate Heller. I saw you in *Life* or *Look* or something."

She had a heart-shaped face, a bright red-lipsticked kewpie-doll mouth, a pug nose, and drawn-on eyebrows over big blue eyes that had seen it all and not been impressed. Her hair was black and hovered over her forehead in a pompadour Elvis Presley would have killed for.

"'Private Eye to the Stars,'" she said with a smirk. "Somehow I don't think you're here for that kind of client."

"I'm not. But any kind of client of mine gets the same confidentiality."

She produced a cigarette from somewhere, the way Bugs Bunny can a carrot. She stuck it in her kewpie lips and waited to see if I'd light it for her. I told her I didn't smoke, which seemed like disgusting news to her, and she got a Zippo from a pocket of her uniform.

"Here's the thing," she said, firing up the smoke. "I can use a hundred bucks right now. My fat fuck of a husband has a new wife, who is about twelve and comes from Iowa of all the stupid places. Why she's still alive after he climbs on top of her, I couldn't tell you."

"One might say the same thing about you, Mrs. Baker."

"Make it 'Mollie,' and I'll call you 'Nate,' just to keep things friendly. I'm not as delicate as I look, Handsome." She made "Handsome" sound like an insult. Of course, this was a doll who could put sarcasm into "Hello."

I said, "So we've established you can use a hundred bucks."

Somebody started the jukebox up and it began blaring Berry's "Roll Over Beethoven," which was a nice gesture if redundant.

"Yeah," she said, letting smoke out, "we have. Here's what else we need to establish. If you're working for the Teamsters or any of those underworld creeps either side of the river, this conversation ends now. I got a little girl to look after, and I know what these people are capable of."

I raised a courthouse palm. "I don't represent anyone who means to do you harm. You have a little girl, huh? I have a boy of eleven."

"Spare me the soft soap. I'm a mommy and you're a daddy. That supposed to make us two of a kind? A woman reduced to waiting tables and a guy who gets movie stars out of jams?"

"No, but we're both parents and don't have to work at it to remember what happened to Bobby Greenlease."

She drew on the cigarette. Held in smoke, expelled it, adding to the foggy atmosphere. "Is that what this is about?"

"That's what this is about."

When she frowned her forehead somehow stayed smooth. "All I've ever said to the FBI or that Rackets Committee investigator was Barney told me once he knew something about the Greenlease money. That's all. Ever since then, the FBI treats me like *I* got the damn dough, in the attic or under the bed or something."

"You think Barney had something to do with what became of that money?"

Another drag. "Barney's no angel. I think I could have straightened him out if I got him away from Hoffa and the rest of those Teamster bums. I mean, he's not such a bad guy, but he was always ready to let big shots lead him into trouble. He likes to feel like a big operator. Which he isn't."

"You're still fond of him."

Her smile was slight but it was a smile. "You should have seen him when I met him. He was tall, good-looking. Not fat at all—and a real charming guy. I can tell you one thing—I'm the best wife *he* ever had."

That information wasn't worth a hundred bucks. I almost told her so, but instead put on a smile and applied a needle.

"Have you heard anything from Barney, Mollie, since he married that young blonde in Iowa? Her father Jake is the state Democratic chairman there, and that's how Barney met her, working for Harriman."

W. Averell Harriman, governor of New York, had made a bid for the presidential nomination in '56. You don't have to be much of a student of history to know how that came out.

Steam damn near streamed out of her ears and nostrils. "He'd better not let that child bride keep him from making his payments for his little girl! If he doesn't keep up, I'll track him down wherever he is and put a gun in his big, fat belly and blow his guts out."

That seemed fair.

She was raving: "Do you know that flabby son of a bitch sent word to me he wanted to get back together at the same time he was planning marriage to that Iowa brat?"

"Well, that's just not right, is it?"

"That dumb little broad will live to regret it. She doesn't know that man the way I do. He used to beat his first wife! And I took my share of knocks, too. He's mean when he's crossed, and I've been around some pretty rough crowds in my day. I've seen that man go crazy. He threatened to kill my brother once! Held a knife to his throat."

"Oh dear."

Her eyes showed white all around. "And the violence, the *terror* tactics he'd go in for, for those Teamster slobs. You know, I could blow St. Louis wide open if I told what I *really* know about the Greenlease money!"

"You're very close to earning this," I said, and I gave her a glimpse of the folded one-hundred-dollar bill I had palmed.

Her mouth dropped and her eyes got smaller. "Look, I was just blowing off steam…"

"It's good to get things off your chest."

She put her hand over my clenched one, which held the hundred. She wiggled the painted-on eyebrows. "Maybe that could be arranged."

There'd been a time. But this broad was tougher than a nickel steak and my middle-aged teeth couldn't take it.

So I just withdrew my hand from hers. Gently. But withdrew it.

Her voice softened, barely audible above the jukebox blaring Berry's "Almost Grown."

"All I know is," she said, trembling with desire for that hundred, "Barney had something to do with it. I can't be more specific than that."

I unfolded the C-note. "Sure you can."

She swallowed. "Okay. Barney told me Joe Costello got the Greenlease money."

Mollie snatched the bill from my open palm and put it with the Zippo. Stood. Before she hip-swung off, to show me what I was missing, she said, "That's all I fucking know. I have to get back to work. Break's over."

So was Chuck Berry's. He came on and did "Sweet Little Sixteen."

Like Barney, he liked them young.

On the other side of the Eads Bridge, I headed for the DeBaliviere Strip just north of the Jefferson Memorial in Forest Park in the Central West End. The Strip, St. Louis's only real rival to the neon playground across the river, offered an unlikely mix of supper clubs, niteries, and strip joints. The latter included the nationally famous Stardust Club at 309 DeBaliviere, where owner Evelyn West—her chest insured by Lloyd's of London for $50,000—headlined a burlesque show of comics, singers, chorines and stripteasers. The other strip joints, like nearby Little Las Vegas, were more openly raunchy, and I knew from prior St. Louis jaunts that most bars hosted either a gambling joint or a betting parlor in back or upstairs.

I parked the loaner Caddy half a block down from my destination. Joe Costello's joint at 317 walked a fine line between
upright and lowdown, its reflective black plate-glass facade
with TIC TOC CLUB in white neon compromised by cheesy
sandwich-board signs out front. These sported glossy 8x10s
touting the imminent appearances of such artists as George
Shearing and Errol Garner, pianists, but also Miss Sylvia
Albana, the Flame of New Orleans, and Tinker Bell, the probable Toast of Never-Never Land, ecdysiasts.

Inside, the air-conditioning was working almost too well.
Costello's reputation as a dapper dresser befit the zebra booths,
pink walls, and black-and-white tile floor. But compared to the
Cosmo Club, the Tic Toc was barely ticking. A couple of probable bookies were going over figures in their notebooks in one
booth, an older guy with a young woman probably not his wife
(or his daughter) were in another, and two teenage boys with
bottles of beer sat giggling in their pew. Serving underage
clientele was one thing the Cosmo and the Tic Toc did have in
common.

Moving across a small uninhabited dance floor, I headed
toward the rear of the room where a black chrome-trimmed
bar with high-backed stools curved around its black-vested bartender and his impressive inventory. Looming over all this was
a raised recessed stage where a pianist could create a mood of
intimacy, or a stripper a mood of debauchery, neither having to
be worried about the customers getting too close.

No musician or stripper was on stage at the moment. The
barstools were empty but for a tall beefy guy off to my right
who might have been a bouncer. In a pale yellow sport coat and
an Aloha shirt, lacking only the lei, he was younger than me
though not young, forty-five maybe. He wore a small amused
smile but his gray eyes weren't laughing, as he paid me more

attention over his glass of beer than I deserved.

Ignoring him, I said to the bartender, "Is Joe Costello in?"

The bartender—mustached, bald, and until now bored—thought about the question, as if I had asked him what number pi was equal to, approximately. Before the barkeep could come up with 3.14159, the maybe bouncer intruded, saying, "Who's asking?"

I looked at him like he was a Jehovah's Witness on my doorstep. "Who's asking," I said, "who's asking?"

While he was parsing that, I said to the bartender, "Tell Mr. Costello it's Nathan Heller from Chicago."

He had a phone back there by the bottles and he used it, passing the information on in a near whisper as if afraid one of the paucity of patrons might hear. "Yes, sir…I will, sir."

Two doors were at the end of a short hallway past the restrooms—one was marked FIRE EXIT, the other PRIVATE; being a trained detective, I knocked on the latter.

The office was small, differing little from the one at Ace Cab, just a little classier—painted within the decade, carpeting and wainscoting. The desk was metal, not beat-up wood, and colorful framed posters of past Tic Toc attractions were on the walls—again, a mix of name nightclub talent (Buddy Greco, Jerry Vale) and striptease gals (Blaze Starr, Tempest Storm).

And hanging right behind his desk was an oversize framed photo of himself and his late partner Leo Brothers, shaking hands in front of Joe's previous night spot, the Clover Club.

Like the other time I'd seen Costello, he was sharply dressed, his cream-color sport coat flecked pink and black, his tie silk, dark brown with a white-and-tan geometric design. Maybe I should ask *him* about pi. The intervening five years, since we'd last met, had not been kind—he looked a decade older, easy, and the curly sandy hair was going gray. He'd reminded me of Crosby back then, and he still did. But Der Bingle was getting a little long in the tooth to be making another *Road* picture with ol' Ski Nose.

He stood behind the desk and stretched his hand across and I took and shook it. The massive gold-set diamond ring remained on his left hand. He was three or four inches shorter than me and his slenderness had turned bony, his cheekbones as sharp as his clothes.

A visitor's chair was waiting for me and I filled it.

He worked up a smile. "What brings you back to town after so long, Nate? And how did you know to look for me here?"

"I'm doing a job for a client that may involve you. You're the first person I'm touching base with in St. Louis. I called Ace Cab and they said you were at your new club."

His quick frown said he'd have to talk to somebody about giving out information so freely. Like I'd known not to mention I'd phoned Ace Cab from a booth in East St. Louis after talking to Mollie Baker.

"Who is your client in this, Nate?"

Since we seemed to be on first-name terms, I said, "Can't tell you that, Joe. Could be any number of people. No shortage of folks might take an interest in the missing Greenlease money."

His jaw went tight; his cheeks glowed red and I didn't think it was good health. "I had *nothing* to do with that, Heller! I live in the same house I did back then. I have two businesses that generate all the income I need. Hard work allowed me to put paneling in the basement and stonework around my fireplace. Before that money went missing, I would buy a new Cadillac every two years and I still do, which is about my only goddamn extravagance!"

I stayed cool. "I didn't ask about your finances, Joe. But the

FBI told the press you were the main suspect in the disappear-
ance of the ransom money."

His eyes flared. "Fucking FBI. For months they tailed me
day and night. They tap my phones, they question my friends
and relatives and even the fucking guy who put in my new furnace! They harass my drivers at Ace. It's only been lately they
backed off. And now *you* come around?"

"I'm not harassing you, Joe. You're just my first stop."

He reached down and flung open a desk drawer; my hand
went to my unbuttoned suit coat, where I could reach the nine
mil easily. But what he withdrew was a quart bottle of Cutty
Sark; he reached again and brought out a glass. He looked at
me with his eyebrows raised—*would I like…?*—and I shook my
head. At least the offer had been for a shot of Scotch whiskey
and not from a handgun.

He poured himself three or four fingers and took a sip that
really should be called something else. He tasted it a while and
swallowed it down, closing his eyes.

Then he sat back, calm now or pretending to be, and said,
"Chicago sent you, I take it."

"Joe, I didn't—"

He raised a palm. "You tell them Buster Wortman and I are
tight. They don't need to send Nate Heller around with a gun
under his arm. Yeah, I know a tailored suit when I see one. Tell
your 'client' to have Buster ask me about anything they want to
know…or should I just go to Chicago and talk to them myself?
Is it Accardo? Or Humphreys maybe? Or both?"

"I did not mention Chicago."

He finished his glass. Quickly. Then he lurched forward,
clutching the empty vessel like a grenade he was ready to
throw. "Those FBI pricks don't care *where* that money went!
They're just looking to frame somebody. They want a fall guy!"

Suddenly it was 1941 and I was in *The Maltese Falcon*.

"Joe, settle down..."

"You think I want anything to do with that kind of money? Me, a father who loves his son! I built a model train set for him, goes from room to room. I bought him a little replica Model T to ride outside around in. The thought of what happened to that Greenlease child makes me want to..." He swallowed, his eyes shining wet. "I'm a *father*, for Christ sake!"

"I know, Joe. I just want to know what *you* know—for example...did your friend Buster Wortman get that money?"

He looked hurt. "I don't know. Why does everybody think *I* know something?"

I kept it matter of fact. "Because you and Lou Shoulders go way back. You introduced me to him five years ago at Ace, remember? He was a bent cop, and you have what might be called underworld connections."

Now he was pouting. "I'm an honest businessman."

"You run a fleet of pimps on wheels, Joe. You've done hard time, you plan heists, then middleman swag to fences, especially jewels, except maybe those you cherry-pick, like that big-ass diamond ring on your finger. Don't shit a shitter."

He didn't look at me. "I can't tell you what I don't know."

"Then tell me *this*, at least. Let's say for the sake of argument, Shoulders brought you the money because you could get it washed in Chicago through Buster Wortman, the Outfit's man in this part of the world."

"Nothing I can tell you."

"Then why is it you think *Chicago* sent me? If they did the laundering, why would they think there's something being held back from them?"

He still wasn't meeting my eyes. "This is all pointless speculation. Jack Carr out at the Coral Court coulda snatched it before Shoulders even got there! As far as anybody knows, that worm Carl Hall buried it. I got it on good authority he had mud on a pair of his trousers!"

I'd seen that mud myself, of course.

"So go get yourself a shovel, Heller," he went on, pouring himself another glass of Scotch. "And start digging." His upper lip curled. "Knock yourself out!"

This was going nowhere. Maybe later I could shove my nine mil in his yap, for the good old-fashioned Chicago lie detector test. But for now I'd take my leave.

When I was at the door, he said, "Hey, Heller!"

I glanced back. He was holding up his left hand with the diamond on it. "This baby is six carats, and it's not boosted. It was a gift. You know who from?"

He jerked a thumb over his shoulder at the picture of Leo Brothers.

Sucker-punched, I shut the door behind me, sighing, shaking my head. Something poked me in the back. Something hard. Hard as metal.

Metal.

A voice rasped, "Take the fire exit."

It was right in front of me. I shoved the push bar and then we were in an alley alongside the building enveloped in a warm night and a darkness that swallowed shadows; and the neons of DeBaliviere Street seemed a world away at the other end.

Someone was waiting for us and grabbed my arm as I stepped through. The newcomer was a burly blond guy of maybe thirty-five in a black-and-white bowling shirt and jeans; he seemed familiar, but I couldn't place him, though that wasn't my biggest concern at the moment. He came around behind me and gripped both my arms. The guy who'd stuck the gun in my back was in front of me now—he was the bouncer in the yellow jacket and Aloha shirt, taking my nine millimeter out from under my left shoulder. He tossed it and it skittered away on the alley brick. The only good news was he stuck his own gun, a .38 with a four-inch barrel, in his waistband. The bad news was his fingers came back as a fist that he buried in my stomach.

I didn't puke—I hadn't eaten for a while. But he drove all of the wind out of me and incidentally it hurt like hell.

"I don't care where you came from," the Aloha-sporting thug said, "just as long as you go back there. Anywhere but St. Louis."

I nodded. Then I kneed him in the balls, or tried to; he saw it coming and mostly blocked it, but he twisted doing so and lost his balance.

"Hey!" a voice called from the end of the alley.

A bizarre figure came trundling down, clothes flapping on him like a thousand flags, a big man, tall, with a tiny head. I kicked the stumbling Aloha shirt guy in the side, hard as I could manage, even as I tried to twist away from the burly blond behind me.

Then Barney Baker was on top of us, and he plucked the blond's grip off my arm like a cartoon giant picking a daisy. He yanked the blond by the forearm and the guy let loose of me and Barney pushed him against the side of the building and did the belly-busting routine he was known to use when he was "organizing" reluctant potential union members—shoving his massive middle and all the weight that went with it into his prey.

"Gonna leave my pal alone? In future? Gonna do that for me, huh, you little prick?"

"Yes, sir! Yes, sir!"

The Aloha shirt was running away already, heading for the mouth of the alley.

Barney flung the blond by the arm and seemed to propel him halfway to the street before the guy's feet got working and then he was out the mouth of the alley, too.

"Nate," Barney said, a big grin on the front of his little head, his hand on my shoulder, "what's the idea of not letting me know you were in town?"

CHAPTER THIRTEEN

A waitress in an orange uniform with a white apron and cap set the basket of hamburgers and a second one of onion rings in front of Barney Baker, who already had a bottle of beer going. And I had the glass of Coke I'd ordered. I was against the wall in a half-booth with Barney in a chair opposite me—he still couldn't fit into one of the orange upholstered booths proper. Hovering behind us was a cartoon mural of customers rushing from all directions to get into the Parkmoor.

Which was a restaurant across the street from the Tic Toc and a block up DeBaliviere. As we'd approached, I wondered if a Midwestern twister had, Oz-style, lifted up the Tudor-style brick cottage and dropped it in the midst of the street's gaudy neon-lit businesses and onto a big, mostly empty parking lot.

Parkmoor drive-ins with dine-in service were spotted around St. Louis—their owner was the inventor of the tray carhops attached to car windows—and this branch stayed open a few hours after the drive-in service had ended, to handle the late-night crowd after an evening of strippers, cocktails and back-room gambling. Earlier the Parkmoor on DeBaliviere catered to after-school teens from nearby Soldan High and grown-ups stopping in after golf or tennis, and anybody on their way to or from the zoo or the Muny outdoor theater.

Barney and I were just two of perhaps a dozen patrons, none teenagers, who were looking for something to soak up the booze they'd consumed. Or top it off with a bottle of beer, like Barney. And hamburgers and onion rings. Pat Boone was singing "April Love," despite it being August, on a jukebox whose selections and volume were designed not to offend. The bedraggled adults in booths and at tables were like predictions of how the town's teens would turn out.

If that blow to my stomach hadn't made me lose my appetite, watching Barney eat would have.

"You just happened along?" I asked.

"Not exactly," he admitted, taking a bite of hamburger that reduced the sandwich by a fourth. He chewed and swallowed, either polite or considering his answer; he had a paper napkin tucked bib-style in his sport shirt under his suit jacket. "I was on my way to see Joe. I just stumbled onto those two, roughing you up."

"One of them was Joe's bouncer. Didn't you recognize him?"

"Sure." He reduced the burger to half of its former self. Chewed. Swallowed. "But I never liked him. Look, I saw some poor asshole getting the shit beat out of him, and then it turned out to be my friend Nate Heller, so I was happy to lend a hand."

He'd lent a belly, really, bumping that blond up against the wall.

I sipped my Coke through a straw like I was Archie and he was Jughead—or Moose. "Why were you dropping by Joe's?"

"Well, now there's a coincidence." He dipped an onion ring into a puddle of ketchup. "I'd only just heard you were in town, asking questions, and thought I'd give Joe the ol' heads up."

"Which turned out not to be necessary," I said. "Since I was already there."

"Right." Chewed and swallowed half an onion ring. "But how was I to know that?"

I leaned on my elbow and smiled. "Now let me tell you what really just happened."

"What really happened," he said, with a shrug, and bit into another ketchup-dripping onion ring, "really happened."

"Well, that's hard to argue with. But let me share the larger story."

"By all means. Who doesn't like a good story?"

"You have somebody who works at the Cosmo Club who keeps an eye on your ex-wife for you. Somebody who called you and told you a guy, who was definitely not a Cosmo regular, was talking to her, and maybe passed her some money. Asking questions obviously on a subject other than what-time-do-you-get-off tonight. Maybe he described to you what I look like. Or maybe he recognized me."

Another quarter of a burger disappeared. He nodded and chewed. "You *do* get too much publicity. Being recognized is not good for an individual in your line of work."

I looked around. "You probably live somewhere in the area…"

"Apartment on DeBaliviere."

"…and thought you better go over and give, like you said, the ol' heads-up to Joe Costello."

"Why wouldn't I just call?"

"What does the FBI have in common with Fred Astaire?"

He chuckled. "Tap tap tap." About a third of a burger went down this time.

"That's right, Barney. So that whole routine in the alley was a set-up. To make you look good while I was getting the fear of God put in me."

He waved what was left of the current sandwich at me. "There you are *dead* wrong, Nate. And none of what you say contradicts what I told you. I walked over to see Joe and happened to see some poor bastard getting beat up, and I just waded in to help."

"If you're the Lone Ranger, I feel sorry for the horse."

He looked a little hurt by that. He finished the hamburger, then shrugged elaborately as he helped himself to the final of three burgers. "Believe what you wanna believe. I cop to wanting to let Joe know you were in town, sniffing around. Question is, sniffing around about *what*, Nate?"

"The missing Greenlease money," I revealed. No need not to. "What did you think?"

He batted at the air. "Ancient history."

"Three hundred thousand unrecovered bucks is like Abbott and that other Costello doing 'Who's on First.' "

His eyebrows went up. "Yeah?"

"Never gets old."

He touched his face with the tail of the napkin around his neck, daubing away stray ketchup. "Nate, my buddy, my pal, what was done to the Greenlease child was evil and, worse, it was dumb. It stirred up Jake Lingle-type heat, St. Valentine's Day-type heat, and anyway these rough tough mob bozos are sentimental slobs when it comes to family and innocent children. Nobody in their right mind would want anything to do with that dough. Touch that blood-taint ransom money? Jimmy wouldn't..." He meant Hoffa. "...Big Tuna wouldn't..." He meant Outfit capo Accardo. "...the Camel wouldn't..." He meant Murray Humphreys. "...Buster wouldn't." Local mob guy Wortman. "...and Joe? He is the softest hard guy you ever saw, loves his son to the point of absurdity, loves *all* his off-springs, including those from rotten marriages."

"Then why does the FBI see him as their prime suspect?"

He was so worked up, he'd forgotten his food. "The FBI! Those Ivy League losers think the Mafia doesn't exist. Hoover thinks Cosa Nostra's the latest dance craze! The FBI. You *know* better, Nate."

"You told your wife that Joe Costello wound up with that money."

He had the hamburger back in hand, but now he put it down.

This was serious. "First of all, she's my *ex*-wife. Second of all, she is one lying vengeful bitch. She would like nothing better than to wrap me up in that crime and make me look bad. Doesn't need to be able to prove anything, just spread vile talk! I'm a labor organizer, Nate! I deal with rank-and-file folks, guys with families, salt-of-the-earth solid working Americans. She would *love* to smear me with those good people."

"Okay. A woman scorned. I'll keep that in mind."

His smile split the difference between friendly and menacing. "Who's your client in this, Nate? You don't work for free. You're not some bleeding-heart crusader. Is it that punk silver-spoon Kennedy kid? Let me point something out to you—if Jimmy Hoffa was some kind of gangster, some kind of cold-blooded, brutal asshole, why are you still alive? I will tell you why. He respects you. You have never ratted out any of your Outfit friends. In fact, sometimes I wonder if you're really working in that committee's best interests. Maybe you have Jimmy's welfare at heart. Your old man was a union guy, right?"

"My old man was a 'union guy,' yes, but he would've been disgusted with the tactics of corrupt men like you, Barney, and our friend Jimmy."

He did something astonishing—he pushed his unfinished food aside. "Well, my friend, back in the early days, people could afford to be idealistic. Could go through life being unrealistic. But we know nothing is black-and-white, don't we? We got to deal with how gray things are, right?…I gotta toddle off. Where can I catch you in town?"

Not sure I wanted to be caught, I nonetheless told him where I intended to stay, which amused him.

He gave me a wave. "Make sure you stop and see me before you leave St. Loo."

The big man with the tiny head took the napkin from his

collar, dabbed his mouth delicately with it, and tossed it on the tabletop. He snatched up the check, said, "I'll get this," as if my Coke was a real factor in his burger banquet, and headed for the register.

I tossed the straw aside and finished my Coke like a man. It would appear Barney suspected I was Hoffa's double agent on the Rackets Committee, but apparently hadn't had that confirmed by Hoffa—possibly hadn't even broached the subject. Which was interesting, since he and Hoffa were tight. That could mean a number of things, including that Hoffa didn't trust Barney, or simply that the union president knew the wisdom of keeping my inside man status to himself.

Or was Barney keeping something from Hoffa?

I swung the Cadillac up the modest incline between the two welcoming low-slung fieldstone entrance walls in the blush of the pink-and-red neon sign. A buzzing secondary neon promised a VACANCY in white. About two-thirds of a full moon cast its ivory tinge onto the gleaming beige and brown ceramic tiles of the rounded units of the Coral Court, their occasional glass-brick windows glowing—not every couple had gotten round to turning off the lights or else were fine following their desires with the lights on.

Returning to the scene of the crime—and I had to stay somewhere, didn't I?—made a certain kind of perverse sense. Special Agent Grapp had told me Sandy O'Day resided here and of course so did owner/manager Jack Carr, who I'd yet to meet.

But I'd read Grapp's notes. Carr had done a stretch at Leavenworth for armed robbery a decade prior to opening his motel and was rumored to have pushed his first wife down the stairs to her death—that should qualify him for the $300,000 blood-money sweepstakes. And Sandy, now a madam for call girls at Carr's motel, seemed an acquaintance well worth renewing.

The office was just inside those fieldstone walls, facing Watson Road, a building in the same Streamline Moderne style as the double units but twice their size, as it included the owner's living quarters. I pulled in front, got out and went up a few steps into a spacious pink-walled lobby, large enough to accommodate a long ebony registration desk, a desk sign at left saying

BY THE WEEK

BY THE DAY

and another at right announcing

HOURLY RATES—

WELCOME TRUCKERS

and maybe implying something that rhymed with "truckers."

The walls were decorated with framed photos of attractions in the St. Louis area, including the Coral Court itself, and both side walls had elaborate wooden racks of tourist brochures. Modern furnishings, appropriate to the place's styling, were here and there, with a corner coffee station and table and chairs, in case a rush on check-ins was on.

The rush was not on.

A tall slender man in a white short-sleeve shirt and bolo tie stood behind the desk at left; his hooded eyes were a gun-metal blue with heavy black circles, his black hair going white—pushing sixty, he had a weather-beaten handsomeness like the first mate on a ship considering mutiny.

"Welcome to the Coral Court." The voice was a mellow baritone with a sandpaper edge. His smile was slight but it hung around.

I nodded, flicked a smile. "Glad to be here."

We went through the check-in ritual—it was a reasonable $8.50 a night and $39.50 for a week, and I took the latter. I signed my name in the register, but he said, "Thank you, Mr. Heller," without glancing at it.

"How is it you know me?" I said. "I've never been here before."

"Sure you have," he said.

That damn almost-smile kept at it.

"Okay," I admitted. We were skipping a round or two in the game. "Only you weren't working the desk when I checked in, five years ago."

"No, but nothing goes on at the Coral Court that I don't know about. Nothing important, anyway. I own the place—Jack Carr."

He offered a hand.

I took it. "Pleasure, Mr. Carr."

That was a working man's hand, as dry and callused as his attitude.

But his tone couldn't have been more casual. "I could put you back in your old room—50-A, if you like."

Now he was just showing off.

"Not necessary," I said. "I'm not terribly sentimental when it comes to kidnapping cases, especially when they lead to child murder. But I would like to ask you a few questions."

He shrugged, then nodded toward the coffee station. "Okay. Care for some joe?"

"As in Costello? Is that who called you and said I'd be coming? He'd have been told by Barney Baker, who was real casual about asking me where I'd be staying."

The gun-metal eyes were sleepy but they didn't blink much. "So, then, no coffee?"

"Wouldn't wanna be up all night. It's been a long day."

"Nightcap, maybe? What's your poison, Mr. Heller?"

"Any rum, Mr. Carr. Bacardi, if you've got it."

"I do, and I'll join you." He gestured vaguely. "Have a seat. I'll switch off the vacancy sign and then be right back."

As he disappeared through the PRIVATE door behind the counter, I selected one of two seats at a round low table with *Holiday* magazines fanned out.

I was just starting to wonder about how long putting together a couple of nightcaps could take when he emerged with two motel water glasses with several fingers of rum in each. He held both glasses out to me, to make the choice mine—maybe he thought I suspected he'd brought me a Mickey Finn-laced nightcap. I took the one in his left hand, and he sat. His smile was something a guy with no sense of humor had learned to do.

"Mr. Heller, *this*—right here, right now—is your opportunity to talk to me. I am a busy man. I do my own books. I oversee this property, work the desk myself at times, and do all the landscaping."

"Landscaping, huh? You do a nice job of it."

He nodded modest thanks. "Every bush, every tree, is my personal doing. Most guests think I'm the gardener. I find it relaxing. I like creating a pleasant atmosphere for my guests. What I don't like to do is talk."

"That may be the case, but you seem to be doing your share right now."

The smile increased a few millimeters, then settled back down. "You mentioned Joe Costello. We're old friends. We have a few common business interests. But we aren't *in* business together. He has his cab company. And I have the Coral Court."

"I appreciate your frankness."

"I have the kind of establishment that requires discretion. At one time I did have a more serious business relationship with

Joe and also with Buster…Buster Wortman? I have a certain capability with figures. With numbers. I did their bookkeeping for a while, until the Coral Court became so successful I didn't need outside work."

"This capability with numbers of yours?"

"Yes?"

"Would one of those numbers be three hundred thousand? And would that be the number allowing you to stop doing outside work?"

The slight smile stayed right where it was. Behind that face with its black-rimmed *Cabinet of Caligari* eyes and that fucking facsimile of a smile, wheels were turning.

"The feds took this place apart," he said. "It was a fool's errand—that money was like most of my guests—just passing through. The Coral Court's walls aren't stuffed with money, Mr. Heller. Get that out of your head."

"What do you think became of it? The missing half a ransom."

"I wouldn't know. And I don't care." He stood. "Now, I hope you enjoy your stay. Speaking as one well-seasoned individual to another, I would suggest that while you're in the St. Louis area, you ask your questions, get what information you can, and then get the fuck out before you get yourself killed. Oh. One more thing."

"What would that be, Jack?"

"You'll need your room key."

He got back behind the desk and I wandered over to my side of the counter. He handed me the key. The smile grew just enough to show me an edge of teeth.

"You'll get a kick out it," he said. "It's what we call the Red Room. Honeymooners love it. Great for Valentine's Day. And if you act fast enough, before it dries and goes brown, no blood stains."

❖

I pulled the Caddy into the nearest of the side-by-side garages separating the two rooms making up my building. When I entered from the mini-garage into the unit itself, I was indeed in a red room. Not the walls—those were cream-colored—but the furnishings: red bedspread, red vinyl couch, red vinyl-upholstered armchairs, pink-shaded nightstand lamps, red-and-black broadloom carpet, red-framed modernistic St. Louis cityscape over the bed.

My bag went on the wooden luggage rack and I tossed my suitcoat on a chair, got my tie off, and kicked off my shoes. Padded into the red-and-black-and-white tiled bathroom, threw water on my face, dried it off while the mirror told me I looked every one of my years at the end of a long day. Went back out and flopped on my back onto the red spread. A Beautyrest beneath me, I'd bet. I placed my nine millimeter Browning on the nightstand next to the paperback of *Compulsion* by Meyer Levin (a bit of a busman's holiday, I grant you). Thought about the people I hoped to interview tomorrow and considered catching the last half of Jack Paar on the tube when somebody knocked on the door.

Carr?

Or somebody Carr had called in who might not be friendly? It sure as hell wasn't room service.

I got the nine mil and held it, barrel high, as I answered the second round of knocks. Cracked the door.

My caller was female, to say the least—tall with black hair in a Gwen Verdon pixie cut, her voluptuous shape wrapped up in a red-and-white striped short-sleeve shirt (smokes in the pocket) and black capris. Tucked under one arm was a quart of Seagram's and under the other a big bottle of Seven-Up; one hand held a hotel-room ice bucket to herself, the other made a fist in mid-knock. Maybe this *was* room service.

"We have to stop meeting like this," Sandy O'Day said. The

wide mouth, lipsticked candy-apple red, mocked me. She looked younger than her nearly forty years—probably rough years at that. Wearing flats, she could damn near greet me eye-to-eye.

"I'm only inviting you in," I said, opening the door wider, "because you'll go nicely with the room."

She brushed by, noting the nine millimeter in my right hand and said, "Is that any way to welcome an old friend? Maybe I should've worn the Marilyn wig."

"I'm going to take a wild stab and say Carr sent you."

She shook her head, pixie strands bouncing. "No. Jack called and said you were here. Sort of warned me. I took it upon myself to play Miss Welcome Wagon. So…welcome."

She went over and set the ice bucket and two bottles on the low-slung modern coffee table in front of the red vinyl couch. She went into the bathroom and fetched two water glasses. Then she sat, curling her legs up under her, running an arm along the couch's upper cushion; her red lacquered nails went well with the room, too.

"You pour," she instructed me.

I sat next to her and set the nine mil on the coffee table beside the ice bucket and built us a couple of drinks. She was wearing Arpège by Lanvin again. I was surprised that she looked so good, and maybe it showed.

"I don't turn tricks anymore," she said defensively. "I'm not in that business these days."

"Sure you are, Sandy. You're a madam."

She sipped her drink, shivered. "Isn't that an awful word? Makes me sound old and fat. Do I look old and fat?"

"No, but you *are* a madam, aren't you? Working out of the Coral Court?"

"I work out of a little house of Jack's across Watson Road. Three girls live with me over there, and the rest are in town for

me to simply phone. I'm *not* a madam, goddamnit. I make…
referrals. Arrangements. Appointments. It's an escort service."

I swallowed Seagram's and Seven-up. "I don't care either
way."

She set her glass down, harder than necessary. "Well, I do.
And anyway, this madam shit is only for the time being. I have
plans."

"You always were an ambitious girl."

" '*Always*'! We knew each other one *night*, Heller!"

"But it *was* memorable."

She sighed and put her hand on my leg. "Not as memorable
as it could have been…"

I stiffened and not the way she hoped for. "What do you want
from me, Sandy?"

She reared back. "What do *I* want from you? *You're* the one
who wants to talk to *me*."

"I do?"

She moved closer. Very close. Her arm came down around
my shoulder and the red-lipsticked mouth drew close to my
right ear. She seemed to be putting the make on, but I was
wrong: she whispered, "Not safe to talk."

Then she moved back. "Let's not bicker. Hey, Heller, what
would you say to a moonlight stroll, for old time's sake?"

I took a swig of my drink. Said, "Why not?"

I slipped my gun in my waistband. We went out the front
and she hooked her arm in mine. The humidity wasn't bad for
the Midwest and the warm night was mixing with the breeze
like the ginger ale and whiskey in my belly. The three-quarter
moon was filtering down through the many pin pines. Sap was
in the air. And maybe his name was Heller.

"Listen," she said, and her voice had a different timbre, "*of
course* Carr sent me. That room is wired for sound recording."

"I'm shocked."

"Yeah, I'm sure. He might be watching—right now."

"Oh?"

"Would kissing me make you sick?"

"Let's try it and see."

We stood there in a clinch and kissed and it wasn't bad at all. She was a smoker and I could taste it, but the fullness and warmth of those sticky lips made it a nicely nasty experience. A perfect chaser for the Seagram's and Seven.

We walked into the pin pines, back into the taller ones that had been there even before Carr got into gardening. I stood with my spine to one of the thicker trunks and she faced me, her lipstick smeared. Was she frightened?

"You want to know," she said, "if the Greenlease money was ever hidden here. I don't know the answer to that. It *might* have been, briefly. But I doubt it."

"Why?"

"The inner walls at the Coral Court are thin. You've seen the layout—the rooms are adjacent to the individual garages. No need for heavy walls. The brick exterior is so heavy those inner walls don't need much. These wild stories about the place being stuffed with ransom dough are just that—stories, wild, and stupid. Certain rooms are wired for sound, yeah, but the walls are just too thin for storing jack shit."

I frowned at her. "You think Carr helped launder the loot? He freely admitted he does business with Costello and Wortman. Said he was their accountant in the old days."

She shook her head. "But that *was* the old days. When he opened up, the Coral Court was meant to be a mob getaway, a place for Outfit guys to vacation or lie low. But then the motel took off with a straight clientele—cheating spouses and honeymooning couples and families with kiddies. Outfit guys were pissed after that—Wortman even took a shot at Carr, and Jack had to make peace. Does them favors when need be."

"Like moving the Greenlease money?"

She sighed, looked back toward the motel. "We need to get in there and do what Carr expects us to."

"Which is what?"

Her response seemed a non-sequitur. "Around when you knew me, I'd had my fill of men. I lived with another woman till about six months ago. I'm a switch-hitter, okay? But you need to know I haven't been with a man for three, maybe four years."

"Why are you telling me this?"

"Because we have to go in there and do what Carr *expects* us to! Don't worry—you're not going to catch anything. And I haven't had a visit from my friend in two years."

"What friend?"

She rolled her eyes. "Oh, Christ, Heller. Really."

She took me by the arm and dragged me back to the room. She stood in the middle of all that red and demonstrated she didn't have anything on under the striped top and capri pants. Her breasts were full, the nipples in their setting large and erect. She twirled, just to smirkingly show off the dimpled firm globes in back. In front she had an appendix scar and her bush was a black tangled dare against startling white flesh.

I was just taking it all in—she stripped with amazing speed and grace—and then she stood with her fists on her hips like a super woman, feet planted wide. Taking a look at my tented trousers, she said, "Well, I can see you're interested."

She came over and got on her knees and zipped me down and got me out. The black pixie-haired dynamo looked up at me with scary beautiful light-blue eyes.

"I wasn't popular as a whore," she said.

"Oh?"

She had me in her hands. "See, I wouldn't do this for *any* man for *any* money. Only men I really liked. Or loved or thought I did."

"Oh."

Then she took me slowly into her mouth and worked me with expert care, particularly for a woman who had sworn off men years ago, and after a while she walked me by the engorged member over to the bed, like taking a child by the hand.

She put me on my back and climbed on; getting in was tough but worth the effort. At first it was like a fist had hold of me and then it got smooth and slippery and when, after a long, delirious, undulating fuck, I came, it felt goddamn good, and maybe to her, too. Anyway, she shivered and moaned and almost wailed. Maybe for the wired walls.

She rolled off, panting. She got a smoke from a pack of Chesterfields and stuck it between those full lips, the red stuff gone now, and lighted up. Then she grinned at me, mouth seeping smoke, and said, "Now, that wasn't so bad, was it?"

"No," I said. "But I'll hate myself in the morning."

CHAPTER FOURTEEN

The St. Louis Hills neighborhood had its share of single-family dwellings, but more than a few two-stories had become rooming houses, with substantial apartment buildings invading as well. This was one of those areas developed in the 1920s to provide families with tree-lined streets, churches and schools, with bordering businesses and the green open spaces of parks. Then the Depression came along and turned the Hills into a nest of apartments.

The neighborhood did seem to be working its way back. The brick structures dominating streets were lined with tall trees, a peaceful Ozzie and Harriet world of kids, bikes, couples walking dogs, moms pushing strollers. Ex-police lieutenant Louis Shoulders lived here, on Tamm Avenue, in one of four buildings he owned. According to Wes Grapp, Shoulders had several rooming houses during his time on the police department, as well; but those were in neighborhoods not so well-shaded—just shady, serving as they did to shelter whorehouses.

The address on Tamm was a block off the Clayton Avenue business district, a big square two-story white-trimmed brown-brick building with four windows across on either floor. More an apartment complex, then, than a rooming house. I found him in the alley at the rear, wrestling a garbage can to the paving's edge across a slightly sloping back yard, to join its tin-can twins. It was hot today and I didn't envy him. Or feel any sympathy.

The tall, broad-shouldered man in t-shirt, overalls and work boots was huffing and puffing, a guy who'd been almost fat and was now nearly skinny, in a sick-looking way, skin hanging off him like a suit the wrong size. His black hair was threaded silver but his heavy eyebrows were charcoal smears against ghostly-white flesh, the face on the bucket head having the look of a man perpetually wondering who might be sneaking up behind him.

As he set the can down next to the others, heaving a sigh, he provided an easy irony: they had nicknamed him the Shadow, both the cops and the crooks, after the old radio show, because as a young officer he was known to prowl the back yards and alleys, looking for thieves, numbers runners and other evils found in the hearts of men.

Another irony about it came easy, too: Lou Shoulders had really been looking for crooks to shake down, thriving on bribes from pimps, prostitutes and gamblers in the midtown Eleventh Precinct police district on Newstead Avenue, where he eventually was nightwatch commander. Not that he hadn't collared his share of bad guys—he'd killed three, including two prison escapees and a "burglar" who invaded the happy Shoulders home. Whispers had it the "burglary" was a bungled hit on a cop despised by one and all.

"Should you be doing that kind of heavy lifting?" I asked. "Didn't you have a heart attack in stir?"

He looked at me suspiciously. Of course he probably looked at everybody suspiciously.

"Do I know you?" His voice was deep and hoarse.

"Well, we had a memorable fifteen minutes at the Coral Court once. But who in St. Louis hasn't?"

"Nate Heller," he said, pursing his lips like he didn't like the taste. He grunted an excuse for a laugh. "I heard you was around."

"I try not to hide my light under a bushel."

The upper thick lip made a sneer. "You could get in trouble, the things I know about you that night."

"Not as much trouble as you, Lou. Another perjury rap, for openers. Did you really have a heart attack? Or was that just a way to serve out your stretch in a medical facility?"

"I did have a heart attack," he said defensively. "I'm a sick man. I don't wanna talk to you. It's not good for me."

He wasn't wrong.

"Look," I said, friendly, leaning a hand on a tin lid, "just think of it as another visit to the doctor. Something you might as well get out of the way."

His eyes, as black as the eyebrows, narrowed in their pouches. "I don't have to talk to you."

"My client would like you to."

"That right?" The hoarse voice was a growl now. "And who would that be? And why should I give a damn?"

I raised my palms chest-high in mild surrender. "Up to you, Lou. You still involved in union work?"

He shook his head, folded his arms. "Not as much. My son, Lou, is. He's security chief with the Pipefitters. What's that got to do with the price of beans?"

"My client is somebody worried about the Greenlease money getting tied to the Teamsters. The Rackets Committee is sniffing around, which you may have heard. Be a hell of a black eye. He'd appreciate your cooperation."

The heavy brows knit. "You're talkin' about…Mr. Hoffa?"

I raised the palms again, higher. "Hey. I didn't mention any names." I nodded toward the street. "I saw a saloon on the corner, just up the block. Why don't we find someplace quiet to talk?"

We did, in a booth in back of the Tamm Avenue Tap.

We both had beers. He was smoking a Camel. Not really what a guy with a heart condition should be doing, but I wasn't his doctor, despite what I'd said.

"I have no idea what became of that money," he said. "I swear on the life of my wife and my children."

He didn't say which wife—he'd been married four times. The fourth had been the "landlady" of one of his two bawdy houses. Of course, Lou was still married to his third wife then, and the landlady had also been his mistress. Who, after the Hall arrest, Shoulders had taken to Hawaii on a vacation.

I didn't rub any of that in his face. But Grapp had filled me in on this colorful ex-cop, with whom I had briefly but memorably intersected five years ago, and the only question I really had for him was, *Why should I believe anything you say, you lying son of a bitch?*

"If you ask me," he said, after a gulp of beer, "the only person who knows where that money is, is Carl Hall. And haven't you heard? Dead men don't talk."

"He didn't say anything worth listening to," I said, "when he was breathing. Anyway, what makes you think Carl would know where that dough went? What, a little mud on his trousers?"

He leaned in, his big head hovering over the booth's scarred tabletop like a window-peeker getting a gander. "I'm gonna tell you something I never told nobody before, Heller, nobody."

"Please."

One black eyebrow went up. "You remember I said I'd have somebody shadow that creep, once we had eyes on him? That afternoon of the day we got him that night?"

I followed that. Barely, but I followed it.

"Well," he said, still hovering, "I shadowed him *myself.*" *Who knows what evil lurks…?*

"He went to a hardware store on Chippewa," Shoulders

said, as if reading it off a report, "and bought two iron garbage cans."

And the man knew his garbage cans.

"The, what-you-call-it, galvanized type," he said. Settling back in the booth now, he rested his smoke in a Tamm Tap ashtray. "Also two big plastic zipper bags, a can of waterproofing spray, and, yup, a shovel. I watched him watch the sales gal make two trips loading up his car. Then he drove off. He went through a couple suburbs and out into the country and was slowing down here and there, like he was looking for a place to hide something. And I wonder whatever *that* could be?"

"Where exactly?"

"There's a bridge over the Meramec on Route 66, not that far from the Coral Court. Few miles west is all. The banks was a mucky mess. East of that bridge he took a winding road around a bluff—I had to keep way back, because he would slow down then pick up speed and a couple times he almost got stuck. Finally I had to reverse it real quick not to be made. Anyway, he went back over the bridge, and once he slowed down at a farm and was giving it a good long look when some dogs started in barking and spooked him. He turned and headed back and I lost him. I tried driving around the area, but came up empty."

"So he could have buried the money."

Shoulders shrugged his. "He had time. Later we found those garbage cans at a country club that went out of business. Dumped 'em in their clubhouse. But no spray can. No plastic bags."

I frowned. "Why would he bury *half* the money?"

He exhaled smoke. "You spent time with him, Heller. You think that punk had his head sewed on straight? Look, I'm sick and tired of talking about the Greenlease case. Just fed up with it. I would never be so foolish as to steal that money—it had a damn red *lantern* tied on it!"

I was shaking my head slowly. "I don't think he buried that money, Lou. He just drove around looking for a hiding place and never found anywhere that satisfied him."

He leaned in conspiratorially. "Okay, then. I heard it was Jack Carr and gangster pals of his that got that money." Leaned back. "Also, some say it all got burned up, 'cause it was so hot."

"Just burst into flames, maybe? No, Lou. Not that, and not gangsters at the Coral Court, or Carl and his shovel. You and your buddy Joe Costello got the loot. But where did it go after that? Neither one of you is living like a king."

He shook his head emphatically and the skinny man's fat lips were quivering. "You have got it *all* wrong, Heller. I go way back with Joe, that's true, we started out driving cab together. That's why when Joe got a line on that little psycho of a kidnapper, I'm who he called. It was just a tip I got. Nothing more. No good deed goes unpunished, they say, and ain't that the truth. I get the kidnapper. I get the gun he used to kill that poor kid. Isn't *that* enough? So I *didn't* recover the whole damn ransom money. Isn't it enough that...."

He covered his face with his hands. He was crying now. Literally crying into his beer.

"I don't mean...I don't mean to accuse Joe or nothing.... He's a good man. Before June...my wife...would make the drive to the U.S. Medical Center in Springfield, to see me? He would make sure our car got topped off with gas. He and his wife had June over for supper all the time, while I was away. People say terrible things about him, like *he* took that money. Let ye who is without sin cast the first stone, I always say."

He dried his eyes with a paper napkin. Found a hanky in a

pocket to blow his nose, which he did louder than Satchmo hitting a high note.

When he'd composed himself, I said, "When all is said and done, Lou, there are still two things missing."

That seemed to confuse him, the eyes under the heavy black eyebrows squinting at me.

"Half the ransom money," I said, "and an hour. The hour after you booked Carl Hall and before you turned over the other half."

"I accounted for that time," he said indignantly.

"Oh, that's right. You had to drop your car off to your 'landlady,' who had an appointment. The rest was kind of vague. 'Personal errands.' And all the while three hundred grand is in the trunk."

He lifted a palm. "Well, we had to load up Dolan's car. Elmer followed me to June's to drive me back." Then, as if it were a point in his favor, he added, "And that footlocker and that metal suitcase, they weren't *in* the trunk. They were in the back seat."

"Ah, well, then that's different. So while you and Officer Dolan dragged Hall into Newstead station, you left three hundred grand in the back seat of your car? I hope you locked it up, Lou."

He shrugged. Waved that off. "People don't steal stuff from in front of a police station."

"You are a very stupid man, Lou."

The little black eyes popped big. "Fuck you, Heller! I was a *good* cop. They gave me medals and promotions. I did a great thing and I'm proud of it. I got that child killer put in the gas chamber, him and his scummy little honey. I got six kids! You think I would touch money with that...that little boy's *blood* on it?"

He started weeping again.

Oh, brother.

He dried his eyes with his arm and he found some room to blow his nose on the hanky. He finished his beer. He plucked his smoke from the ashtray and had a few final puffs.

Then, softly earnest, he said, "You will not believe this, but I am not the man I was. I don't just mean physically speaking. I mean where morals go. I was a good cop, but it's true I sometimes...stumbled. In prison, in the prison hospital, I read the Bible. I read it before, of course, but this time...I *really* read it."

"Did you."

"I did. I regret certain things in my life. But I would swear on *any* Bible that I had nothing to do with what happened to the Greenlease money. I pray...I pray for that poor child often. Just *think*, as a parent, what they been through! Breaks my heart. But I read that Mrs. Greenlease, she's very religious, too. And she understands God works in mysterious ways."

"You mean like shooting a little boy in the head?"

He got choked up. "Please...please. I know you don't think I'm sincere, but I swear I am. That's why I've become a deacon of the church."

Fuck you, Heller, I'm a deacon of the church.

"I've even begun my studies."

"What studies are those, Lou?"

"To become a minister."

I laughed. I went over to the bar and paid for our beers, then went back to the booth and said, "Let me preach to you, Lou, from the gospel of Who the Hell Do You Think You're Kidding. You're not crying for that dead kid. You're not even crying for your lost career. You're crying because you threw it away for a fortune that slipped through your goddamn fingers."

And I left him there in his pew.

*

The storefront in the shopping district at Chippewa Street and Hampton Avenue wore white neon letters on a pale green background—

D & S Dry Cleaners

—and various hand-lettered signs all but blotted out the windowed front: "ONE HOUR" SERVICE, QUALITY "QUICK" DRY CLEANING, PRESS WHILE "U" WAIT and the like. All those quotation marks were troubling—desperation merged with hedging a bet.

As I went in, the kerosene-like odor of dry cleaning welcomed me. The slender man behind the counter didn't; his face was a blank space waiting for an expression to happen, his smock as white as a doctor's, with D & S stitched in red on the breast pocket.

I'd only seen him that one time five years ago at the Coral Court, but I knew the ex-uniformed cop at once. At the time, Elmer Dolan had reminded me of a younger version of Shoulders, as if he were the man's son—similar dark hair, high forehead on an oblong head, bushy grown-together eyebrows and small, full-lipped mouth. His eyes were dark too, but lacked the shifty quality of the older man's.

While even now he was boyish-looking, Dolan was no kid anymore, though Shoulders had still referred to him as such. Yesterday's twenty-five-year-old rookie patrolman was today's thirty-year-old businessman now, draped in melancholy much as the clothing in hangers on their rack, awaiting pick-up, wore plastic bags.

"Mr. Heller," he said, with a nod. As if the last (and for that matter the first) time we'd met hadn't been briefly, five years ago.

"So your partner called you with a heads-up," I said, crossing to the counter and leaning there. "He'd be the 'S' in 'D & S.' "

"And I'm the 'D,' " he said. "But it doesn't stand for dumb. Lou says I don't have to talk to you."

Behind him, past a narrow barrier, the dry-cleaning business was singing its percussive, tuneless song: hiss of steam, presses opening and closing, metal pedals squeaking.

"Lou's right," I said. "I'm no cop. Of course, you aren't either, anymore. I'm a Chicago private investigator working for a client."

"I know who you are. I read about you in the papers sometimes. Who's the client?"

Shoulders had talked to me because I invoked Hoffa. That wouldn't work with Dolan.

Now and then you just have to play a hunch. Mine was an educated one, based upon a framed family portrait on the shop wall—a pretty young wife, a beaming boy of maybe three, and a proud papa with an arm around her and a hand on the child's sleeve. The papa was Elmer Dolan, of course.

I said, "My client is the Greenlease family."

An expression finally happened: the eyes tightened, the brow furrowed, the mouth quivered. "I suppose…I suppose they want their money back. Well, I don't have it."

"It's not that they want their money back," I said with a shrug, as if this were the most casual subject in the world, "it's that it sickens them thinking of anybody profiting off their little boy's death."

His mouth was quivering so much he had to cover it; his eyes were going moist with something like genuine human feeling, not the self-pity that characterized the crocodile tears of Lou Shoulders.

"Give me a second, would you?" he said. "I have to get a girl to cover the counter."

He slipped in back, past the hanging garment purveyor, and soon returned with a pleasant young colored woman in a D & S smock to take his place. He summoned me to follow him and I did, through the work area where an all-Negro crew in white was at presses with the exception of an older gal who was hand-ironing. The kerosene-like smell was much stronger back here. Not a big set-up, but an efficient one.

Dolan walked me into a cubbyhole office with metal furnishings, desk with chair, visitor's chair, one four-drawer file cabinet. The desk was cluttered, centered with an oversize account book. He shut us in, then from a small refrigerator of bottles of Coke, he got us each one; I liked the boyish man's taste in soda pop. He got behind the desk and gestured for me to sit opposite.

"The FBI," he said, after swigging some Coke, "have been after my story for a long time. Why should I give it to you?"

"You wouldn't be giving it to me," I said. "You'd be giving it to Robert Greenlease, Sr."

"Spare me the violins. If you hadn't already pulled my heartstrings, we wouldn't be sitting here. It makes me sick what happened to that boy, and what his parents got put through."

"Are still going through."

"I know. I know. But I have two children of my own now, and they are of more concern to me than, with all due respect, Mr. Greenlease's late son Bobby."

"You're afraid to talk." Why sugarcoat it?

His eyes hardened. "You are goddamn *right* I'm afraid to talk. Not so much for myself—like you said, I was a cop. Every day when I went to work, I did so knowing I might not come home. Plenty of officers in St. Louis have been killed in the line of duty."

"You weren't."

"No, I wasn't. And I don't want to be killed as a civilian, either, because that leaves my wife and two kids to fend for themselves."

My turn to swig some Coke. "Well, at least you have your mentor to look after you."

"What mentor?"

"The former Lieutenant Louis Ira Shoulders. The honored cop who killed bad guys dead and won all those honors. I mean, you're in business with him aren't you?"

Of course I knew exactly what reaction I was after. And got it.

"Fucking Shoulders!" He slammed his half-full Coke bottle on the desk and the liquid fizzed. "My *partner*, you call him! My mentor!"

"Well, isn't he? The 'S' in—"

"In 'D & S,' yes! The Shadow! He's *my* shadow, is who he is—keeping an eye on me. Making sure I stay mum." He sat forward, elbows on the desk. "Let me tell you how my life got ruined. I'd already made my mind up to leave the department. The St. Louis PD is a nest of thieves! I don't know why my father never warned me. Maybe he was one of them."

"Your father was a cop?"

He nodded curtly. "And my uncle. But I wound up at Newstead Avenue station, the dirtiest district in town, and Shoulders ran it. I'd tried putting in for a transfer and got slapped down. That day...that very goddamn day that all the shit happened...I planned to sneak off to deliver my filled-out application to the Triple A."

This was news to me. "You were going to quit?"

Now came some vigorous nodding. "I'd made up my mind. Then right after roll call, the 3 P.M. to 11 P.M. watch, Shoulders calls me over and says his regular driver is sick. He wants me to fill in. Now, he already knew about Hall and the money and everything, I'm sure of it. But not a word to me."

"You weren't his regular driver?"

"No. Without cluing me in at all, he yanks me into the dirtiest mess in St. Louis history."

A wave of recognition went through me: *in 1932, I'd been a young off-duty dick when the two most corrupt cops in Chicago grabbed me and pulled me unaware into a hit on Frank Nitti. They shot Capone's successor twice in the neck but somehow Nitti hadn't died. I quit the force and went private, staying alive by forging a surrogate father-and-son relationship with Nitti that connected me, unwillingly, to the Outfit to this day.*

"Mr. Heller? I lost you there for a moment."

"Sorry. Go on."

He sat back. Folded his arms. Shrugged. "Well, that's all I can give you…without certain conditions."

A steam press out there hissed at that.

"That is," he said, "if you want to know what *I* know about the Greenlease money."

"Certain conditions."

"Yes. You can *only* share this with Mr. Greenlease. I don't even want his *wife* to know. You have to say that it's…what's the word? Hypothetical. This is what *might* have happened."

"You won't go on the record."

"No."

I crossed my legs and my arms and sighed. "Then what good is it?"

"It means he'll know. The boy's father will know. And maybe someday the world will, if I can outlive Lou Shoulders and Joe Costello. Maybe then I'll tell the FBI—God knows they won't have stopped asking me. Until then, this is all you get. Do I have your word?"

"…You do."

"Are you a father?"

"I am. I have a son."

"Swear on your son's life."

I nodded. Sighed again. "I swear."

He told me. He left out what I already knew, including what I gathered but hadn't witnessed, specifically the transfer of Carl Hall to that apartment at the Town House within St. Louis PD jurisdiction. That cabbie Hagan had been around for most of it, but hadn't been there when Shoulders directed Dolan to load up the lieutenant's car with the footlocker, the metal suitcase and a briefcase that collectively included the entire ransom but for the free-wheeling spending Hall had done on his day of binge drinking. Shoulders drove Dolan and all that money to the home of Joe Costello on Gurney Court in a nice, quiet South St. Louis neighborhood. Helped them down the stairs with the three heavy pieces of luggage into a paneled basement, where the money was counted on a coffee table.

"Shoulders pointed to the stacks of money," Dolan told me, "and said, 'Half of that is ours. You'll wind up with fifty grand. What are you going to do with your share?' I told him I didn't want anything to do with that crap. And I didn't even know, at that point, that this was the Greenlease ransom!"

"But Shoulders did?"

He nodded emphatically. "Yeah, I'm sure of it. From things he said that night, and other things he said over time. He knew. And when I said I didn't want any part of the money, he said, 'You really don't have anything to say about it.'"

"You never took any of the ransom?"

"Not really. We took half back to the Newstead station. I pleaded with Shoulders all the way there not to take so god-damn much—it *had* to come back on us. And I was scared stiff, scared we'd be caught, scared if I didn't go along with them, Costello and Shoulders would kill me. I should've pulled my gun and arrested them right there in that rec room!...But I didn't."

"What did you mean—'not really'?"

"Well, to protect myself and my family, I backed up whatever story Shoulders was telling at the time—it shifted all over the place. And that landed me in prison on that perjury rap. I got two years. Maybe you know that."

"Go on."

"When I got out after fifteen months—it was December '55 —Joe Costello wanted to meet with me at Ruggeri's restaurant. He said he'd sold my share while I was inside, and offered me ten grand. I turned it down, but...I'm not proud of this...it was Christmas and I'd been doing time and had no job. I asked for fifteen-hundred dollars for living expenses and...to buy presents for the wife and kids."

He started to cry.

Him I could feel for. Shoulders could go fuck himself.

I said, "Is that everything, son?"

"N...no. Not quite. A guy was already there when we got to Costello's that night."

"What guy?"

Steam hissed, a librarian asking for quiet.

He obeyed, keeping his voice down, saying, "A big guy with connections. You know? *Connections.* He helped Joe count the money. And was good at it, like a banker. Then he took the money with him, the other half of it, before we left with the rest, to turn in at the station."

I leaned forward and put an edge in my voice. "*What* guy, Elmer?"

He shook his head. "Can't tell you, Mr. Heller. Not even if

Joe Costello and Lou Shoulders were dead and gone. Not even…not even if this big mob guy *himself* was dead and gone, because he's *so* connected it would come back on me, sure as hell. My kids would not have a father and my wife would not have a husband."

"Okay, Elmer."

"The rest of it? You can tell Mr. Greenlease, but *not* before he swears on his life to keep it to himself. Maybe someday I'll go public. But till then, he has to *swear*. On his daughter's life, 'cause I read he has one. On *her* life, Mr. Heller."

He was getting worked up.

I said, "All right, Elmer."

"Because if you don't keep your word, I'm a dead man."

And he probably would be.

As he walked me out of the work area, I said, "You have a solid crew working back there. Business good?"

"I thought it was. But we've just sold the place."

I frowned at him. "Why, if you're doing well?"

He shook his head. "Our silent partners are people in Chicago who know the laundry business. They insisted we sell. They were disappointed with how we were doing."

He opened the gate in the counter for me and we stepped through and I said, "Would one of those silent partners be named Humphreys, by any chance?"

"Murray Humphreys, yes. His people came in and set everything up for us, when we started out last year."

And that explained it. The Murray Humphreys chain of dry-cleaning establishments laundered more than clothes.

At the door I asked, "Tell me, did the feds take an interest in your books?"

He laughed, once. "Oh, they've been all over us. But they didn't find a thing. We're squeaky clean. It's disappointing, 'cause we were really making a go of it. Now I start at a service station next month, pumping gas."

We shook hands and I went out.

Had the Outfit backed Lou Shoulders, as partial payback for bringing the Greenlease money to them? And had it proved a bad investment when federal scrutiny prevented them from cleaning up in a new market?

CHAPTER FIFTEEN

Extending over a carport and glassed-in lobby, the sign said in yellow-edged red neon, with the "M" and the "B" in white-edged pink—

STAN *Musial & Biggies*

—a neon baseball dotting the "I" in Musial, a floating star over "STAN," and a toasting drinking glass near the "B" (Julius "Biggie" Garagnani had been a well-known St. Louis restaurateur even before bringing Musial into the business). The rest of the modern brick two-story restaurant loomed behind and to the right, the central windowed area of both floors dramatically spotlighted. All in all, aglow in the dusk, the restaurant made a gaudy eye-catching monument to a local hero, Stan the Man, the Cardinals' beloved batter. And in a town noted for Italian fare, Musial's was not a bad place to catch a plate of spaghetti and meatballs, although I was having the filet with mushroom sauce and Sandy O'Day a shrimp salad.

After such a spectacular exterior, the dining room proved something of a disappointment, just a bland sea of linen-clothed tables-for-four with subdued lighting, and organist Stan Kann quietly playing show tunes, all overseen by an endless mirrored bar. On a weeknight, business was slow and the prices high— $4.75 for my steak, a la carte, side dishes sixty cents—with mostly tourists taking the bait.

"I was at the other location once," I said to Sandy, as we noshed on a buck's worth of toasted ravioli, "when Musial himself was going table to table. Signing autographs, ruffling kids' hair."

"Sweet guy," she said between nibbles. "But he's usually only around in the off-season."

She was in a creamy white silk blouse with pearls. Her gray pencil skirt and low heels weren't apparent, seated, but when I'd picked her up at the little house across the highway from the Coral Court, I greeted her with a low wolf whistle, despite her insistence that she'd selected her wardrobe not to draw attention. Her short dark hair had an Audrey Hepburn look that shouldn't have suited her but did.

In the little living room of the nondescript frame house, the three younger women living in had been lounging around in various states of partial dress and curlers, a blonde reading a comic book, a redhead a movie magazine, and a brunette sitting cross-legged in front of a rabbit-eared TV watching *My Little Margie*. They looked barely out of high school but a hardness at odds with their Bobby Soxer tastes was setting in already. Sandy had that hardness, too, the full-blown variety, but like her hair, she wore it well.

We were seated against the restaurant's far wall under a row of baseball paintings—I'd asked for some privacy and we'd got it, at least as much as possible in a big dining room—and as we waited for our meals, I started by asking her about the owner of the Coral Court, a subject we'd largely danced around last night.

I said, "Carr claims not to be involved with hoods like Costello and Wortman, beyond the occasional favor. Is that on the level?"

"More on a slant," she said. "It's true he stopped doing their books for them and, like I told you, the place got too successful for mob guys to use to cool down or hide out—you know, beyond an hour or an overnight with their piece on the side. But Jack still has business ties."

"Like your, uh, escort service?"

She nodded. "Wortman gets an overall slice—I started out with him, years ago. I was his…special girl for a while, and he still has a fondness for me. Costello gets a kickback when a cabbie lines up a john. Those Coral Court rooms wired for sound have made any number of politicians, of whatever persuasion, cooperative. Sometimes at the No-Tell Motel not telling costs you."

"But Carr is not Mafia."

"No. He's nothing in the greater scheme of things."

"Who *is* something?"

A cocktail waitress stopped to ask if we wanted another. Sandy ordered a second highball but I was fine with my first rum and Coke.

Sandy said, softly but unblinking, "Well, for one thing, Joe Costello got the Greenlease money."

Almost exactly the words Mollie Baker had used; and confirmation of what Elmer Dolan had told me. Also, calculated shock value on her part.

I asked, "How is it you know that?"

She had a little speech ready; she put it across with a tiny wicked smile and an admirably droll delivery: "I don't mean to be crass, Heller. But you already had one on the house, last night. I'm sure you'll be picking up the check tonight, and I appreciate that. Still, it's what any gentleman out on the evening with a more or less respectable lady is expected to do."

"No argument."

She leaned closer, spoke softly. "I put you off, last night, before getting into anything you really wanted to know, because I had to talk to somebody today. Somebody who owes me money. I'll be frank with you."

"Please."

"If this party had come through, you and I wouldn't be

having this pleasant evening out together. But he didn't come through."

"If I might ask—with what?"

"I'll get to that. We need to back up a little. Actually…more than a little. Say…five years?"

The hair on the back of my neck prickled.

She was saying, rather archly, "After I came to your room that long-ago night…and you found me less than irresistible…"

"Hey, you were sexy as hell. I just had a drunken kidnapper on the brain."

"No apologies necessary. What's done is done. But back then? Turned out my evening was just beginning.…"

Very quietly, interrupted only by the arrival of her second highball, she told me how she had caught a cab and gone back to her aunt's apartment, to borrow the woman's car. She had a pal in Buster Wortman's second-in-command, Elroy "Dutch" Downey, and caught up with him in East St. Louis at the Paddock Lounge, a sleazy bar of Wortman's. But Buster was out of town, Dutch said; and after a moment or two of soul-searching (had she found one, I wondered?), she filled her pal Dutch in about the drunken big spender at the Coral Court with luggage full of loot. Dutch's eyes got big and then he went off to use the phone.

"When he came back," she said, "he told me I'd get a nice finder's fee, if anything come of it. I said, so you got hold of Buster? And he said, no. He'd called Joe Costello. The Coral Court was Costello's turf. So, obviously, was the cab business, and of course that cabbie Hagan was involved."

"And *did* you get a finder's fee from Joe?"

"No. And when it became obvious Costello and Shoulders had taken that ransom dough, I told Joe I wanted a piece. I *led* him to that windfall! He scored three hundred grand—ten percent for pointing him to it was a bargain. I said I wanted thirty grand or I'd turn his pale ass in."

I sipped rum and Coke. "Where that money came from didn't bother you?"

The wide red mouth twitched. "Money doesn't know where it comes from."

I'd said that myself enough times; how could I judge her?

But she was sitting in judgment on herself, somewhat at least, saying, "I wanted that money. I was human, poor and desperate. I had my own kid, who was alive and hungry. And I wasn't really thinking past the payoff."

"You're lucky to be alive, you know."

"Oh I know," she said, embarrassed. "But I always got along with Joe Costello pretty well. He'd been decent to me. I was one of his Ace Cab girls. And he's the one who set me up at the Coral Court with the...escort service. I've never had to do much but make phone calls and play house mother to a few of the younger girls, till they get broke in."

"So him setting up the service, that was how he paid you off?"

She shook her head and the short dark hair bounced. "No, he still me owed me. And here I was kicking back money to him and his cabbies on their, you know, referrals. Not that my cut was unfair or anything. But, Heller, man, I'm *sick* of the life. I'm gonna be forty. No. I'm *already* forty. Fuck, I'm already forty-two."

"You're a swell-looking forty-two, kid."

"Thanks. But I don't wanna be part of the life anymore. I got my eye on a cozy restaurant back east. Medium-size burg with nice people, nice schools for my little girl. Not so little now— junior high."

"So then it was Costello you went to see today, huh? To ask for what he owed you?"

The gray-blue eyes flared. "No!…Yes. I, uh, said I'd settle for ten grand. I can secure that little restaurant for that and stay with some people till it gets going. I said I'd turn the whole escort business over to him."

"And he said?"

"Joe told me he didn't owe me a damn thing. And that the escort service was his and Carr's, and go to hell. So. Is me coming forward with this worth ten grand?"

"Is it?"

Our food came. It was delicious. We said not a word. Not even pass the salt. Coffee came.

Then she said, "Or am I reading this wrong? I figure you're working for the Greenlease family. They want the rest of their money back, but it's probably gone and I can't help with that. But if I came forward and told the FBI what I know, they would have Joe Costello by the short and curlies. Dutch Downey would *be* in dutch. That creep cop Shoulders, too. And maybe Buster, which I kinda hate, 'cause I like the guy. Anyway. This whole *thing* would come out."

"Dangerous for you."

Her eyes tightened. Her mouth dropped like a red-rimmed trap door. "Or…are you working for somebody who doesn't *want* this to come out? I…I can do that, too. Ten grand would seal these lips forever. I'll work with you, Heller. I *will* work with you."

How desperately unhappy she was, behind her glib tough-girl facade, was clear. She was filled with needs that were over-riding caution.

I said, "Look. You're a smart kid, and—"

"I'm not a kid and I sure as hell am not smart." She got a deck of Chesterfields from her purse and started lighting one up, nervously.

My whispered words were like terrible sweet nothings. "Honey, I'm afraid you know just enough to get yourself killed, but not enough to change anything in the Greenlease case. Do you have family you can turn to?"

She laughed and smoke and bitterness came out. "Well, I'm the product of a rape, Heller, what do you think?"

I put a hand on one of hers. "Maybe I can help you out. You've given me an important piece of the puzzle and that's going to be worth something. I can't promise it's worth the ten grand you're after, but you won't have to go public. Listen. I *will* help."

Her eyes were moist. She squeezed my hand.

"I wish I'd met you a long time ago," she said.

"I wish I could say I'd have done right by you."

A waitress came around with a dessert menu. I ordered us a dish of spumoni to share, so we could sit here and talk some more. Before it arrived, however, the host himself, bald, chubby, cheerful Biggie in a tux, leaned in with a smile. I figured he was going to ask if we'd enjoyed our supper, but I was wrong.

"Mr. Vitale requests a few moments of your time, Mr. Heller. He's in the Red Bird Room."

"Uh…certainly. Tell him I'll be there shortly."

Biggie patted me on the shoulder and was gone.

Sandy clutched my sleeve. "Heller…what's going on?"

"No idea. I've done enough business in St. Louis over the years to know Vitale's one of the town's top Mafiosi. Second only to Tony Lopiparo."

"Tony Lap is ailing," she said, a frantic edge in her voice. "He's fucking dying."

"Yeah, well, Vitale is dining. I better pay my respects."

She clutched harder at my sleeve. "Nate, he's Joe Costello's protector. Those two are tight. He's probably who Joe turned that ransom money over to! And if he knows you and I are here together…"

"I'll handle it."

The waitress positioned the dish of spumoni on the table between us. With two spoons. I was on my feet.

"Work on this," I said, putting the colorful ice cream in front of her and handing her a spoon. "Save me some. I'll be back before it melts."

"Don't be fooled by his nice-guy bull! Vitale's a smiling snake. And goes *everywhere* with bodyguards."

"They all do. Anyway, what's he going to do to me in a big busy dining room?"

The Red Bird Room was big, all right, adorned with red velvet drapes on one wall and on another a mural of Cardinal ballplayers in action. Busy it wasn't, however: it was entirely empty but for two central tables. At one, a couple of thugs were eating a spaghetti and meatballs dinner; they wore cauliflower ears and off-the-rack suits, the jackets a little too big, to help conceal their armaments. A table was between them and where sat two men both about fifty, well-dressed, in sharp suits and ties. They were either waiting for their meals or, more likely, had already eaten; they had a carafe of coffee with cups for each, sugar and cream handy.

I recognized these latter two, from the papers. The more conservatively attired of the pair was Morris Shenker, the mob lawyer of choice in St. Louis and a counselor utilized nationally by the Teamsters union. The other was John Vitale, whose heavy black eyebrows recalled those of Lou Shoulders, but otherwise reminded me of that smiling, pleasant, deeply self-interested straight-man, Bud Abbott. If only Joe Costello from Ace Cabs was here, we'd have the full team.

Both men stood as I approached—the two thugs just kept

eating—and I shook hands first with the smiling Vitale, a warm lingering grasp, and then with the unsmiling Shenker, a quick catch and release.

As I sat and the two men resumed their seats, Vitale said, "I don't believe we ever met, Mr. Heller, but we got many mutual friends in Chicago. I hear you knew Frank Nitto well."

This insider's use of Nitti's actual last name seemed purposeful to me.

"We got along," I said. "What can I do for you, Mr. Vitale?"

He threw a casual wave. "I won't keep you long, Mr. Heller. I'll let you get back to your pretty companion."

He didn't say whether he recognized that pretty companion or not.

"But actually," Vitale continued, leaning in chummily, "this is about what *I* can do for *you*."

"Oh?"

He nodded, then the black eyebrows lifted. "Coffee or a drink or maybe wine?"

"No thank you. Please go on."

He grinned, shrugged. "I like to pride myself on bein' on top of things in my little corner of the world. Uh, excuse me, I don't mean to be rude or anything. This is my attorney, Mr. Shenker."

I gave Shenker a nod and got back half a nod for my trouble. Then, risking a grin, I said to Vitale, "I hope you don't feel you need legal counsel, chatting with me."

He laughed a little, more than the remark deserved. "No, no way…though I *do* need to get into some dicey territory."

"How so?"

"Like I said, I stay on top of things." He gave me a mock scolding look. "So what's this about you goin' around talking to people about a very old, very sad crime? The Greenlease kidnapping?"

I leaned back in my chair casually. I could sense the eyeballs of the spaghetti eaters nearby landing on me occasionally, like flies cruising for a meal.

I said, "Not the kidnapping so much as the ransom. Or anyway, the missing half. Why, did you have some information for me?"

"I do. And this'll save you a trip, lookin' me up. What I got for you is this: I never in any way, shape or form had nothing to do with that missing money. Not a goddamn fucking thing."

"That's good to know." I put a confused frown on. "But why would I *think* you did, Mr. Vitale?"

He glanced at the attorney, who gave him another barely visible nod. Then Vitale said, "There is a rumor that Joe Costello, who is a good friend of mine going way back, was on the receiving end of that dirty money."

"You don't say."

"And," he went on, after receiving another tiny nod from the attorney, "that I paid him ten cents on the dollar for it, then sent that hot cash to Havana for the casinos to put back in circulation."

Shenker spoke for the first time, a rich courtroom baritone, and it damn near gave me a start.

"Mr. Heller," he said, "may I remind you that your client confidentiality pertains here."

"My, uh, client…what?"

"You and I," he said smoothly, damn near smiling, "both represent an individual whose name we don't need to be bandying about in public."

This was in public? A mob guy, his mouthpiece and two bent-nose meatball munchers? A waiter who stuck his nose in now and then to check if anybody seemed to want something? What the hell?

Then I wised up—since the client Shenker was referring to obliquely was hardly Bobby Kennedy, or Robert Greenlease either, a certain Teamster came to mind.

"Understood," I said.

"May I continue?" Vitale asked.

That query was not issued to me.

Shenker again barely nodded.

The mobster went on, "For there to be any truth in such a foul goddamn rumor, you would have to figure Joe Costello felt on the hook to me for *any* big score he made. That if he had fell into any kind of heavy-duty dough, I would expect him to come to me with it."

I squinted at him. "Not the case?"

He shook his head, firm. "Not the case, no. Joe is what you call an ally. Really, a friend. And a sometime business associate. But he is not…one of us. More a, uh…"

"Friend of the family?"

Vitale's smile this time was sly. "Friend of the family, that's good." The smile slipped away. "Anyway, he could be a made man and I still would not feel I had any right to any part of that money unless I helped bring about how that money happened."

He was implying something that had been nibbling at the back of my mind; but I let it sit.

I asked, "And you did *not* provide any help in how that ransom came to be in Costello's hands?"

Another firm head shake. "No. *If* it came into his hands. I didn't say it did! But the one thing I want you to take away from this little talk of ours: I had not a damn thing to do with any of this, and the fact that you and me, Mr. Heller, never did business before is the only reason why I don't take offense."

"Offense at what, Mr. Vitale?"

"Offense that you would think I'd ever have *anything* to do with that kind of blood money! What happened to that kid makes me sick. I have a son myself. And daughters, and making a profit off the death of some little boy…pulled out of the hands of a goddamn *nun*…that's what you burn in hell for."

Said the drug-dealing, gun-running gangster.

Still, I felt he was sincere.

"I appreciate hearing this," I said.

"Good. Good. You know, my people…Frank Nitto's people, Alphonse Capone's people…went in the kinds of businesses that was available to us, as immigrants and sons of immigrants. Now time passes and we make money and inroads into more respectable things. Like backing the working man in unions— my friend here helps in that area. I think you'll find, if you talk to our mutual Outfit friends in Chicago, that even the hardest-ass men don't want nothing to do with foul evil shit like the Greenlease snatch."

So quick it startled me, Shenker stood and said, "Thank you for your time, Mr. Heller."

Vitale stood as well, but sat right back down. The thugs just kept eating. I'd been dismissed, so I gave the mobster and the lawyer a nod to share and got the hell out of there. This was one red room too many, as far as I was concerned. But I had learned things that helped bring a fuzzy picture into focus.

Back in the main dining room, I joined Sandy. The dish of spumoni had been taken away—melted and uneaten, judging by the grim look the woman wore.

She clutched my right hand. "What did Vitale want?"

I saw no reason not to tell her. "To let me know he had nothing to do with the Greenlease money."

"Do you believe him?"

"I do. I wouldn't bet the ranch on it, but, yeah."

Her words came quick: "He's not as important as he used to

be, you know. He backed down when Buster muscled in on the pinball racket. And the Syrian mob has taken over the South Side. Well, they're Lebanese but everybody calls them Syrian."

Her nerves were getting to her.

I said, "Let's get you out of here."

I took her by the arm through the lobby, past a big oil painting of Musial at bat and a display case of memorabilia, trophies, and autographed baseballs. As I was paying the check, Sandy stepped through the glass doors into the warm night under the roof of the carport. A gentle sirocco-like breeze riffled her short dark hair and creamy white blouse.

A taxi was waiting and the driver called out to her. I heard him just as I was going through the doors: "Did you call a cab, ma'am?"

She walked closer and bent down to talk to him through the open rider's side window, and said, "No, I'm sorry, must be someone else," and he shot her in the head.

Even before she fell, the cab squealed off. Some of what had been inside that pretty head splashed on my suit coat and drops spattered my face. When her legs went out from under her, she collapsed in a surprisingly graceful pirouette, the blue-gray eyes large if unseeing and yet staring right at me. The black hole in her forehead stared at me, too, and then she was on her face on the cement with the exit wound a cavernous thing, a carved-out red room of its own.

She'd finally got that payoff.

CHAPTER SIXTEEN

As would be expected, I was first questioned at the scene by uniformed officers followed by plainclothes homicide detectives. Then I drove the loaner Cadillac—under police escort, as if I were a visiting dignitary, but thankfully without sirens—to police headquarters at the corner of Twelfth Street and Clark Avenue.

Somewhere in that massive six-story gray limestone cube of a building (where Carl Hall and Bonnie Heady had early on been held), I was further questioned, but not until after I'd been given my phone call. Someone on duty at the nearby FBI office, also on Twelfth Street, arranged to have a big football coach of a special agent named Don Hostetter come over to Police HQ.

Hostetter worked on Greenap with Wes Grapp, who was in Kansas City right now. Despite our never having met, the Special Agent vouched for me as an investigator for the Senate Rackets Committee. He informed one and all that the late Sandra O'Day was a potential witness I had been trying to groom for Senator McClellan and chief counsel Robert Kennedy.

That name-dropping, and an assurance I would make myself available as a material witness, got me shaken loose from the noble department that had brought the world the likes of Lieutenant Louis Shoulders and Patrolman Elmer Dolan. I was to let them know when I returned to Chicago, my contact information collected.

Walking me out into the warm, windy night, Hostetter—a

no-nonsense six-three in his mid-forties—said, "You have blood on your face and gory dried shit on your suit coat."

"I know."

"It's not a good look."

"I don't plan to go out."

He walked me to the Caddy in the police parking lot and said, "Stop by the office tomorrow. I'll see if I can get Wes in from K.C. Seems like you may have some things you'd like to share."

"Thanks for springing me."

"No problem. The Chief always likes it when we can add to your package, Mr. Heller. It's about four inches thick now."

I was back at the Coral Court in twenty minutes, snugging the Cadillac into its little private garage. When I stepped from there into the Red Room, I found the TV going and a guest watching it. On the red vinyl couch, in a yellow sport shirt and brown slacks and moccasin slippers with no socks, sat the motel's proprietor—Jack Carr, smoking a cigarette, an ashtray on the coffee table before him, from a pack Sandy had left behind the other night. A book of Coral Court matches was nearby.

He glanced at me with his dark-circled gray eyes. "Sandy made the news but you didn't," he said, sounding like an all-night D.J. who smoked too much. "Blood on your face."

"Yeah."

"Crusty shit on your jacket."

"Not the first to notice."

"Brush it off and take it to a dry-cleaner."

Unintentional irony.

I went into the bathroom and got out of the suit coat and wadded it up and stuffed it in the wastebasket. Richard Bennett could make me a new one. I looked at myself in the bathroom mirror. My tie was loose but I didn't remember making it that way. The blood spots on my cheeks were like freckles applied for a high school play. I ran cold water and splashed it on my face. Soaped up my hands and rubbed the stuff off. Brownish water swirled down the drain.

I went back out there in my short-sleeve white shirt and shoulder-holstered nine mil. I said to Carr, "Any special reason you're here?"

He didn't answer me. The TV was heading into the national anthem, signing off for the day, and he got up and shut it off, the cigarette dangling from that not-quite-a-smile. We stood facing each other in the open area between the foot of the bed and the door. He brought his ashtray along, nursing the cigarette's gray residue.

"I liked her," he said. "She was a tough broad but she wasn't mean. That's not a bad combination."

"No it isn't."

He took some smoke in. Let it out. "And she really held onto her looks. Always a pleasure doing business with her. See who killed her?"

"Somebody in an Ace Cab."

"Almost anybody could be driving an Ace Cab. They all have records, you know. You could hire any of those crumbs to do about anything. Still. Doesn't mean Joe Costello was behind it."

"Is that right."

The zombie eyes slitted. "I heard stories about you, Heller."

"Have you."

"I wouldn't be surprised if you went out and did something about this."

"You wouldn't."

"From one old soldier to another, it's not worth it. I liked

Sandy fine. I am gonna miss her sweet ass and salty talk. But she knew what she was getting into. All these people do. It's like my son."

"You have a son?"

"I did have. He was wild. I tried to put him on the straight and narrow, but that's hard when you don't set a good example. He made it out of Korea alive. Came back and, here's a funny coincidence, drove cab a while. Then he got involved with some East St. Louis lowlifes, and the next thing you know, Bobby…that was his name, Bobby…"

Another unintentional irony.

"…turns up dead in the trunk of his car. Stab wounds, gunshot wounds, tortured first. People said some assholes figured his old man hid the Greenlease money and maybe he knew where. He was twenty-four. People would come up to me all sorry and sympathetic, tell me how terrible it was. I told them, he was dead to me long before that. After that, I could've cut ties with every crooked son of a bitch on both sides of the river, but I didn't. My boy made his bed. Like Sandy. Not telling you what *to* do or *not* to do, Mr. Heller. Just one old soldier to another."

I said nothing.

Going out, he paused to say, "They're going to be crawling all over this place again, the cops and the feds. I've already found a new home for those three girls who lived with Sandy. But, uh, you need to be out of here tomorrow morning."

He gave me a little salute and was gone, door shutting gently behind him, as if trying not to stir any ghosts.

I shut off the lights and sat on the foot of the bed in the dark and tried not to cry. Worked hard at it. I would be goddamned if I'd blubber like Shoulders and Dolan and everybody else on this fucking job. Carr was right: Sandy knew what she was getting herself into. The scent of that Greenlease money had made her crazy. What did I care if she lived or died? She was just another whore. I barely knew the bitch. Then the fucking tears came.

A two-rap knock came to the door. My palms took away the wetness and I wiped them on my trousers. I glanced around as the double knock repeated. Carr had forgotten Sandy's pack of smokes on the coffee table. Not hitting the light switch, I cracked the door to make sure it was Carr, but it wasn't, and a big guy who was mostly silhouette shouldered his way in. Behind him was another male shape. He came barreling in, too, as I backpedaled, going for the Browning under my arm, but my arm got batted away and somebody snatched out the gun and gave it a toss that made a thud somewhere on the carpet. A hand on either side gripped my biceps from behind as the guy in front of me lifted a hand with white cloth in it, and he poured liquid from a can that infused the cloth with the antiseptically sweet-smelling liquid that was chloroform, and clamped the damp cloth over my nose and mouth.

It took longer to take effect than you might think, and I fought it, flailing, kicking, for what must have been two or three minutes anyway. Which is a long fucking time. And it took two good-size strong men to hold me down, the cold and oily feel of the damp cloth the last sensation I experienced before I learned that the lights could go out in a room where the lights were already off.

The chirring rumble, and occasional jostle, of wheels on pavement told me I was in a car before my eyes came open and confirmed it. My arms were handcuffed behind me and my ankles were bound with heavy twine, the cuffs making me wonder if the fedora-sporting, gorilla-shouldered pair in the front seat were cops. My mouth tasted oddly sweet. My face around my nose and mouth burned a little.

I was lucky to be alive. If you called living being cuffed and ankle-bound in a back seat driven somewhere by a couple of possible cops, probable goons, not that those are mutually exclusive categories. But my head hurt, worse than if they'd sapped me, and the nausea had what was left of the Musial's meal churning, wanting out.

Like me.

The driver, a forty-ish hood, said, "Jesus, I thought he was supposed to be tough. Is he still under?"

A pale oval with a double chin and tiny eyes looked back at me. My slitted eyes would, I hoped, look closed as I sat there slumped.

"Still under. What do you expect, Mel? He's over fifty."

"Hell, so are you, Dutch."

Wortman second-in-command: Elroy "Dutch" Downey.

"Fuck you very much, Mel. Anyway, I wasn't the one who got dosed. If this bastard dies on us, Buster's gonna be pissed. He already ain't in the best of moods."

"It was your idea. You said this Heller was tough! And you're right about the boss—he's half in the bag. That's when he gets mean."

"Not good news for our line-load back there."

Line-load: taxi jargon for passenger. Was every St. Louis mobster a former cabbie?

I knew where we were now. Not far from East St. Louis—Collinsville, Illinois. We were cutting through another sin strip, the neons of taverns and night clubs like welcoming fires in the night, the Oasis, the Mounds Club, the Horseshoe Lounge, Diamondhead, Red Rooster. A scummy little Las Vegas that stayed open all night in this extension of East St. Louis.

Soon the bright lights turned into rural Collinsville and then we were turning onto a graveled drive.

"You awake back there?" Mel asked the rear view mirror.

"…Yeah."

"Just behave yourself and this won't be a one-way ride."

"What's the occasion?"

Dutch said, "That would spoil it."

Up ahead, spotlighted like a premiere, loomed a pair of intersecting square brick buildings with flat roofs, the main two-story adjoining an add-on single story, a Streamline Moderne castle. Between this place and the Coral Court, all that was missing was a rocket ship. As we drew closer, I could make out the wide moat that surrounded the island on which the castle perched, the two-thirds of a moon making an ivory shimmer out of the water. Something silver and scaly broke the surface on the jump.

I said, "That thing has *fish* in it?"

Dutch said, not unfriendly, "Best-stocked private lake in Illinois."

And the only one with a gangster living on an island in the middle of it.

For all the modern majesty of the castle and its well-manicured grounds, the bridge that crossed the moat was a wooden, rickety thing. It led to a macadam driveway that curved around right to a three-car garage, which is what the one-story add-on structure turned out to be. My buddy Dutch used a remote control gizmo to open the triple door, which slid overhead to admit their car, an Oldsmobile, into the garage next to a silver Cadillac. Yes, another Cadillac, and if you're keeping up with your irony scorecard, every Cadillac in this part of the world emanated from a Greenlease-supplied dealership.

The door closed behind us at the push of a button on the

brick wall shared with the house. My ankles were cut loose but my hands remained cuffed as we entered a big white hospital of a kitchen that only made the lingering sweetness of chloroform seem more distinct in my mouth. Through there I was nudged in the back with a gun into a hallway merging into a cavernous foyer whose marble floor was as pure white as the money that paid for it was not. A limestone central fountain with a September Morn nude wading in it was overseen by wall-hugging potted plants on pedestals with leaves like green swords.

The foyer fed not the promised pretentious interior decoration but various doorless rooms furnished out of a Sears-and-Roebuck catalogue—an office with modern fixtures, a dining room, a living room, and a large well-stocked library indicating Buster might be the best-read gangster around (maybe the best-read Buster around, period).

A matching marble staircase with a black wrought-iron rail extended either to the afterlife or the second floor. The gun urging me on indicated it might be both. The rooms up here had doors and I was shown through one into what appeared to be a guest bedroom that might have been in a Holiday Inn. Pompous here, prosaic there, Buster Wortman's moat castle definitely sent mixed signals, even if his gun-toting emissaries did not.

As he uncuffed me, Dutch Downey said, "Strip."

"What?"

"See that towel on the bed?"

"I'm not blind."

"Strip and put it on. We'll collect you in ten minutes." It sounded like I was a butterfly about to go into an album.

The door shut. The double bed had a towel neatly folded on the pink nubby spread. Above the bed was one big frame of shots of the house and moat under construction. A big picture window had its curtain drawn halfway back. I went over and looked out. Fish jumped in the moonlight. I watched this a while. One missed and hit the grassy shore and wriggled there, dying. Don't ask me what kind of fish. I shut the curtain.

The bedroom had its own bathroom and I went in and bowed before the porcelain god and finally got rid of the Musial's meal. Not near as good on the return trip. I sat on the edge of the tub and worked at feeling human, breathing like a guy who'd just been saved from drowning.

Then I was wearing the towel like Sabu in a picture with dolls in sarongs, not guys in baggy suits and revolvers. At just about ten minutes on the dot, Dutch and Mel returned for me. They walked me down the hall and into a big nightclub-ish room with a full bar along one wall and black leather uphol-stered sofas and chairs scattered around in little groupings, with glass-topped tables for ashtrays and drinks. The lighting was indirect but not dim, canceling any notion of me playing loin-cloth Tarzan on these fedora-sporting apes.

I was shown through a big bathroom, with a shower that would have accommodated enough chorus girls to keep any dumb-ass hood from getting bored, and into an adjacent steam room, which at least explained the towel.

This was no small sauna, however, but more like what the Sands or Flamingo in Vegas might offer—three tiers of slatted wooden seating in a tiled space big enough for the top Romans to gather and discuss how the Lions Vs. the Gladiators game came out.

One small moderately hairy man in a towel and a pearl-gray fedora on loan from George Raft sat perched on the middle row of the facing wall as I entered. He had his hands folded on his lap. He had a kind of long, deadpan face that made me wonder if he'd been nicknamed for a resemblance to a famous comedian.

"If I don't wear a hat," Frank "Buster" Wortman said in a second tenor, "I get sweat in my eyes. I know it looks stupid, but you know what? It's my house."

That was his greeting to me.

He gestured toward the side wall with a cigar he had going, its smoke mingling with the steam. "Take a load off."

The seating right next to him was taken up by a folded towel over something that made a lump. I had an idea that it might be a .38 caliber lump. On the other side was a phone on a long cord and an ashtray.

I sat on the second tier on the side wall to his left. You could have fit a dozen guys in here comfortably. And frankly, I'm not sure why, but the heat felt good. Seemed to make my splitting headache recede.

"I know it was bad manners," he said, "pulling you in, in the middle of the night. Thanks for coming."

Thanks for coming? Bad manners?

"Sure."

"I don't think we ever met." He leaned over and offered a hand and I met him halfway and we shook; then he and his loin-wrapped towel settled back where they were.

"I know it sounds stupid," he said, "but this cools me down when I get hot. And I got very damn hot, earlier, and I suppose I tied one on a little."

That didn't seem to call for a response.

"You were a friend of Frank's," he said.

The "were" meant Nitti not Sinatra, or anyway I was pretty sure it did.

"I was." I played a card that wasn't entirely an exaggeration. "I was fond of Mr. Nitti. He could be like a second father to me."

"I know you been here a couple days," he said, "asking about the Greenlease money."

I gave him a nod.

"Who are you working for?"

No hesitation: "Jimmy Hoffa."

That impressed him. He didn't even try to hide it. "No shit. He's, uh, concerned about these rumors that half the Greenlease ransom wound up in the Teamsters Pension Fund. Am I right?"

"You're not wrong."

Abruptly, he changed the subject. "Did the fellas show you around at all?"

The fellas?

"Did you get a look at these digs?" He gestured with the cigar like it was a magic wand. "Too bad it's after dark. Even with outside lighting, you miss things. And I got a twelve-horse stable, a swimming pool out back. Rathskeller in the basement."

"Impressive."

"I hardly ever leave this place. Since my divorce, I let the world come to me. This steam room is perfect for meeting with other guys in my line of work, and with politicians and local business leaders. I got a phone in every room, including this one."

"I noticed."

He went on: "The steamfitters piped in a heating system no hotel could beat—those union guys are great—and since not everybody loves me...hard to believe I know...they put in a steel plate. Not in my head!" He laughed. "Coverin' the roof, I mean. People drop things from planes these days, y'know. So. I made this place like a castle 'cause I'm the king of my little kingdom."

"I would imagine you are."

He pushed at the air. "Now, I'm not full of myself. I don't

have no big head or nothing. It's a *little* kingdom, East St. Louis. But my 'subjects' are happy as clams. Taxes are low, city coffers overflowing with all kinds of revenue, and I keep the worst elements out. With the help of the local John Law. I'm mostly vending machines now, and I never put up with the dope trade. Sure, we run wide open in the entertainment districts. But drive around my town and see—streets in good repair, beautiful parks with no trash scattered around, grass at public buildings tended like a goddamn golf course. Good schools."

Why was he telling me all this?

"It's a fine place to raise a family, Nate...I'll call you Nate, and you call me Buster. Okay?"

"Okay, Buster."

"Why, there's less street crime here than any other city its size in the whole damn country! And less than St. Louis itself! *Real* crime, I mean. I can see you wondering why I care about your opinion. Somebody in my position can't be swayed by people who don't understand what we are trying to accomplish for the community."

I nodded.

Something sharp came into his tone. "You listen to me. I wouldn't touch that Greenlease money with a ten-foot pole. When that kid was snatched, I told one and all, everybody around me, that it was the most stinking no-good thing a man could do, steal a kid. I got three of my own! And when that boy turned up dead..."

He crushed the cigar in a fist and flung it to the floor.

"...everybody in my world *knew*: I would strangle those who did it with my *bare* hands, my bare fucking *hands!* I made no secret of it, Nate."

"I believe you, Buster."

A slow nod of the fedora-topped head. "All right. Okay. Just so you know. And *know* this, too: nobody offered me that money. Nobody was dumb enough to. If Joe Costello got it, and some people say he did, he did not bring it to my attention. And I have stayed out of it because there is disagreement about such things."

I frowned. "What kind of disagreement, Buster?"

A sigh. "Well, over whether handling that money is just as damn bad as ransoming and killing that poor child. To me, it's blood money. It's filthy, wicked, ill-gotten gains. And again, I let that be known. But not everybody sees it that way. So I am telling you right now...and would suggest you believe me... that my hands never touched that money."

"Your word's good enough for me, Buster." Particularly sitting in a steam bath with him with that towel settling over what was definitely a .38, and considering the less than gentle way I'd been brought by his emissaries into the court of the king of East St. Louis.

"Now what prompted me," he said, "to bother you in the wee hours was a phone call I received...actually several phone calls, including more than one from St. Louis police officers who are friendly to me...about the sad event of earlier tonight. Yesterday evening, actually, as we are past the witching hour, aren't we, into a new day?"

"We are."

He shook his head, somberly. "Sandy O'Day was a special gal to me. We had some nice times together, and then when she wanted to go in business for herself, I helped set her up through Joe Costello. Of course I'm aware she was part of that fucked-up mess involving the arrest of the psycho kid killer...the night that half the ransom money walked away somehow."

"Sandy didn't take it. But she knew things."

His eyes tightened. "What things, if you don't mind my asking, Nate?"

Under these circumstances, how could I mind?

"When Sandy learned that Carl Hall had several suitcases full of cash," I said, "she took a midnight ride to the Paddock Club."

The eyes were big now. "She went to *my* club?"

"Yes, but you were away, weren't you?"

"I was, when all that happened. Out of town, visiting my kids at my ex-wife's, if that's important."

"Where you were isn't. But when Sandy couldn't find you, she talked to your man Downey."

"*What?* Dutch?"

"Dutch Downey called Costello. The short answer is, Costello and Shoulders took half the money and turned the rest in, hoping that'd close the books. They were wrong and they were stupid. It looks like the money went to Chicago to be washed. Possibly in the Humphreys laundries. Probably partly in the Southmoor Bank."

He was shaking his head. "Come on, Nate. The Camel would never in a million *years* deal in money that hot...that...that *rotten.* And Accardo would blow his stack! They are all family men!"

That was "family" with a lowercase F.

I said, "Now, Buster—you and I know there are plenty of guys in Accardo and Humphreys' world who would happily deal with hot money. And in yours. Who wouldn't give two shits where it came from."

He came over and sat beside me. He did not bring the towel with the gun. "You're sure about this, Nate?"

"I heard it from Sandy herself, not half an hour before she got shot down by somebody driving an Ace Cab. There can't be much doubt Costello was behind it. When I went to the Tic Toc, night before last, he stonewalled me and then two of his boys jumped me in the alley."

His eyes were moving fast. "Sandy said she went to Dutch?"

"She did. She was with him at the Paddock when he called Costello. Does Downey have any good friends in the Outfit? Particularly in Murray Humphreys' organization?"

He looked whiter than the steam surrounding us. He said, "It was good of you to come."

I'd had it. "Good of me to *come*? Your boys Dutch and Mel jumped me, shoved a chloroformed rag in my face, and that shit can *kill* you! They handcuffed me and tied me up like a calf and dragged me here. Good of me to come!"

Aghast at this news, he leaned over and clutched my arm. "Not my doing, Nate....Go get dressed. Tell my boys to meet me with you in the garage."

I nodded, and went out, where Dutch and Mel were sitting at the long bar having bottles of beer. I conveyed what their boss had told me, then I was returned to the guest bedroom.

I got dressed and walked to the window. I looked out and didn't see any fishes jumping now. I considered climbing out and jumping myself—two stories wouldn't kill you. But there was a moat, and I didn't particularly want to go swimming; and somebody might see me head for the bridge. I had no idea how many other Wortman minions might be here in the castle. And he'd seemed friendly enough, even grateful for what I'd told him. Why run?

Dutch and Mel walked me down to the kitchen and back into the garage, where the Oldsmobile and a Cadillac were parked, and Buster—hands in the pockets of a terrycloth robe, feet rocking in sandals—was waiting.

Dutch said, "What do you want us to do with him, Buster?"

"This breaks my heart," Buster said, and his right hand came from the robe's pocket to train the .38 revolver on Downey.

His number two looked astonished. He raised his hands, palms out, nodded at me and glared at his boss. "You're not going to believe *this* asshole?"

"About what?"

Buster shot him in the head, and bone, blood and brains spattered the brick wall like a giant bug against a windshield.

"Jesus!" Mel said, wide-eyed, terrified.

"Calm down," Buster said. "You're in charge of clean-up."

Now I was a witness, but before I could do anything about it, Buster dropped the .38 in a pocket of the terrycloth robe. Looking nothing at all like a comic in an old movie, he said, "Nate, I'll call you a cab."

"Okay," I said. "Just don't make it an Ace."

CHAPTER SEVENTEEN

By the time I got back to the Coral Court, I figured I'd been up eighteen hours. The only sign of a struggle in the Red Room was my nine millimeter on the carpet where it had been tossed by either Dutch or Mel—their entry had been a blur. I picked the weapon up and placed it on the nightstand by the phone.

I didn't feel tired—more like overwrought. I took a warm shower, to help come down from that high a guy can get surviving a kidnapping by hoods after his dinner date got killed and two chatty gangsters made him the center of their attention. You've had evenings like that I'm sure.

My head still ached from the chloroform dosing and I got a bottle of aspirins out of my shaving kit and shook out five or six. Took them. Pajamas seemed wrong somehow and I just crawled under the cool sheets in my boxers and settled my head into an equally cool pillow and waited for the wings of Morpheus to flap down and carry me off.

They didn't.

Pieces were floating inside my head like a Dali painting trying to make sense of itself; but after a while the fragments assembled into something more on the Norman Rockwell order, minus the saccharine Americana. I had caught the barest glimpse of the cab driver who'd fired that bullet into Sandy O'Day's forehead, but he might have been the blond from the Tic Toc alley who'd seemed vaguely familiar to me.

What do you need, Heller? An engraved invitation?

I switched on the bedside lamp and got the phone book out of the nightstand drawer. Looked to see if Joe Costello's home number was listed and it wasn't. I called the FBI office and asked if Special Agent Hostetter was available and he was.

"Mr. Heller," he said in his gruff, businesslike way, "don't you ever sleep?"

"Not lately. I need a favor."

"Always a pleasure to accommodate a taxpayer."

"Can you give me Joe Costello's unlisted number?"

"Any special reason?"

"I'm thinking of sending him flowers."

A long pause. Then: "Stay on the line. I can get that for you."

About a minute later, he kept his promise, and then I was dialing my buddy Joe at home. It rang a long time. I was hoping to rouse Costello himself, but the voice…"Yeah? Hello?"…was female and sleepy and properly irritated.

"Mrs. Costello?"

"Yes?" It sounded like she wasn't sure.

"Sorry to call at this hour, but it's important. Could I speak to your husband?" I had cooked up a reason for bothering Costello about being questioned at Police HQ on the cab-driving shooter. Which was basically true.

But she said, "He's still at work," and hung up.

The Tic Toc stayed open till three A.M., and it was just past that. When I called their Yellow Pages number, somebody was still there, cashing out or cleaning up. A male, probably the bartender, said, "I think he's over at Ace Cab, workin' on the books. He's a night owl, Joe is."

I got out of bed and into a *Playboy*-approved ensemble— sports shirt by Viyella, navy slacks by Corbin, and sports jacket by Cricketeer, one size up to allow for my holstered nine-millimeter semiautomatic pistol by Browning.

I felt good. As refreshed as if I'd just had eight hours of sleep and not twenty minutes of brooding. I snatched up Sandy's pack of Chesterfields and the book of Coral Court matches on the coffee table. I only smoked in combat and certain civilian situations mirroring combat. So somebody was in trouble.

Maybe me.

I sucked smoke into my lungs and held it there and embraced it like an old friend I wasn't afraid to hug just because we were both real men. I dropped the pack of smokes in my left-hand pocket, the matches, too. In my right-hand pocket I slipped a spare magazine of nine-millimeter cartridges.

Heading back into St. Louis on a morning that still thought it was night, I kept the Cadillac's front windows down, letting the smoke out and the warm wind in. It rustled my hair like Stan the Man with a Little Leaguer visiting Musial and Biggie's with his dad. Right now, the city was just a stray scattering of insomniac windows, neon signs and the dark husks of sleeping businesses; occasional headlights ahead and behind reminded me I wasn't the last man on earth.

At this hour, empty taxis slept shoulder to shoulder in the smallish parking lot in front of the dingy white-brick vertical building with ACE CAB COMPANY on its picture window at right and two closed garage doors at left. As before, I parked across the way in front of the Swiss Chalet-style shopping arcade. My jacket was unbuttoned. When I reached the other side of the street, I tossed the butt sparking into darkness to sizzle in a gutter, then slipped the slumbering nine mil quietly from its cradle, ready to wake it up.

No one was around in the parking lot and no sounds emanated from behind the twin closed doors of the double-bay garage. I moved quietly to the big picture window. The switchboard where a good-looking dye-job redhead had been seated on my previous visit was just her empty chair now. At left, however, that burly natural blond dispatcher was sitting at his microphone like a disc jockey waiting for a song to be over; his big wall-mounted map loomed before him, with only a small scattering of magnetic pins dotting it in these wee-small skeleton-crew hours.

He was snoozing in his tilt-back chair, or anyway loafing, arms folded. I hadn't been able to place him in the alley—the one time I'd seen him was five years ago, after all—but that glimpse of the shooter behind the cab's wheel who leaned over to fire a round into Sandy's head finally sealed it.

If the EMPLOYEES ONLY door was locked, I would have to shatter that picture-window glass with a gunshot; but it opened just fine.

As I went in, the blond turned in the swivel chair and his eyes got big and his mouth, too. He was in a white shirt with a black bow tie and navy slacks and his cabbie cap was on the desk. Here's the cute part: a revolver was angled in it, a small .32 Remington, pre-war I thought. Didn't figure this for the gun he'd used at Musial's.

But he'd brought a pistol to work, so he must have known the coming hours might not just be another day at the office. His fingers were almost on the gun when I slapped him with the nine mil barrel, hard, along the right side of his face. It bloodied the ear and ripped the cheek like a red Christmas package a kid was getting into, and then he slid from the chair, hitting his head on the edge of his desk, and folded up like a big stillborn fetus on the wooden floor.

He'd made just enough noise going down for me to pause a few seconds with the nine mil in hand, ready for anything. Beyond his dispatcher's workstation were double doors open onto the adjacent repair garages, one big room despite the overhead door above each of two bays. No one seemed to be in this area, its lights off, though a mid-'50s Chevy sedan with Ace Cab markings was on the nearest of two lowered hydraulic lifts.

Nothing but silence followed. From the cabbie cap, I collected the revolver, a .32, and emptied the cylinder of bullets onto the floor and tossed the little gun out the door into the parking lot, where it skittered away on the cement. I knelt and checked the blond—he wasn't dead, because the red juice in him was still flowing, making a puddle actually; but he was out colder than Jersey Joe after Marciano finished him.

In the recess between the dispatcher's area and the switchboard, between men's and ladies' rooms, an edge of light ran along the bottom of the closed unmarked door. I went into the little office and found the proprietor of the Ace Cab Company indeed hunkered over a ledger book. But also on the beat-up old desk was a .38 long-barreled revolver, a Smith & Wesson Police Special. I crossed the short distance, plucked the gun from his desk and dropped it into his metal wastebasket. The metal-on-metal made a satisfying clunk.

His smile was as immediate as it was nervous. As always, he was sharply dressed, a black sport shirt with a white-and-pink diamond pattern. His sandy, curly hair was combed over and his hooded blue eyes looked bloodshot. "How did you get past Howie?"

"Is that his name?" With the hand that didn't have a Browning in it, I pulled up a chair opposite him and sat, hefted the pistol. "Love tap with the barrel of this. He may live."

"Hope he does," Costello said, "or I'll never hear the end of it. My wife's nephew. Kind of late to be calling, isn't it, Nate?"

"Or early. Of course there's no tomorrow for Sandy O'Day. You heard about that?"

He nodded and put on a sad face that wouldn't have convinced a six-year-old. "I did. Hell of thing, in this day and age. Too bad. She was a good kid. Good earner in her day, and did very well for us out at Carr's."

"Your nephew was the shooter."

"No, that can't be," he said, waving it off, the gold-set diamond on his hand catching the meager overhead light and winking at me. On the wall, in the framed photos of Joe and his late partner at Ace, Leo Brothers seemed to be winking at me, too, as he grinned at the camera.

"I *saw* him shoot Sandy, Joe," I said. "I didn't mention it to the cops. Or that he jumped me in the alley alongside the Tic Toc. I mean, we're friends here, right? So how about you cut the bullshit."

I put the nine mil on the desk. Close to me. But right there on the desk. He couldn't keep his eyes off it, a man trying not to look at his wife's sister's tits. I got out the Chesterfields and shook one loose and lighted it up.

"Question is," I said, "did you send him? Howie doesn't look bright enough to have too many of his own ideas."

He showed me surrender palms. "Hear me out. Sandy O'Day came around to my house...my *house*, where I live with my wife and son—"

I stopped him with a raised forefinger. "That's the wife with a nephew, right? Right. Go on."

"She wanted ten grand. Said she worked up a story she was going to peddle to the FBI about me getting the Greenlease money."

"Just another dirty blackmailer, huh?" I let a serpent of smoke curl out. "And here we both thought she was a good kid."

His voice turned apologetic. "What happened to her outside Musial's, that was probably my fault, partly—my bad judgment."

"Oh?"

He sighed. "Y'see, after I talked to Sandy, I got pretty hot around the collar. I blew my top about it to Howie and a couple of the other guys, how she was putting the squeeze on me so tight I might have to shutter Ace Cab. And these are ex-cons who *need* the work. Who in St. Louis but Joe Costello pays good money to bad eggs just outa stir? It's what I get for trying to give 'em a helping hand and a leg up. All I can think is, Howie musta got it in his stupid head to remove the problem. Without my urging, mind you."

"Rash of the boy. Your wife's nephew needs a good talking to. If he ever wakes up."

He just sat there looking at me and trying not to look at the gun I was tempting him with. Then: "Heller...I'm willing to let it go."

"Let what go?"

"You bashing my wife's nephew."

"Howie? What if he doesn't wake up?"

"These things happen." He sat forward. His mouth was twitching a little. "I, uh, understand you've been going around talking to people on both sides of the river."

"I have."

"Come up with anything?"

I flipped my left hand casually. "Just that one crisp fall evening in 1953, you and Lou Shoulders spent an hour at your house...you know, the place where you and your wife and son live?...counting that 'missing' three-hundred grand. That kings-in-the-counting house routine covers the missing hour between when Carl Hall was booked and the other half of the ransom finally got logged in."

"You have no proof that meeting took place."

"You mean, I have no proof because Johnny Hagan is bought off and afraid? And Lou Shoulders is lying his ass off and bawling his eyes out, tossing in the occasional heart attack as a convincer? Then there's Sandy O'Day, with a baseball-size hole in the back of her skull at Stan Musial's. Good thing Stan the

Man has an alibi—he's on the road with the Cardinals. Everybody else's alibi seems kinda on the shaky side. My smoking isn't bothering you, is it? This is a small space."

"No," he said coldly. "I don't mind."

I shrugged. "But proof is beside the point, in a way. I'm not a cop. Yes, I am an officer of the court, and as a licensed private investigator, I have a responsibility to share information with the authorities. Theories, however, I don't have to share."

The hooded eyes were boring through me now. He studied me for maybe ten seconds, which is longer than it sounds. "How much?"

"Oh, this isn't blackmail. I was out with Sandy O'Day earlier, remember? I know how you dealt with her, and really all she wanted was a share of the spoils. No, I have no interest in your money. But I do have a client who will pay to hear what I learned."

"Some you talked to," he said, "come away thinking your client is Jimmy Hoffa. Others that you're working for the Rackets Committee. Or maybe Robert Greenlease."

"Why not all three? Everybody and his dog is interested in you, Joe. You're a popular man. I don't think anybody will be hard to convince that you and Shoulders and poor scared Dolan were divvying that dough up in your rec room back in September '53. But the sad thing is, I don't think any of you got much for your trouble. That money was so goddamn hot, it cost so much to launder it, only dribs and drabs came back. And nobody approved of what you'd done—not Vitale or Wortman, and sure as hell not Accardo and Humphreys…all of them saw that three-hundred grand as drenched in the blood of a child."

"Easy for them," he muttered.

"Easy for them is right. They're making big money off the public's little sins—pinball machines, gambling halls, slot machines, bookie parlors, union racketeering. Of course, there's also loansharking, handbooks, prostitution, and some people traffic in narcotics…but nobody's perfect. Kidnapping is something out of the Lindbergh past, the kind of ill-advised, out-of-date venture that in the '30s got Ma Barker and her boys riddled with lead and made J. Edgar a household word. And these Outfit bigwigs, like Accardo and Humphreys, and field lieutenants like Wortman and Vitale, they see themselves as good old-fashioned American businessmen, standard bearers of capitalism, and all of them are working toward the day they'll be wholly legit. More or less."

"What do you want from me, Heller?"

"I want the name of the other man who was there that night."

"What night?"

I slammed a fist on the desk and the nine mil jumped; so did Costello. "What night do you fucking think? Some big shot with Outfit ties who connected you to the Southmoor Bank and suggested how to avoid attracting the attention of the top dogs by using second-tier Outfit players, who didn't have the luxury of being moral about blood money—the big man who said he'd buy the laundered money, when it finally made it through the wash."

He thought about that, but not for long. "I think you already know that name."

"I think I do," I said, and spoke it.

He just nodded. "So then we don't have other business to discuss, do we, Nate?"

It had gone from "Nate" to "Heller" and was back to "Nate" again.

"Really, just one other little thing."

He clearly had no idea. "What?"

I leaned into the desk, the nine mil very nearby. "Johnny

Hagan wasn't with you in your rec room when you and Shoulders counted the money that night...or maybe the end buyer actually counted the money, but...anyway, Johnny wasn't there. Yet he's still on your payroll. Why?"

He shrugged that off. "I don't pay him all that much."

"Oh, I know. Mostly he's just afraid. Doesn't want to die. Who does?"

"What's your point?"

I used an ashtray on the desk to dispose of the butt and lit up a fresh Chesterfield. "Just that I think Johnny knows something... and I think maybe Sandy learned about that something from him...which would change everything. *Everything.*"

He recoiled but then recovered: "I doubt that. We're done, Heller. You should leave before Howie wakes up."

"*If* he wakes up. I hit him pretty hard. Where was I? Oh, yeah. Here's the thing—you played a much bigger role in all this than anyone knows, even though you were at the center of the Case of the Missing Ransom Money from that very first night. Only, really, this all began long before that."

"That makes no sense, Heller."

"Sure it does, Joe. Because Carl Hall came to *you,* months ahead of time, with a plan to take down the biggest ransom in history. He had an insider's knowledge of the Greenlease family because he was friends with Bobby's older brother, Paul, who Carl knew at military school. Carl may have oversold it to you... I don't think Paul and Carl remained close or anything, Carl was just a guy who could get the cadets booze and maybe reefers and, who knows, even girls...but the kind of payday Carl was talking about was worth considering. Greenlease was maybe the richest man in the Midwest. The plan was to kidnap the daughter, who was eleven. She'd be easy to handle. Maybe you backed Carl in what looked like a potentially big, easy score, plowing a little money into the scheme. But for sure you told him to come to you with the money, after the snatch came off. You could get it laundered for him."

"You're out of your goddamn mind. You need to go."

"Where you really went wrong was not taking a harder look at Carl Hall. He was another of your ex-cons, right? But he was a big talker, a dreamer who lived on a diet of booze and dope, with a blowsy girlfriend who hooked out of her house and was as big a boozer as her boyfriend. They wound up taking the young boy, not the almost-teenage girl, and the part of his plan Carl hadn't shared with you was that he would shoot that child in the head, rather than have to deal with him. And *then* go after the ransom."

"You...should...*go*."

"But at least Carl did stick with the rest of the plan. He drove to St. Louis. Rented a room for his dipso sweetie and himself. And connected, as prearranged, with your cabbie, Johnny Hagan. The Coral Court was a good place to hide out for a while because Jack Carr was pliable for this kind of thing. You were not in a position to alert any cops about all this money rolling into town, except the crooked likes of Lou Shoulders. It was a pity, a goddamn shame, that boy had been killed. But that money...so much money...."

He was trembling; you could barely see it. "It...it *was* a pity. Killing that child. Horrible. I still picture my own son being driven into that field...."

"Don't cry! Everybody's been crying and it's starting to piss me off."

Shaking now. "I...I don't sleep...I take pills...every night, Nate, I take pills. You're no saint! You know how things can get out of hand. It got away from me, is all. It just....got away from me."

They came in the door all at once, four cabbies still in their fucking caps and bow ties, like I was a car getting full service at a top-notch gas station, *We are the men of Texaco, We work from Maine to Mexico*. Only what was happening was they were yanking me off the chair and dragging me by the arms out through the dispatcher's area and into the double garage. Howie was leading the way, walking backward, grinning as his buddies shoved me onto the cement floor and started working me over, the smell of oil and grease in my nostrils. Costello's nephew-in-law was holding a bloody hand towel to the side of his face where I'd whacked him. He had a monkey grin going.

The saving grace was they were idiots. The place was filled with tools and implements designed for fixing but that could break you; only these were cabbies, ex-cons with scarred faces and cauliflower ears and assorted missing teeth, and all they knew to do right now was hit me with their fists, and bending down like that did not give them their full power, making for mostly glancing blows and the occasional bread-basket punches I could tense my muscles against. My nine mil was back there on Joe's desk but at least, apparently, none of them had grabbed it. I protected my face and took as much of it on my arms as I could.

Finally I kicked one in the balls and he howled as if the steel-beamed ceiling was the moon and he tumbled back and took another dumb shit down with him. Then I scrambled through the hole I made like a desperate linebacker and cut around that Chevy on the hydraulic lift, almost running into a metal cart that I pushed back into the four men coming at me, hard enough to make the two in front stumble into the other two, and then something wonderful happened: one of the assholes slipped in grease and landed on his back but his head slammed into the lip of the lowered lift. He sprawled as if taking a sudden nap, either out cold or dead and I didn't give a damn which, my only regret that I didn't have time to laugh.

Up ahead was a wall of hammers and wrenches and I started pulling them off their pegboard hooks and flinging them, randomly at first, but targeting as the attackers slowed and began bouncing off each other as they danced in place when the tools struck home, yowling with pain appropriate where each hammer and wrench hit.

I hadn't seen him come around the other side, but suddenly there he was, having circled the sedan on the lowered lift, Howie with my nine mil in his hand. When he aimed it, I aimed, too, flinging something as hard as I ever flung anything—a hammer that flew straight and true and sank into his forehead, so deep only the rounded peen of the ballpeen hammer showed.

And the best part was the hammer found purchase pretty much in the same spot where his shot had taken Sandy down.

I scavenged the Browning and turned on my attackers, who were already scrambling away, one dragging the guy who hit his head on the lift edge, leaving a red snail trail. Then they were gone. A few had left their caps behind.

I found Joe Costello sitting at his desk with the revolver I'd dropped into his wastebasket in his hand now, angled toward his head. Toward his temple.

He said observationally, "Well, you look like hell."

He was right. I was bloody and my clothes were torn and splotched with grease. But unlike his cab drivers, I had all my teeth.

I kicked the chair aside—he flinched—and walked to the edge of the desk. "Where did those pricks come from?"

His smile had a crookedness. He lowered the revolver, rested his hand with it on the desktop. "You're not so smart, Heller. You cold-cocked their dispatcher. They came to see why he wasn't responding." He shrugged. "Least that's how I make it."

"So." I nodded toward the revolver he still held. "What's this? You gonna kill yourself now?"

"Why? You want to watch?"

"Best offer I've had today. But it isn't even dawn yet."

His lips were trembling. "I haven't had a good night's sleep since September 1953. I nap, but I'm up all night. I have a son, Nate."

"So you said."

"How can I live with this?"

To cool things down, I said, "You didn't mean for it to happen. You just...set the stage. It went sour because you didn't size up that psycho Hall right."

He raised the gun, pressed the barrel to his head and his finger was on the trigger when I lurched across the desk and yanked his hand away from his head and it went off between his shoulder and his chest. Not near enough to his heart to matter. I already knew he would live. So did he. Maybe that's why he skipped yelling in pain as the blood bubbled and went straight to crying.

There was no getting away from tears on this fucking thing.

CHAPTER EIGHTEEN

Jack Carr, trimming hedges along the curved honey-color exterior of the Coral Court office, saw me coming and put his clippers down. In a sweat-stained t-shirt and shabby jeans, he might have been the motel's gardener at that, or maybe a drifter in a James M. Cain novel planning to help some bimbo kill her husband.

"Checking out?" he asked, not unpleasantly.

"As requested," I reminded him.

"I'll get you myself," he said. "Desk girl's on her break."

I followed him in and he got behind the counter, that almost smile still hanging around and not turning into anything. The black-circled eyes might have indicated he'd had a rough night too, but I knew they were nothing new.

"Normally I don't do a refund," he said, "when somebody who pays weekly rate leaves after only a few days. But seeing as I asked you to go, you have fourteen dollars coming."

Considering that fair, I signed the receipt he gave me, and slipped the cash in my billfold.

"Seen the papers?" he asked, leaning on the counter, looking like a friendly emissary of the undead. "Catch the TV news maybe?"

"No. I slept right through to my wake-up call."

That had been eleven A.M. It was noon now—checkout time on the dot.

"Very lively day yesterday," he commented. "*Dispatch* gives the O'Day shooting a lot of play. Some other juicy stuff didn't make it in before deadline, but the TV had it. Seems Joe Costello shot himself cleaning his gun at home—in his rec room. He'll live."

"How about an Ace Cab employee who didn't?"

"Nothing that made the TV news. Afternoon paper may have it. Oh, there's a message for you." He went and got it from the Red Room's slot on the wall of key cubbyholes.

I opened the folded note "*If you're still around, call me,*" then the number and the caller: "*Barney.*"

"Hope you had a pleasant stay," Carr said.

"Call it memorable," I said.

But as I pulled out onto Watson Road, AKA Route 66, I didn't bother giving the array of yellow-glazed and glass-brick bungalows, shining in the sun, a last look. I remembered what happened to Lot's wife.

Barney and I arranged by phone to have an early supper at Pelican's, the massive gothic three-story, turreted red-brick building at South Grand and Shenandoah. Just what I needed— another castle. At least this one wasn't modernistic with a moat.

The pastel blue-and-pink dining room, however, with its horizontal wall mural of Disney-ish aquatic animals and plants, had a definite Streamline Moderne feel. Though at four P.M. the venerable restaurant had just opened, a customer was already seated and digging in at a bowl of soup. Looking like a tourist in his tent-like pink sports shirt with pants baggy enough for a clown, Barney Baker was spooning thick, dark soup into the hole under his nose on the tiny head.

Normally that might have been enough to make me lose my appetite, but all I'd had today was a cup of frozen custard at one of the ubiquitous Ted Drewes stands. That had been between stops at the PD and FBI, both on Twelfth Street, letting the cops know I'd be back in Chicago by tomorrow afternoon, and sharing my investigative findings with federal agent Herb Moss and (on speaker phone from Kansas City) Wes Grapp. Like the ransom money, my account was laundered.

"Nate!" Barney burbled. "Sit down, kid. You've *got* to try this."

"What is it—chili?"

"It's the house specialty—turtle soup."

"No thanks."

"Don't you have any adventure in your soul?"

"Fresh out."

He waved that away. "Well, you got plenty of other choices. The Pelican menu's ridiculous. German here, seafood there— but I recommend the stewed chicken and dumplings."

That's what I ordered, and it was delicious, all right. I didn't say much for a while, since it was Barney who'd called the meeting. I passed on dessert while Barney took his time with a dish of orange sherbet ("Watching the ol' weight").

"That hooker turned madam," he said, "kinda owned today's headlines. Nice-lookin' woman and I never heard bad things about her. You knew her?"

"You know I did. Sandy was at the Coral Court with Hagan and Carl Hall that night. So was all that cash."

He didn't rise to the bait.

"Judging by what I see in the papers," Barney said—the afternoon editions were on the stands, "our pal Joe Costello had a rough-as-a-cob night. Wound up in the hospital, lost a lot of blood. Seems he was cleaning his gun before sun-up. Kind of a funny time to decide to oil up Old Betsy."

"Isn't it."

"Or maybe he got depressed and tried to pull a Dutch act." He narrowed his little eyes. "And speaking of Dutch, seems Wortman's boy Elroy Downey turned up shot dead in his merry

Oldsmobile. Over on the Illinois side, Huntswood Road? Him and his buddy Mel Beck, also dead by gunshot."

Apparently after Mel dealt with the mess at the moat castle, the boss had decided to include him in the overall house cleaning.

"And," Barney said, after another taste of sherbet, "an Ace Cab Company dispatcher named Howard Ratner was found bludgeoned in the boonies north of Belleville, also over in Illinois. Do I detect your fine hand at work in all this?"

"Do you?"

He shrugged. "Nice and quiet in our little river communities till Nate Heller come to visit. You sure do stir things up, buddy."

"I get around. But then so do you."

"Union organizing knows few boundaries."

"Not the way you do it, it doesn't." I leaned back, folding my arms. "You know, you probably didn't courier that money to Chicago yourself. I'm guessing you let Downey, working with somebody on the Outfit end, handle getting that bundle to the Southmoor Bank."

He flipped a pudgy hand. "No idea what you're talking about, son."

"*You* were the big shot in Joe's rec room. You saw all that money, Barney, and were the only one smart enough to know just how hot it was. You knew damn well the likes of Hoffa and top Outfit guys like Accardo and Humphreys would not want *jack shit* to do with the bloodiest blood money to ever come down the pike. They have kids of their own, and like to think they got lines they won't cross. And even any who maybe could stomach where that dough came from, knew if it ever came out? The public blowback would be disastrous."

He had a lopsided grin going. "I'd *cry* if it wasn't so goddamn funny, what you're saying!"

"Well, please don't cry. There's been enough of that."

He leaned forward, patting my sleeve. "Nate, buddy, pal, amigo, *come on*. This is good 'ol Barney you're talking to. Barney Baker, friend of the working man. Barney Baker, Civil Rights activist."

"You mean, Barney Baker who showed up at the President Hotel just in time to shove me in the middle of Joe Costello's plan to make a big score?"

He shook the tiny head; it was like the lid on a big bottle trying to screw itself off. "Hey, I was just on the fringes! I do what I *always* do—open doors, grease the wheels, you know, facilitate."

Now I leaned in. "I don't think you were on the fringes, Barney. I think you were either down out of sight with your hands jammed up the puppets' asses, or else up in the theater flies working the strings on the marionettes."

Finally he scowled at me. "What the fuck are you talking about?"

"You know *exactly* what I'm talking about, Barney. You're a smart guy, self-educated. Hell, you know words like 'facilitate.' You have nothing to worry about from me. I can't put you in that rec room. And the other players are too fucking scared of you...good old jolly Barney."

He raised a forefinger. "You wanna back off on this now, Nate. Right now."

I grinned at him. "The one thing I *don't* know...the one thing I'd *still* like to know is...were you in on it from the start? Did you know about the kidnapping all along? How could you not be hungry for a nice big pile of that Greenlease green? Then that psycho screwed you and Costello and everybody by putting a bullet in that sweet little boy's head. Did you, Barney? Know all along?"

He reared like a bull elephant at its trainer. "What the hell *difference* does it make, Heller? Does it bring that kid back? Who made you the fuckin' conscience of America all of a sudden?"

"Tell me, Barney. How do you sleep at night?"

"Like a baby, Nate. Like a goddamn baby."

I pushed back on my chair and got to my feet. "Well, then— you better hope nobody snatches you from your cradle some night."

I let him pay the check.

But for all my bluster, I wasn't sure this ton of lard would ever *really* pay.

Once again, I was in the Greenlease mansion in Mission Hills, sitting on the leather-upholstered sofa beneath the mural of hunters and hounds heading toward the trees. Bobby Green-lease's father, seated next to me, was dressed much as he'd been at the beginning of all this, five years ago—a dressing gown (this one black and orange) over pajamas with slippers. I was in a short-sleeve sport shirt and slacks, having just made the four hour-plus drive from St. Louis. At almost ten o'clock P.M., his wife was in bed. He was having bourbon, and had made me a rum and Coke.

His manner was as quiet and friendly as ever. Behind the white-haired, strong-jawed countenance of a successful man of business, he had a kindness, a goodness, that had made him the perfect prey for the slimy likes of Carl Hall and Bonnie Heady.

My host wanted me to be frank about my investigation and I was. In detail, but not in writing. Client confidentiality covered us both, so even last night's brutal fight in that Ace garage got recounted.

"I don't know if it's any consolation," I said, wrapping up, "but everyone who came into contact with that money had about as much luck as those guys who dug up King Tut."

His thin lips formed a thin smile. "The Greenlease curse?"

"You could call it that. The money went through so many hands, diminishing each time, nobody made much. That cop Shoulders lost his job, went to prison, and is having heart attacks for a hobby, when he isn't bawling his eyes out in self-pity. Dolan is a guilt-ridden wreck, living in fear, going from promising police officer to gas station attendant and with a growing family to support. That cabbie Hagan is eking out an existence, afraid of his shadow. I saw the O'Day woman shot and killed right in front of me. Two mob guys are dead because they tried to move that money. And the bank used in the laundering is in trouble with the feds, with the top mobsters feeling the heat. Again, if it's any solace to you."

He sipped bourbon. "It would not be to my wife. She is a tender soul, a loving, Christian woman. I, however, am a businessman. A capitalist, unashamed, and for me—who has spent so much effort making money, pursuing money—I cannot stomach the thought of anyone profiting off my boy's murder. It just leaves too bitter a goddamn taste."

"I understand. I love *my* son, too."

He rested his hand on my arm. Squeezed. "So what you've done, what you've learned, Mr. Heller…Nate…*does* provide solace. To me. I can accept the plague of locusts these bastards have brought down upon themselves as their due punishment. I only wish the money that went into the Teamsters coffers could have led to the fall of this Hoffa creature."

I shook my head. "Probably not possible. The laundering process protects them. Too many hands. Money came into their pension fund through a bank. Legal, aboveboard, just good old-fashioned business."

I had told Bob Kennedy the same thing on the phone today. That the Greenlease money was a dead-end unless his accountants were miracle workers at exposing dirty laundry.

Stoic in his disappointment, Kennedy had said, "We'll, uh, get him next time."

I'd called Hoffa, too, with the "good news." He laughed at "Booby" coming up empty again. But to put it in context, when I spoke to Bob, he was on a secure government line; Hoffa had to go to a phone booth.

I said to Greenlease, "I hope you don't take this the wrong way, but you've probably made more money off these sons of bitches than they ever got out of you."

"How is that?"

I shrugged. "Every damn one of these St. Louis gangsters drives a Cadillac."

Initially that hit him like a punch; then he began to chuckle and finally outright laugh. He stood, as did I, put his arm around my shoulder and walked me out. Told me he'd again made arrangements at the Hotel President, where I could leave the loaner Caddy.

At the door he said, "I hope you won't consider this overly, well, uh...bloodthirsty of me to say."

I half-smiled. "Bloodthirsty?"

"Yes. Perhaps I allowed myself to take too seriously the, well, stories about you that one hears. About the bad people who sometimes disappear when they come into your sphere of influence."

"Some of that's exaggeration, sure."

"But, Nate, I just would like to know...that Costello character. When he had a gun to his temple—*wanting* to die...why not let him pull the trigger?"

I shook my head. "I couldn't do that, sir."

"In heaven's name, why?"

"He hadn't suffered enough."

*

In 1959 Joe Costello tried to kill himself with pills before being sent to prison for two years on gun charges. He ultimately self-destructed in a more imaginative way. After selling out to his ex-partner at the Tic Toc Club, a drunken Costello lost his head when the new owner refused to give Ace cabs exclusive loading privileges at what had been Joe's own club. He shot and killed the ex-partner outside Tic Toc there on the DeBaliviere Strip. Facing trial on a murder charge, Costello—seeing a psychiatrist regularly and suffering from hypertension, liver trouble, and diabetes—died in July 1962 at age 53 of a heart attack at home. A Cadillac was parked out front.

A bitter, depressed Lou Shoulders, 63, had a fatal heart attack a little more than a month earlier. This freed Dolan up that same year to finally make a statement echoing what he'd told me in 1958; but the ex-patrolman still did not identify Barney Baker, though his description of the fourth man counting money in Costello's rec room fit the big, tiny-headed Teamster thug perfectly.

Elmer Dolan never returned to law enforcement, instead working for a building materials firm and then a liquor distributor, both in St. Louis. In July 1965, with the FBI acknowledging his perjury had been out of concern for his family's lives, Dolan received a full pardon from President Lyndon B. Johnson. Dolan died of a heart attack at 45 in 1973.

I had no idea what became of Johnny Hagan, but in preparing this memoir, I asked my son Sam—who runs the A-1 now—to do a full search. In 1972, John Oscar Hagan died in the gutter in Los Angeles—Central City East, Skid Row.

Murray Humphreys' lieutenant, Fred Evans—Dutch Downey's insider at the Outfit, who aided in laundering the Greenlease money—was heading for his Cadillac outside his West Lake Street office when two men approached and riddled him with slugs. I knew him a little—just starting out, he ran a popcorn stand for Capone at the 1933-'34 Chicago World's Fair. Asked about the murder of his second-in-command, Murray Humphreys said, "He was no friend of mine."

Jack Carr died of a heart attack on April 21, 1984, the year Route 66 was decommissioned and removed from road maps. He had been obsessively attentive to the Coral Court even after its fortunes began to fade. His wife, however, a former prostitute with a potential new husband in the wings, had no such sentimentality, selling out eight years later. She even had the iconic neon sign destroyed. Though preservationists worked to save the Art Deco motel, it was torn down and replaced by a subdivision of single-family homes. The distinctive low-slung front gates are now all that survive at Oak Knoll Manor.

But at least the Museum of Transportation in St. Louis includes a Coral Court Motel exhibit: the exterior of a bungalow built from salvaged 1946 glazed brick and glass blocks. It's part of an exhibit of car culture in the USA with a vintage Fleetwood Cadillac ready to pull into the unit's garage. Bobby Darin's Dream Car, a space-age fantasy from the year Lou Shoulders died, perches close by.

Still ruling East St. Louis at age 63, Buster Wortman died August 3, 1968. He was in intensive care, suffering complications after larynx surgery; but some said his death was due to a liver ailment from heavy drinking. After Buster died, his son subdivided the land around the moat; last I knew the Art Moderne castle was standing, still surrounded by water but also suburban homes.

Attorney Morris Shenker, who represented both Vitale and Wortman, came also to represent Jimmy Hoffa and the $700 million Central States Teamster's pension fund. He borrowed two million personally from the Outfit and bought the Dunes Casino and Hotel in Las Vegas, promising a kickback he never delivered. He died of natural causes, as mob lawyers often do, in 1989.

John J. Vitale took over the St. Louis branch of the Outfit after the death of Anthony "Tony Lap" Lopiparo. He was "manager" of heavyweight champ Sonny Liston, and likely arranged Liston taking that famous dive in the championship rematch with Mohammed Ali. He dabbled in coin-machine rackets, firearms trafficking, and informing the FBI. The St. Louis mob boss died in his sleep in 1982.

Wes Grapp became head of the L.A. office of the FBI, but left the Bureau under a cloud. He had borrowed from the Beverly Hills Fidelity Bank headed by Stanley M. Stafford, whose young son in 1968 was kidnapped and rescued by Grapp and his agents in a highly publicized $250,000 ransom case. He subsequently joined the budding Federal Express as their world security director until retiring in 1982. (EDITOR'S NOTE: Grapp died in 2011 at the age of 93.)

Barney Baker, having clowned past Bobby Kennedy with dialogue out of *Guys and Dolls*, gained notice in the press as a comically corpulent thug who somehow managed to attract good-looking women. He next came to national attention as a connected Teamsters guy who'd been on the phone several times with Jack Ruby in the days before the Kennedy assassination (and Ruby's killing of Lee Harvey Oswald). He claimed not to know Ruby and that these lengthy calls had come out of the blue ("We just had mutual friends"). He served time on labor racketeering charges and wound up in a small office at the Teamsters' Central States Pension Fund building in Chicago, sitting at an empty desk usually reading a racing form. In later days when I saw him, he looked unkempt and disoriented, though he was driving a new Cadillac with a CLERGY sticker on the back bumper. He died November 1995.

Robert Kennedy and James Hoffa would come into my life again.

Bobby Greenlease's parents sought counsel from a Jesuit professor of philosophy and theology at Rockhurst College, where they funded a library and art gallery, as well as donating land for a high school to be added to the college campus. Robert Greenlease died at home in Mission Hills in September 1969, near the sixteenth anniversary of his son's kidnapping and murder. Virginia, 91, died in 2001, leaving one million dollars each to the Rockhurst college and high school in her son's and husband's names.

The Greenlease daughter, Sue, haunted by her little brother's death, developed an adult drug problem, dying in 1984. Paul Greenlease, whose success with his own Cadillac dealership made his father proud, lived only to 47. Yet both fared better than the children of several other of the tragedy's principals.

Dolan's son Brian, following in his father's footsteps, joined the St. Louis Police Department. In 1998, he was one of three officers charged with misdemeanor assault of a man who had taken them on a high-speed chase. Brian resigned and signed on with another department and soon faced similar charges, looking on while another cop beat up an informant. He seemed always to be quietly complicit in the crimes of other officers—like father...? He wound up a security consultant in the Middle East, dying at 53.

In 1972, St. Louis hoodlum Louis D. Shoulders, 41, was blown up in his new Cadillac in the Missouri Ozarks in apparent retaliation for the murder of a Pipefitters Union official. Deep in the *Tribune* coverage was something I hadn't known but probably should have: in 1955, at just 26, the son of the notorious late disgraced police lieutenant of the Greenlease case had been a prime suspect in the vicious murder of Jack Carr's son, Bobby.

And now, as a man well beyond middle age, taking stock of my life, I realize how big and yet so very small my cast of characters is…and I know how vital it is to look both ways when I cross the street.

You never know when the next Cadillac or cab might be coming.

I OWE THEM ONE

Despite its extensive basis in history, this is a work of fiction; some liberties have been taken with the facts, and any blame for historical inaccuracies is my own, mitigated by the limitations of conflicting source material.

My usual practice, in the Nathan Heller memoirs, is to use real names as much as possible. That remains generally true here, but I have employed composite characters in several instances. For example, Sandra O'Day is merged with madam May Traynor (O'Day survived, Traynor was shot and killed); I retained "Sandy O'Day" because I liked the sound and got used to it. "Sandra O'Day" was just one of many aliases used by the woman born Mary Ann Redd. Johnny Hagan is a fictionalized version of cab driver John Oliver Hager. Will Letterman is a composite of Robert Ledterman and several other business associates who came to the aid of Robert Greenlease in his hour of need.

With several real-life persons named John involved in the Greenlease case, referring to John Carr as "Jack" made sense; and partly because two players were named Elmer, Elmer Dowling has been fictionalized into Elroy Downey. For the Greenlease daughter, Virginia Sue, I used "Sue" to avoid confusion with her mother, Virginia. Those kinds of liberties, designed to lessen disorientation for readers, have been taken throughout. The wonderful *noir*-ish name Lou Shoulders, however, is real.

Characters who appear here under their true names must also be viewed as fictionalized. Available research on the various individuals ranges from voluminous to scant. Whenever possible, newspaper and magazine interviews, and transcripts of courtroom and hearing appearances, have been used as the basis of dialogue scenes, although creative license has been taken.

Time compression has been employed, sparingly. While most of the events of the second section indeed took place in 1958, I have included material from somewhat earlier and somewhat later. The depiction of the arrest of Carl Hall taking place at the Coral Court—and not in a St. Louis apartment house—reflects an inconsistency in the research material. The official record insists on a St. Louis arrest, but numerous articles and books give the Coral Court as the location. For my narrative purposes, the latter was preferable; and surely I can be forgiven for doubting the official record coming from the St. Louis police of this period.

Though the Greenlease kidnapping was a significant crime of the Twentieth Century, and at the time rivaled the Lindbergh case in public perception and interest, few books on the subject have been written, of which only two can be considered substantial. *Zero at the Bone: The Playboy, The Prostitute, and the Murder of Bobby Greenlease* (2009) by John Heidenry is a straightforward, well-written account, and the book I would recommend for readers interested enough to seek out a nonfiction account. *A Grave for Bobby: The Greenlease Slaying* (1990) by James Deakin arguably covers the case in more depth, but was a frustrating research tool, archly written, nonlinear in presentation, and lacking an index. Nonetheless, I am in debt to both authors.

Of several self-published books on the Greenlease case, *The Kidnapping of Bobby Greenlease* by Wayne Hancock is the best I encountered. More of an overview than *Zero to the Bone* and

A *Grave for Bobby*, Hancock's book runs only 106 pages (some of which covers other cases), but I found it a worthwhile read.

Difficult to find (and when you do it will be pricey) is the gloriously color-photo illustrated *Coral Court Motel 1941-1995* (2000) by Shellee Graham, filled with factual mini-articles, rare photos, and reminiscences by guests of the greatest No-Tell Motel in American history. Graham also wrote a frank, detailed article largely focused on the mysterious John Carr, "A Stylish Lair," for *Route* magazine, at this writing available online.

The Greenlease case is well explored in Don Whitehead's *The FBI Story* (1956) with the expected emphasis on the federal response to the crimes. An insider's experiences are shared in "Greenlease Kidnapping Case (GRENAP)" by Robert V. Harman in *Society Of Former Special Agents of the Federal Bureau of Investigation* (1998), no author given. *The Outfit: The Role of Chicago's Underworld in the Shaping of America* (2002) by Gus Russo has excellent Greenlease coverage in the context of organized crime. *St. Louis Crime Chronicles: The First 200 Years — 1764-1964* (2009) by Bill Lhotka includes a brief but solid chapter on the case as well as one on gangster Frank Wortman. *The Frank "Buster" Wortman Story* (2013) by Bill Nunes, a massive self-published volume, is a treasure trove of interviews, news clippings, documents and photographs pertaining to Wortman (and his moat house); not really a biography—it includes a novel by its retired teacher author—the eccentric volume is, like *Coral Court Motel*, an expensive out-of-print book to obtain.

The Big Bundle follows a trilogy of John F. Kennedy-related Heller novels (*Bye Bye, Baby*, 2011; *Target Lancer*, 2012; and *Ask Not*, 2013) and is the first of two projected Robert F. Kennedy-related novels (the second being the forthcoming *Too Many Bullets*). I won't list my entire library of Kennedy brothers non-fiction books—or of James Hoffa ones—but will focus on the sources I leaned upon here.

Vendetta: Bobby Kennedy Versus Jimmy Hoffa (2015) by James Neff—whose Sam Sheppard book *The Wrong Man* (2001) was vital to the writing of the previous Heller novel, *Do No Harm* (2020)—was the key work in this area. Others consulted include *Bobby Kennedy: The Making of a Folk Hero* (1986), Lester David and Irene David; *Crime Without Punishment* (1962), John L. McClellan; *The Enemy Within* (1960), Robert F. Kennedy; *Harold Gibbons: St. Louis Teamsters Leader and Warrior Against Jim Crow* (2018), Gordon Burnside; *The Hoffa Wars: Teamsters, Rebels, Politicians and the Mob* (1978), Dan E. Moldea; *In Hoffa's Shadow* (2019), Jack Goldsmith; and *The Teamsters* (1978), Steven Brill. *Tentacles of Power: The Story of Jimmy Hoffa* (1965) by Pulitzer Prize-winning *Des Moines Register* reporter Clark Mollenhoff was particularly helpful. As an Iowan, I was frankly pleasantly surprised to find my home state entering a narrative focused on more likely locales, i.e., Kansas City, St. Louis, and Washington, D.C.

Those settings were in part brought to life for me by two local publications, the 1950s-era *Kansas City Area of Missouri* (undated) published by the Missouri State Division of Resources and Development; and the wonderfully photo-illustrated *The '50s in St. Louis* (1980) by Lonnie Tettaton. Also helpful were *U.S.A. Confidential* (1952), Jack Lait and Lee Mortimer; two *St. Louis Today* articles by Bill McClellan, "Following in Dad's Footsteps" (2017) and "In St. Louis' Story, Everyone's Linked" (2012); and the article "The DeBaliviere Strip" by Jo Ann Vatcha in the September–October 2013 issue of the neighborhood newspaper, *The Times of Skinker DeBaliviere*. In an undated article from *Illinois Heritage,* William P. Shannon writes about Chuck Berry and Club Cosmopolitan in "Music History Made in Illinois," available at historyillinois.org.

Much information about the Greenlease family, and in particular the charitable work of Bobby Greenlease's parents, can be found at the Greenlease Family Website (greenlease-family.com).

Also referred to were the WPA guides to Kansas, Missouri, Illinois, California, Los Angeles, and Washington, D.C. Disneyland references include *Disney's Land* (2019), Richard Snow, *Walt Disney's Disneyland* (2020), Chris Nichols, and material at Mouseplanet.com, specifically "Disneyland 1958" (Parts One and Two) by Jim Kortis. I drew upon *Los Angeles's Bunker Hill: Pulp Fiction's Mean Streets and Film Noir's Ground Zero!* (2012), Jim Dawson, as well as *Kiss Me Deadly* (1955), which I nod to in a borrowed line of dialogue, and half a dozen other classic films *noir*.

Among a plethora of postings on You Tube about the case, two stand out: "The Bobby Greenlease Kidnapping and Murder Sites Now!" on *LandumC Goes There*; and "Coral Court Caper" Parts 1 and 2, *History of the Mother Road—Route 66*, by Insane Sam Allen. Two episodes of true-crime TV programs center on the Greenlease case and I screened both: *A Crime to Remember*, "Baby Come Home" (2014) and *Deadly Women*, "Under His Control" (2010). Online I looked at news stories of the day in the *New York Times* and the *St. Louis Post-Dispatch*, among many others. Also available—thanks to the Freedom of Information and Privacy Acts—was *The Greenlease Kidnapping Summary Report* from the Federal Bureau of Investigation.

One tidbit I did not find a way to include in the novel is Bonnie Heady on Death Row reading Mickey Spillane's *The Big Kill*, a book that concludes with a child killing an evil woman.

Due to Covid lockdown and other factors, I did not work extensively with my longtime research associate, George Hagenauer, but we did discuss aspects of the case.

Thanks as always to my great friend and agent, Dominick

Abel, and my always enthusiastic, understanding editor Charles Ardai, who made a new home for Nathan Heller. The gang at Titan Books—including but not limited to Vivian Cheung, Nick Landau, Laura Price, Paul Gill and Andrew Sumner—has been similarly supportive. Nate Heller and I thank you.

Barbara Collins—my wife, best friend and valued collaborator—read each chapter even though she was working on her drafts of two collaborative projects of ours. No one ever had a smarter, more beautiful cheerleader to act as sounding board and editor. Even with the haunting resonance of a six-year-old grandchild, she was able to provide her usual expertise to this project.

MAX ALLAN COLLINS

is a Mystery Writers of America Grand Master and four-time winner of the Private Eye Writers of America "Shamus" Award. His Nathan Heller historical mystery series was presented the PWA "Hammer" for its longevity and contribution to the genre. His graphic novel *Road to Perdition* (illustrated by Richard Piers Rayner) became an Academy Award-winning Tom Hanks film, and his produced screenplays include *Mommy* and *The Last Lullaby,* based on his Quarry novels, which were also the basis of a Cinemax series. He has developed thirteen Mike Hammer novels from Mickey Spillane's files and (with wife Barbara as "Barbara Allan") writes the award-winning *Antiques* mystery series. His comics credits include scripting *Dick Tracy* and *Batman,* and co-creating *Ms. Tree* and *Wild Dog* with artist Terry Beatty. His *New York Times* and *USA Today* bestsellers include *Saving Private Ryan, American Gangster, Air Force One,* and various *CSI* titles.

The
NOLAN
Novels

by MAX ALLAN COLLINS

Skim Deep

The first new Nolan novel in 33 years! The veteran thief finds himself in hot water when he's entangled in a plot to steal the skim money from a Las Vegas casino.

Two For the Money

Back to where it all began: after years on the run, would Nolan bury the hatchet with the Mob…or would they bury him first?

Double Down

Stealing from the criminal Comfort clan is risky enough without a skyjacker complicating matters.

Tough Tender

Their cover blown, Nolan and Jon must pull a job a second time for a blackmailing bank exec and the femme fatale behind him.

Mad Money

Can even Nolan pull off a heist of every store in a shopping mall at once? If he can't, the woman he loves is going to pay…

Available from your favorite bookstore.
For more information, visit
www.HardCaseCrime.com